Hi

I thought you might need a good to read on your out west.

stories from an Island Author.

Island Author.

enjoy Aston & remember your Roots.

love Grama & Papa
:S

P.S. - xxooxo 2007
Don't stay away for ever.

MW01173626

MURDER
at Mussel Cove

MURDER
at Mussel Cove

Hugh MacDonald

www.looninballoon.com

A LOON IN BALLOON BOOK

MURDER AT MUSSEL COVE

Library and Archives Canada Cataloguing in Publication

MacDonald, Hugh, 1945-
    Murder at Mussel Cove / Hugh MacDonald.

ISBN 0-9737497-0-9

    I. Title.
PS8575.D6306M87 2005   C813'.54   C2005-903075-5

Published by: Loon in Balloon Inc.
               Suite #3-513
               133 Weber Street North
               Waterloo, Ontario
               Canada   N2J 3G9

Cover and interior design by Steve Penner

Printed and bound in Canada by
Friesens Corporation
Altona, Manitoba, Canada

FIRST EDITION
987654321

"For my parents and grandparents,
their fascinating poems and stories."

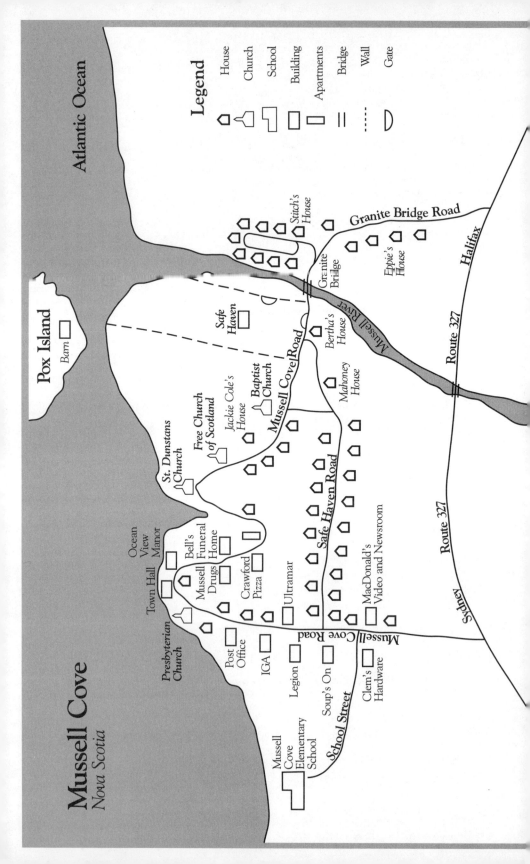

Mussell Cove
Nova Scotia

Pox Island

Barn

Atlantic Ocean

Legend

House
Church
School
Building
Apartments
Bridge
Wall
Gate

Stitch's House

Granite Bridge Road

Granite Bridge

Eppie's House

Halifax

Mussell River

Safe Haven

Bertha's House

Baptist Church

Jackie Cole's House

Free Church of Scotland

Mahoney House

St. Dunstans Church

Mussell Cove Road

Route 327

Ocean View Manor

Town Hall

Bell's Funeral Home

Mussell Drugs

Crawford Pizza

Ultramar

Safe Haven Road

MacDonald's Video and Newsroom

Route 327

Presbyterian Church

Post Office

IGA

Legion

Soup's On

Mussell Cove Road

Clem's Hardware

Sydney

Mussell Cove Elementary School

School Street

CHAPTER ONE

1

On the horizon, the underbelly of dusky clouds glowed red. Sara Miles slowed down enough to read the battered sign: "Mussel Cove—pop. 403." Some luckless hunter had blasted its worn plywood face with a shotgun, adding to its look of general neglect.

She glanced in the rearview mirror and felt reassured that no one was following her. She flicked on the interior lights, glanced again at her face and was reassured that there was no obvious swelling around her eyes. The bruises on her body would soon heal. But Tony had injured her deeply, in a way he would never get to know.

She smelled burning wood as she gradually applied the Civic's brakes and coasted along the narrow paved road that snaked through the dense white birch and alder skirting the village. As she left the dripping trees behind, public works barriers appeared in the rain-filled light from her headlights, blocking the roadway. Beyond them, fire engines painted the same luminous green as the barriers straddled the hose-strewn lawn of a two-storey wood house now in ruins. Flames licked out past the broken glass in the upper windows. From the frying pan into the fire, she thought ruefully.

Suddenly the same gut-wrenching feelings she had experienced only a few short weeks ago—as she drove across the border into Canada at Houlton, Maine—were back. I'm no longer home, she had thought then, and now I'm going to live and work in a foreign country. But she was surprised at how quickly she had settled in. Halifax, Nova Scotia, had turned out to be a lot like

Portland, Maine. She had felt safer and more comfortable than she had in years. But soon afterwards Tony, with his bad temper and brutal fists, had caught up to her at the apartment in Halifax. At that point she had longed to go home to the comfort and security of her father's house. But her dad was gone now. The heart attack had come with no warning and it was just another thing her mother, somehow, managed to blame her for. Now here she was, on the run again, entering a small, remote Cape Breton village and once again she was feeling isolated and alone.

She struggled to shake it off. I must focus on my work, she thought. She had taken a temporary job as a reporter for *The Halifax Loyalist*, a small weekly newspaper, until she could find permanent employment as a teacher. Preferably an English teacher. She raised her eyebrows and sighed, grabbed her camera—sheltering it as best she could under her blue jacket—and stepped from the car. The heavy rain had eased to gentle drizzle. She crossed the street stepping around the deeper puddles as best she could, and approached two young men with close-cropped hair. They were flopped down on the bench seat of a rusty, olive-colored pickup, which was parked under a street light. The driver, the taller of the two, drank noisily from a can of beer. He was in his twenties, perhaps, about her age, with a vacant, gap-toothed grin that almost made her smile. His eyes seemed full of mischief.

Jake Abbott watched her step toward him into the light of the street lamp under which he and Carney were parked. She looked young, maybe even younger than he was. She moved easily, like an athlete, her body slim and boyish but not quite. He liked the way her hips moved underneath those jeans, and the roundness of her breasts. She held her head high, her strawberry blond hair cut short and fashionably spiked. He noticed her clean smell even with the acrid bite of the wood smoke. Her face was stunningly feminine, her eyes penetrating and perhaps brown—it was hard to tell in the distorting flood from the street light. He felt an immediate attraction.

"Was anybody living in there?" Sara asked them, nodding toward the house.

"A family from Newfoundland: father, mother and a kid—a girl, I think."

"That's right, Jake," said the other man, whose gelled hair resembled a badly mown lawn. It bothered Sara how his loose leather boots with their huge Stetson buckles muddied the truck's cluttered dash, so she shifted her gaze to his grinning face and noticed that his right ear was much larger than the left. She wondered if someone had tugged on it too much, a parent, or a teacher perhaps. The thought struck her as funny and she found herself smiling back at him.

Jake continued, "Anyway, I hope they get them trucks out of the way. It's been a long day. Where you from, pretty lady?" By the sound of his voice he'd been drinking all day.

"Halifax ... I'm on holidays."

"Oh, a tourist. You don't sound like Halifax. More like a Lunenburger or a Yankee. Where you staying at?" asked the driver.

"Safe Haven," she said matter-of-factly. Her assignment included free accommodations at Safe Haven, a large manor house belonging to the publisher of her paper. He and his family had used it for a single season and then placed it suddenly on the market. Apparently they were still having problems selling it. She decided to tell these guys nothing more. They didn't need to know she was American. The village would be content thinking she was a tourist. Certainly, no one needed to know that Laura, her editor, had sent her here to get away from Halifax for a bit. This business with Tony was entirely a personal matter. The excuse had been that she should investigate the claims made in a bizarre letter the paper had received; namely, that there had been a string of unexplained arson cases in Mussel Cove, and rumors were going around that the house fires had been set by children. Sara had confirmed there had been arson cases, and so Laura promptly dispatched her, smelling a story with lots of local content and color.

"Safe Haven? Jesus H. Christ! Not by yourself," exclaimed the passenger. He took a final swallow from his beer and with a resonating wet double burp tossed the empty can, which clattered behind the seat.

"What's wrong with Safe Haven?"

"Nothing," said Jake, the driver. "Don't pay no attention to Carney."

Disconcerted, she shrugged. "All right ... Just tell me how to get there."

"Okay," the driver continued. "Stay on the main drag until you cross the bridge. Watch for a tall stone wall on your right. You'll come to a wrought iron gate. You'll know it when you get there. The caretaker is a bit odd, too. It is a real creepy place. On second thought, maybe you should listen to Carney; get a room somewhere else and wait for morning."

"Big stone wall after the bridge, with a gate in it. Thanks for the help."

"No problem."

Sara noticed a quick movement close to the left side of the burning house near the trees. She could have sworn she saw something like an animal running, perhaps a deer attracted by all the commotion.

"Did you see that?" she asked the men.

They looked puzzled. Now they were staring at her.

"I didn't see nothing," said the driver. The other man shrugged.

"I'm Sara Miles," she said to break the silence. The driver shook her hand. She was surprised to find his grip warm and soft, but then he tightened his hold on her hand until she felt compelled to pull away from him forcibly. As a result she almost dropped the camera she had been sheltering inside her jacket. She took a minute to remove the jacket and wrap it around the camera. The rain wasn't heavy but it might be persistent enough to damage the Minolta.

The driver was now staring at her white blouse, which was quickly getting wet in the rain. He made no attempt to disguise what he was doing. She crossed her arms in front of her breasts, holding tight to the camera, and blurted out, "My boyfriend will be here in a day or so."

How ironic, she thought, to be using Tony to ward off strangers when he likely posed more of a threat than they ever would.

"Jake Abbott," the driver said. "My buddy here is Carney Moffatt." The passenger reached a long-fingered hand to Sara. Carney's cold, muscled hands were callused but thin, like a surgeon's. Their hands had only briefly touched when Jake roughly shoved Carney back against the passenger side door. "Don't crawl over me, you faggot," Jake snapped.

"See you later, baby," he said, winking at Sara. He turned the key in the ignition, slammed down the accelerator and fishtailed down the street, tires squealing on the wet pavement. In the misty wake of the pickup Sara watched an elderly pedestrian in black, who had been drenched by the sooty water from a puddle beside him, gesture in obvious frustration at the disappearing tail lights.

Sara returned to her car and shivered when her wet blouse made contact with the back of the seat. The Honda's tires chirped as she pulled away. The old man on the curb was wearing a Roman collar, some kind of a clergyman, she assumed. He nodded when she caught his humorless eye.

Heavy rain once more began to spatter her windshield. It stained the face of the few wooden farm buildings she passed whose dim lights made them seem all the more distant and unapproachable. She left the security of the final yellow street lamp on the southern end of the granite bridge and plunged into the deepening gloom.

...

The cast-iron gate needed paint, but the key Laura had given her turned in its lock with surprising ease. She wiped the water from her eyes and saw that someone had scrawled, "Your dead meat. Rot in Hell, Bitch," on the gatepost in white chalk, probably stolen from a local school. "You're" she corrected in her mind, always the teacher. She laughed at herself and, remembering how much she resented goons who wrote such garbage, shivered in her drenched blouse, swung the gate wide and drove inside.

After locking the gate quickly behind her, she drove slowly up the lane, her tires crushing the tips of willow branches that had strayed onto the crumbling concrete driveway.

The huge house was built of the same dreary Nova Scotia granite as the wall and bridge. Patches of gleaming, wet stone—where ivy chose not to cling—reflected her headlamps. The rest looked black and impenetrable, including dark-paned windows with black, solid shutters spread like the wings of giant bats. A light glowed beside the front door. Someone was waiting up for her.

A large cheerful woman opened the front door. Aunt Bertha—as she insisted Sara call her—took her suitcase and offered her coffee. Sara held on to her briefcase, which contained her notebook computer. Sara accepted the offer of coffee, noting, as it was served, that the silver-haired woman, with her large-cheeked, round face and triple chins, had a smile that appeared permanently pasted on. She was considerably overweight, probably in her late fifties, and moved slowly by shifting her weight consciously from one foot to the other. Most surprisingly one of her large arms—which were pushed away from her body like wings by a huge bosom—ended in an artificial hand.

Sara drank the hot coffee hastily and then yawned. A long day. The stout woman showed her to a high-ceilinged room with a canopied bed and obligingly left her alone. Sara had always wanted a canopied bed for herself. Against the east wall of the well-appointed bedroom sat an altar-like table that somehow frightened Sara. It didn't belong in a bedroom, really, such a large, long table. But who was she to complain about the décor? She was dead tired and the room was fresh and clean, smelling of detergent. She yawned, undressed quickly and crawled into the huge bed. A soft, damp Atlantic breeze ruffled the drapes. Despite her fears, it took only moments to shake the looming presence of the "altar" from her mind and to drift into dreamless sleep.

...

Jake and Carney sat in the disarray of Jake's cramped apartment. Carney was eating the last cold slice of the pizza Jake had bought for supper three nights ago and loudly drinking orange juice directly from its cardboard container.

"I told you to use a glass for that juice," said Jake.

"They're all dirty," answered Carney. "Besides, I'm finishing it."

"It's still disgusting watching you eat." He paused a moment. "You know what Carney?"

"What, Jake?"

"I think we're going to pay a visit to that new Sara girl, soon ... real soon."

CHAPTER TWO

2

The lights inside the house had now gone out. She had watched fat, old Bertha lock the door behind her but the light in one up-stairs room had stayed on a short spell after that. Someone else was inside. Little Eppie was so sore and tired she didn't care as she groped for the spare key under the mat by the kitchen door. It wasn't there. She would have to go in the other way. She sighed.

The cover of the garbage container was ajar. The child climbed the tin-lined chute to the kitchen pantry, trying to protect her yellow dress from whatever old Bertha might have tossed out after preparing tea for herself and her guest. At the top of the chute she unhooked the heavy mesh screen as she had done so many times before. The screen had been installed to discourage rats from entering the house. It wasn't difficult to unfasten if you knew how. Bertha opened it every time there was garbage to toss down the chute. Ira had shown Eppie the easy way to unhook it from below. Eppie needed a place to sleep and this old orphanage would do just fine.

She was not afraid of the darkness, nor of the huge old home. She was a friend to the ghosts. She knew that the living were the real enemies of the children of Mussel Cove.

She climbed the stairs to the second floor. The first bedroom she came to had its door open wide, and, on the big bed inside, a tall, slim, blonde-haired woman lay asleep. Eppie intently watched the woman's chest for signs of breathing. She didn't want this pretty woman to die, like her mother had died tonight in the house fire. Eppie stared, mesmerized, until reassured by the gentle rise and fall of the soft flannel nightgown that the woman was merely sleeping. A few tears silently trickled down Eppie's cheeks.

She tiptoed to the dresser and picked up the sharp-pointed scissors, the kind her mother had always used to cut her hair. She held them in her fist—just in case—and climbed onto the bed. On top she brought her knees up against her bird-like chest and listened wide-eyed to the pretty woman's breathing. The point of the scissors cut into the center of her palm. Eppie didn't even flinch. Moonlight caressed the woman's neat, spiky hair and made her skin white, like raw piecrust. She's so pretty and sweet, thought Eppie.

Eppie wished she, too, owned a flannel nightgown. She wished she were pretty, too. Maybe now she could be. Maybe now that he had been burned up in the fire she would have a chance. Holding the scissors tightly, she leaned across the woman's body and kissed her softly on the forehead.

Sara recoiled slightly, half-smiled, then woke with a start.

"Oh, my god," she yelped, her voice betraying alarm and fear. As her eyes adjusted she saw a dirty-faced young girl outlined against the moonlit window. "Who the hell are you?" she asked. The child before her had a mop of dark brown curls. Her eyes were small and also dark, her face freckled, not exactly pretty but almost, and very scared. Her pale face and hands, especially her fingernails, were black and grimy like a garage mechanic's. She smelled of wood smoke.

Eppie quickly pulled back to the edge of the bed ready to spring in one direction or the other. "I was afraid," she pleaded, her voice full of terror and confusion. "There was nowhere else to go. Our house burned down."

Sara recalled the burning house on the outskirts of the village and what the young guys in the truck had said about the family dying.

"Your parents ...?"

"Burned," the girl answered. She looked to be ten or eleven. Sara tried but couldn't imagine how frightened the child might be, or how she came to be here in her bed. She wondered what to do. Bertha, the woman who had been here to greet her, had gone home. Sara was simply too tired to start phoning anyone now. And she didn't want to jolt the child any further.

"You poor darling," Sara said. "You must be so tired. Would you like to sleep in one of the other rooms? We'll make some calls in the morning."

"Can I stay in here with you? I don't want to be alone."

Sara felt a tightness in her chest. I could have had a daughter like this, she thought. If only Tony had been a different man. She knew then she couldn't send the child away. Not this late at night. Not on this night. And she was so tired.

"I guess that would be all right. Climb under the covers and try to get some sleep. We'll make those calls in the morning. Good night."

"Good night."

"What's your name?"

"Eppie."

"Good night, Eppie. I'm Sara."

"Good night, Sara." Eppie relaxed her grip on the scissors, which she had managed to conceal. She was satisfied. The woman had passed the test. Eppie curled up beside the pretty woman, feeling so cozy and safe she almost purred.

CHAPTER THREE

3

Sun electrified the air. Sara woke up alone in the room. She yawned, lifting her arms above her head, enjoying the morning's first stretch in the elegant bedroom. Lazily she glanced at the quilt and was startled by the sooty outline she saw there. The room smelled of burnt wood. Then it hadn't been a dream. The child must have been covered in soot. Her name was Eppie, she recalled. Where had Eppie gone?

Sara stepped from the bed and peered underneath, threw on her blue fleece housecoat and hurried downstairs.

The smell of coffee and bacon met her part way down. Someone was in the kitchen. Tiptoeing a bit nervously to the door, she peeked inside. Bertha stood, large and red-faced, over a huge kitchen range, her wide back to the kitchen doorway. "Good morning, Sara," she said without turning around. "How are we doing?"

"A bit shaken, thank you. Someone visited me in my bed last night. A little girl."

"That was the McNeil child," said Bertha matter-of-factly. "I sure was pleased to see her alive."

"Yes, she was lucky she wasn't in the house. She told me her name was Eppie."

"So you know it was her house that burned last night."

"Yes. Where is she?"

"When she came downstairs this morning, I called Children's Aid and two women came over and carted her away. Funny you didn't hear all the ruckus."

"Ruckus?"

"The child didn't want to leave. She told the social workers she'd come back to Sara first chance she got. She said nobody could stop her doing what she pleased. She was so angry ... like an old house cat gone wild."

"Poor child. How old is she?"

"Eleven, they thought. She wouldn't say."

"Why would she want to come back to me when she doesn't even know me?" Was it possible that Eppie had experienced the same powerful feelings Sara had, recalling how comfortable and protective she had felt with the child asleep beside her? "How terrible it must be to have your parents burn to death. I can't imagine ... She's lucky she didn't die in the fire. Thank goodness she wasn't in that house."

"I'm not so sure she wasn't inside. Her hands were red, and sore-looking, and her eyebrows and hair were all singed. My nephew the pharmacist and volunteer fire fighter—well, he's not really my nephew—anyways, he told me the house was pretty far gone when the pumper trucks arrived."

"Look here, now," Bertha continued, leading Sara away from the pantry door toward a large table that was laid out for breakfast. "You set yourself down and have a bite. That's the best thing for you now. There are fresh biscuits and eggs. I brought jam I made from rhubarb I picked out behind the Haven." Bertha paused, reflected and sighed, "This place wasn't ever much of a haven."

"Oh?"

"Not for the kids that lived here."

"I don't know much about this house," Sara said, interested.

"It was an orphanage. Not a great place. But that's a long, sad story." Bertha ambled to a frying pan on the range from which she spooned scrambled eggs onto Sara's plate.

"You shouldn't wait on me, Bertha. Is this a Bed and Breakfast? I can't afford to pay too much."

"This is no B & B. The owners wrote me to say you'd be using the house. I'm just being neighborly. Around here that's normal but I suppose it's hard for people from away to understand. It gives me pleasure to host visitors from time to time. If you want the house to yourself—if you know what I mean—I'll make myself scarce."

As she spoke, Bertha shoveled a mound of pan-fries and bacon beside the eggs and brought a plate of buttered soda biscuits hot from the oven. Once again Sara noticed the artificial hand. It was covered in an ugly yellow plastic that had developed a green tinge over time. She wondered how Bertha had lost the hand.

"Thank you," she said to Bertha who had been emptying cupboards and wiping walls and shelves before carting the contents to the sink for washing.

"I'll finish up and get out of your way," said Bertha. "I have to get home to my nephew Philip. The lad's not used to fending for himself."

"Can I drive you home?"

"Oh, no, dear. I like to walk. Does me good. It's just a lovely stroll up the hill to our house."

Twenty minutes later, after a hot shower and short inspection of the interior of the house, Sara opened the heavy front door and stepped onto the veranda. The lawn was like an unkempt rural cemetery minus the headstones. She stepped into the long grass and looked back toward the house. Though the grounds were in disarray, the building had apparently been solidly built and well maintained. The window trim had been recently painted the color of heavy cream and there was, at least on the surface, none of the decay one would expect in a vacant house of this vintage. Even in its present setting the Victorian house with its dark, functioning shutters retained a formidable dignity. A series of paths wound here and there through the long grass. They led not only around the house and to nearby storage buildings, but meandered off into the distance, crossing one another at various intervals throughout the immense acreage of the estate.

Sara set out to follow as many of these as she could before returning inside the house. The fresh air and warm sun were a comfort. For the first time in days she was beginning to relax, her mind free of Tony, the man she'd attempted to abandon back in Portland. But Tony had refused to stay behind in the good old USA and had tracked her to Halifax. He had broken into her apartment and waited for her return from work. As she stepped inside, he punched her in the face, then threw her down the stairs behind the apartment. When she was able, she had called the police who arrested him but couldn't hold him because of his lies. He had an unscrupulous friend who claimed she had been with him all the time. He accused Sara of lying. Someone may have hurt her and someone may have threatened to kill her, but it couldn't have been him.

What he didn't know and never would—was that his last bit of violence caused her to miscarry his child, the only part of him she wanted for her own. Now that she had lost her baby she wanted nothing ever to tie her to him again. Yet she suspected in her heart that Tony hadn't finished with her yet, so she needed to get away from Halifax for a bit. Laura, her editor and friend, had provided a helpful, if temporary, solution by giving her this assignment in Cape Breton. Sara hoped that by now Tony had given up and returned to The States.

The first path led away from the house to a densely wooded area to the east. She remembered the young men in the pickup last night, warning her about Safe Haven. Obviously they had been trying to scare her. They had failed—for the most part. Still, she shouldn't venture too far from the house. Anything could happen. She could fall and break a bone, or some local pervert could be lurking in the shadows waiting to pounce. Besides, if Tony had found her once, he could find her again. She shuddered.

The air was sweet with the odor of decaying vegetation released from the cold storage of a long Maritime winter. There was the fresh scent of ferns and new leaves, bay laurel and the resins of stunted spruce and pine. What a lovely, peaceful place this seemed to be. She needed to forget her personal troubles and enjoy being here.

The path twisted and turned up ahead and disappeared around a bend, losing itself amid dense, misshapen evergreens.

As she entered the trees she experienced a drop in temperature and a dimming of sunlight. It was like going down into a dark, damp cellar. Overhead the sun sliced through the tangled branches, delivering strobe-like flashes of light and heat. In places she was forced to stoop when branches, heavy with dusty needles from past summers, pressed close to the musty earth.

Before long she smelled the ocean and listened as it raked the shore with growing volume and intensity. She then came into a clearing, and stepped onto the beach itself—into blinding sunlight and a rise in temperature. With gray gravel underfoot she looked out over the Atlantic, past a small tree-covered island a few hundred feet offshore. Nearby she found six canoes lying bottoms-up above the high-water mark. From there she could see the roof of a barn amid the trees of the island. She felt a chill as the sun tucked itself behind a small cloud. She had done enough exploring for her first day. It was time to return.

Sara's pockets bulged with candy bar wrappers and other litter she had begun picking up along the path. But there were too many of them. Lots of people had been out here on the property. Who? She turned toward the house. The gravel rattled under her feet and the sound echoed along the shore, startling her. For just a moment she half-expected Tony to jump out of the bushes. He could hide easily among these trees and all this vegetation. She felt her skin crawl.

Where to now? She didn't want to force her way through those trees again. Off to her left, she discovered a second path that wound through yet another clump of trees and lead her to the north bank of the narrow river that flowed back up, in the direction of the road, along the south of the property. This path was narrow like the first one, but less dense. It was often just as low-slung—more suited to Leprechauns or Hobbits than humans.

The west face of the island with its huge barn was visible on her left. Before long she turned to her right and discovered that she was outside of the tall, stone Safe Haven wall. Now she understood that the wall couldn't completely surround the property, as she hadn't encountered it on the pathway to the shore. She continued to walk between the river and the wall until she came within a stone's throw of the bridge where the wall bent slightly to the right to swing up beside the paved highway.

Moments before, she had spotted a narrow opening in the wall where the stonework had collapsed and tumbled inward. She made a mental note to mention to Bertha that the wall needed repair. For the moment she was glad the opening was here. The break in the wall meant she could return to the safety of the house without going all the way around to the front gate. But it also meant that if she could pass easily through the wall, so could anyone else. Tony came to mind yet again. She despised him now but it had been very different in the beginning.

They had met in the school where she had been assigned to do the practice teaching for her Education Degree. He was a supply teacher, filling in on a maternity leave. They met in the staff room. He was tall and athletic with a red buzz cut. He was broad-shouldered with arms and biceps like a boxer, an enormous smile and deep dimples. He asked her out that first day and they became inseparable. She took him home and her mother loved him. Her father was accepting as always though he never seemed to warm to Tony like her mother did. Sara guessed it was because someone was coming between Daddy and his girl. Time would take care of that, she thought.

He wanted to marry her and have a big family. They spent the first summer camping and he wrote songs about her. They shopped together and were perfect in bed. He bought her a ring and she said yes.

Once she had the ring things began to change. He watched her like a hawk. If another man spoke to her, Tony would be jealous. Any time they were apart, he interrogated her. He never wanted her to go anywhere without him, even with her father.

The first time he roughed her up was following a basketball game at school. Arnold Simms, who taught chemistry at the school, gave her a lift home after the game. He was having trouble at home and wanted her advice. They talked for half an hour in his car. Tony grabbed her when she came inside the door and pushed her up against the wall.

Things went from bad to great, and back to bad. Eventually it became obvious she had to do something. She spoke to her mother who took Tony's side and told her she had to stay away from other men. Men were jealous, that's just the way it was.

But that wasn't the way it was going to be. She resigned her teaching job, giving thirty days notice, and handed Tony back his ring. He threatened her and so she made plans to leave town. Her father went to see Tony and threatened him. Tony, of course, threatened back. It was shortly afterwards that her father had his coronary. Three days later he died in intensive care.

After the funeral, her mother wouldn't speak to her at first. When she did, she told Sara that she had been the cause of her father's death. Her mother asked her to move out of the house. It was too painful, she said, to see Sara every day and remember.

After her final day at school, when she arrived at the house, Tony was having coffee with her mother. Sara turned and left. Tony followed her and climbed into her car. He told her to drive outside of town; he wanted to talk. When they stopped he tried to make love to her. When she refused he dragged her out of the car and beat her with hands and feet until she couldn't stand. "Next time I'll kill you," he said. "Either I'll have you or no one will!" He drove away with her car, leaving it in her driveway. Once she was able, she walked back to her mother's house. Her mother wasn't home. A note said, "Tony and I are out getting coffee. We'll see you when we get back." Sara quickly packed her bags and left. She hadn't seen or spoken to her mother since.

Back inside Safe Haven, exhausted and thirsty, Sara walked past the stove that continued to pour out heat despite the stifling temperature of the room. Bertha had been gone long enough for the kettle to have boiled dry. Sara refilled it and placed it on the hottest part of the surface. A cup of tea would be nice.

She was sitting half in a daze, drinking her tea, when she noticed the phone message tacked on the bulletin board.

The Children's Aid Society called. They are having a deuce of a time with the little girl. She asks for you all the time. They phoned and asked me if I would think of fostering her for a little while with your help. It might settle her, they said. Just a temporary thing. Anyways, it's up to you.

B. Morris

"Shit," Sara muttered to the empty house.

CHAPTER FOUR

4

Sara yawned and tapped on the door. This was the address Laura, her editor, had given her. Earlier she'd called the local police number. She asked for information about any investigation into the recent rash of fires. The officer said the investigation was ongoing. He said he could tell her nothing more for now. It was late evening, the day was nearly over. She hoped the woman had not gone to bed. The badly lit corridor reeked of cabbage, stale fish, fungi and piss. The ceiling above the stairs had begun to sag and in several places the bubbled paint had lost its grip on the wall and hung like the skin of a spent balloon. There was no elevator and the stairway hadn't seen broom or vacuum in weeks. She already pitied Inabelle Coffin, the old woman who, she had been told, lived on the other side of this door.

"What do you want?" a tired voice rasped through the partly opened door.

"My name is Sara Miles. I'm staying over at Safe Haven. I heard about your fire. Do you feel like talking about it?"

After a brief hesitation Sara heard the rattle of a security chain and the door opened. "Come in, if you want," croaked Inabelle.

"How are you doing, Mrs. Coffin?"

"Not so good." Inabelle's hair was almost white, her skin dark and wrinkled like a dried apple. She wore heavy lipstick smeared outside the edges of her mouth, a trick that might have worked when she was younger, and so many layers of clothing that Sara wondered if she was looking at the woman's entire wardrobe. The old woman parked her bony bottom on the outside edge of a tattered armchair and proceeded to blubber. Sara pulled a Kleenex from her purse and eased down next to her, placing her hand on the woman's back, her fingers taking note of the protruding spine. It looked like Inabelle might also be wearing all of her jewelry. Thin fingers held a variety of rings. Broaches and pins were fastened like military decorations across the front of her outermost sweater, a dozen pennants and necklaces circled her wrinkled neck, and numerous pins and combs protruded from the wasp's nest of hair that framed her ashen face.

The apartment was a hodgepodge of worn and battered articles. Sara counted no less than five smoke detectors in the room. Fire extinguishers sat at the ready on top of several pieces of furniture and here and there on the dusty floor.

"Was this your husband?" Sara held up a small photo of a bright-eyed young man in a military uniform. "How handsome he was."

Mrs. Coffin began to cry in earnest, managing a few words between sobs. "I'm so lonely without Calvin. He was my only friend. I only got one picture. I managed to save my jewel box with this photo in it and what clothes I could grab from the closet. We had no money for insurance. This is the only thing of Calvin's that's left." She pulled a gold pocket watch from the apron of her dress and handed it to Sara, who automatically flipped open the cover and began to read the inscription. The old woman suddenly snatched it from her hands, dropping it deep into the pocket from which it came, but not before Sara had read: "Twenty-five years of outstanding service to the children of Mussel Cove. The Cobans—Safe Haven."

Sara paused, somewhat embarrassed, before she managed to speak again. "That's all you saved. How terrible. Do you mind if I get this on tape? I have such a terrible memory."

"Why do that?" Inabelle sat up suddenly, her voice frightened.

"I'm a reporter for *The Loyalist*."

The old woman stood. "You'd best go!"

"Look, I'm sorry if I offended you."

"I should have known nobody would bother with me if they didn't want something. You'd better go. Now!" She picked up a fire extinguisher and aimed the hose at Sara. "You ought to be ashamed of yourself. Why don't you go home where you belong."

Sara shrugged and backed into the corridor. The door slammed. Through it she heard Inabelle's sobs.

"Goddamn," said Sara. "The poor thing." She drove away muttering about her own lack of sensitivity. She, too, was now on the verge of tears. If only she had a home to go to—that might solve a lot of her problems. But the father who adored her was gone and her mother had made her feelings clear. Home for now was Halifax and she couldn't go there because of Tony. She sniffled and then sighed, "Goddamn!"

She got in her car and started away, slowly accelerated and drove past several battered pickups and cars that sat as if abandoned in islands of murky light beneath the street lamps on Main Street. People lived here. They just weren't always visible. She looked forward to touring the village in daylight. Things didn't feel right just at the moment. She had a fleeting thought that the whole village might actually be hiding from her. But that was crazy, wasn't it?

CHAPTER FIVE

5

Jake Abbott and Carney Moffatt slumped on the weathered doorstep behind Jake's apartment. For some reason, neither could explain, they had always been friends.

Jake was in charge. He was taller—about six feet—better-looking, smarter. His hair was a light brown that went blond in the summer, his eyes blue. He might have been an athlete if he could have learned to do as he had been told. He could have been handsome if he had ever taken care of himself, especially his teeth.

Carney was good with his hands but not too smart. He knew that he was odd-looking but he didn't care. He cared about Jake and would do anything for him. The top of Carney's narrow head came even with Jake's chin. His brown eyes were small and close-set. Carney looked thin from the waist up with narrow shoulders but he had the hips and thighs of a fat person. Some of the jocks in high school used to call him Fat Woman. He hated it. Jake punched the quarterback of the football team in the face once because Carney got upset. Nobody teased him after that. Carney never forgot.

Jake took a swallow of beer and lifted a bit of pigeon shit off the step beside him with his grease-blackened thumbnail and flicked it at Carney, who grinned back at him. They were drinking Moosehead. They'd been here since early afternoon, originally to undertake minor auto body repairs on Jake's pickup, but the beer that Jake purchased in order to lure Carney and his skill over to his cluttered yard had become the real focus of their afternoon.

"Nothing like a cold beer, eh, Jake."

"You said it, Carney. Look, I've been thinking we should make our visit to that babe over at the old orphanage."

"You like her, don't you, Jake. What you got in mind?"

"You saw the way she looked at us. Them city babes are just crying out for it, you know. If we go over there she'll fall over on her back and let us ride her to Halifax ... and back."

"Us, Jake? Count me out. I'm not interested. You never know what you'll get a dose of. Especially from city babes. God knows who she done it with the last time."

"Yeah, but she'll be prepared. She'll have some kind of protection and even if she doesn't, I got me a boatload of safes in the old glove compartment. What's the matter with you, Carney? You gone chicken shit on me? Believe me, babes like her are just dripping wet waiting for real men like us to come along. You wouldn't believe the faggots they have to put up with in Halifax."

"You think so, Jake?"

"Fuckin' A-right, Carney. Jesus, you saw her sniffing around our truck. You must have noticed the way she was looking at me."

"I guess so. But I don't want to go prowling around Safe Haven. You said yourself it ain't no safe haven. Didn't you say that the other night, for Chrissakes?"

"Sure I said it, you jerk. But that was to the girl, a city girl."

"When do you want to go?" muttered Carney, twisting off another Moosehead cap.

"After a bit. Let's wait until the town beds down. We still got a few green beer buddies to kill. When we finish them off there'll be time enough."

"Yeah, sure."

...

It was well past two in the morning when a very drunk Jake maneuvered the pickup to a spot just outside Safe Haven's granite wall. The men sat motionless and savored their drunkenness, bodies wavering, while above them the dark mantle of the cloud split, allowing a brief glimpse of a well-rounded moon.

"Let's go in, Carney." The effort to sound sober was lost on Carney who was, if possible, drunker than Jake.

"You got a key for the gate, Jake?"

"Yeah, right. I phoned over and asked her to leave out keys for us."

"Is that right?"

"No, it ain't right, you asshole," Jake snarled, shaking his head. "How come a smooth guy like me ever got hooked up with an asshole like you. Get your fat ass over next to the wall. We're going to climb it."

"All right, I'm coming. Wait for me."

Jake shoved Carney over against the wall and slapped his ears viciously until he convinced him to crouch down. He used Carney as his footstool and, after stepping from knee to shoulder, managed to grasp the top of the wall and pull himself, with enormous difficulty, to the top. He crouched there for a moment between pine branches that reached across the wall from the tall trees inside until the world stopped spinning nauseatingly below him.

Carney found the climb much more difficult. For one thing, he had nobody's back to step on. For another, he had Jake on top of the wall goading and teasing him. Finally, after several failures, Jake got hold of the back of Carney's shirt and dragged him scrambling to the top. Carney was there only a moment before he fell heavily to the ground on the inside, landing with a sickening thud on his back.

Jake then jumped blindly, narrowly missing Carney and somehow managing to keep his feet. He laughed out loud as he looked down at where Carney lay groaning on a mound of dried pine needles. Jake helped his friend up, roughly brushing the needles from his shirt and backside. By this time, the moon had once again burrowed deeply into dark cloud. It wasn't possible to see the house from where they stood.

"What was that?" Carney tugged at Jake's sleeve.

"What?" Jake tried to sound nonchalant but he had heard it too.

"It sounded like a big fucking animal," he whispered. "I used to go hunting with the old man and sometimes we'd hear foxes and things in the woods beside us. It used to give me the creeps knowing they were out there watching us when we couldn't see them. What I just heard sounded like that, but a fuck of a lot bigger. Honest to God, Jake, I heard something."

"Aw, you're drunk as a fucking skunk. Get your arse in gear and let's get over near the house. I'm getting tired. If we're going to visit that sweet piece of ass we better get going."

"No, Jake. Let's go home now. I don't like the sounds I'm hearing around here."

"Come on, fuck-face. I'm not going to ruin my evening listening to a drunk asshole who keeps on hearing things. If you want to go home, then go the fuck home. I don't give a damn. I've got things to do." He turned away abruptly, wrenching his sleeve out of Carney's frightened grip and started off in the direction of the house, leaving Carney peering anxiously into the darkness around him while his heart pounded.

"Wait up, Jake, for Christ sakes, I was only fooling. I'm with you all the way, Buddy." Carney stumbled along the pine needle-covered ground and then into the open where the unkempt grass was lanky and wet. Neither of them heard the catlike footsteps that followed closely behind them. They were easy prey—too drunk and too stupid to make any attempt to move about quietly.

The house loomed above them in the damp gloom. They sensed its presence before they actually saw it. The windows were in darkness except for one on the second floor. Below it, Jake and Carney stood in open-mouthed astonishment.

...

Knowing that the house was well inside the high protective wall, amid tall pines, Sara had pulled the sheers across the windows but left the heavy drapes unclosed. The evening was warm and she wanted to feel the breeze inside. Aunt Bertha had not returned. Until she came up to bed, Sara had been typing her first impressions of Mussel Cove, including the disappointing visit to Mrs. Coffin, into her notebook computer.

Time had slipped by quickly and now she was tired. She yawned as she set her alarm clock, standing naked but for her panties between her bed and the window, gazing drowsily out into the dark and gloomy night. And then, as if she had felt the cooling shadow of some dark spirit, her feeling of safety and security deserted her. She drew back into the room and pulled on a housecoat. A shiver ran up her spine as she changed her mind and jerked the heavy drapes shut. Of course it was only her imagination. The doors were locked and she was safe. Or, was she? Eppie had gotten into the house while she slept. Get those thoughts out of your mind, she told herself. She would sleep now and deal with the world tomorrow.

There was still the decision about Eppie. No matter how much the novelty of having the girl around appealed to her, she ought to say no to these strangers who expected her to care for this strange child, albeit with Aunt Bertha's assistance. Looking after a child would mean her freedom would be pretty restricted. That might interfere with her investigation. Still, she was intrigued and sympathetic. She would decide in the morning. The cool sheets quickly warmed to body temperature and she dropped off into another deep and dreamless sleep.

...

"What did I tell you?" said Jake, pointing up at the window where Sara had stood moments ago. "Did you see those hooters! I figured they had to be smaller than that. They didn't seem nearly that big with her clothes on. Come on! Let's go get some of that."

"Listen, fer fuck sakes, will ya!" hissed Carney as he squinted and pointed out into the darkness behind them. He was still astounded by Sara's silhouette against the bright light in her room. But just then the moon found a space in the dense cloud and peeked through. Carney's gasp was audible and chilling. He stood frozen in place like a jacked deer, pointing out into the tall grass, struggling to find his voice.

A half-dozen humans-in-miniature, wearing grotesque Halloween masks, quickly surrounded them. The small creatures carried round-pointed garden shovels slung casually across their shoulders. But as he watched they brought their shovels forward and held them threateningly above their heads. Carney remembered something from Grade Eleven English. *All Quiet on the Western Front* had been the novel's name. The German soldiers had used their shovels instead of bayonets for close fighting.

"What the fuck's going on, Jake?" Carney gasped. Then he turned to face the creatures and shouted: "Who the fuck are you and what do you want?" The small figures didn't answer. Instead they raised their shovels higher and took a menacing step forward.

"O my God, Carney," said Jake in a thin-voiced whisper, suddenly sober. "Someone's playing some kind of a weird joke on us. Let's get the fuck out of here." He turned and stumbled, Carney at his heels, past the crowd of masked wee people, heading in the direction of the wall. Without a word, the tiny figures hurried after them. Behind him Jake heard the distinct ring of metal on bone. He turned in time to see several shovels connect again with Carney's head, and as Carney fell the creatures surrounded him, their shovels raining down steadily and mercilessly. Jake could already imagine the shovels tearing his face apart. He felt like he would explode. He heard a horrid wailing sound and realized it was coming from his own mouth. He pissed his pants and scrambled toward the wall but found his way blocked by a phalanx of shovel-wielding gnomes. The point of the first shovel cut into his face at the level of his eyes and he felt a warm flow of blood wash down his cheeks. Then there was only pain as blow after blow descended and his legs gave way. Involuntarily he began to pray aloud, "Our Father, Who art ..."

The children stood above the battered, twitching bodies of their victims as the blood pooled around them. Without a word, several of the masked figures reached down and began to drag the battered bodies to a flower garden at the edge of the woods, a few hundred feet from the gazebo. Most of the others stood motionless and unmoved by the scene, but a few whimpered and one of the smallest among them vomited. One of them, who seemed to be in charge, used a small flashlight to look carefully through the contents of the pockets of the dead men, removing keys and identification and a few dollars. All of this would be deposited in the metal box under the floor of the barn on the island. In the meantime, the bodies were pushed into a hastily dug open grave. The good buddies were buried without a word of farewell beneath the cold, damp soil and gravel.

...

No one heard Jake's keys turn the ignition of his pickup. No one saw the tall driver stroll away after the truck dropped into the deep water off the wharf a few kilometers away in Fourchu later that night.

CHAPTER SIX

6

Everything was tucked away. As usual, some of the bigger kids stayed behind until the tall man, known to them as "The Gingerbread Man," carried the masks and shovels into the room under the barn. They didn't approach him too closely. They were quite afraid of him. He always appeared out of nowhere with his heavy brown clothing and ominous hood. Because of the color of his clothes and his shape one of the younger children had called him The Gingerbread Man. It stuck. The older kids knew he was a real person in a mask but the smaller ones thought of him as some sort of monster.

The ghost girl had told them that The Gingerbread Man was not there to harm them. She said he always did what she wanted just like they must always do what she asked. And they believed her because the hooded man never interfered with what they wanted to do. His job was to take care of the barn, she said, and to clean up after the parties. But she warned them never to get too close to the man and they were only too happy to obey.

On the way back from the island, once the canoes were pulled up onto the gravel, Kensey Mahoney and her friends scrubbed themselves in the cool ocean surf. Kensey was eleven years old, tall for her age and thin to the extreme. Her hair was long and straight, a reddish brown. Her thin face with its long prominent nose looked pasty in the intense moonlight.

The water around her turned inky as the sticky stains leached out of their clothing. They were too close to the end to have everything ruined by curious parents finding blood on somebody's clothing. If anyone found out too soon, the ghost girl would be angry.

Kensey felt better when the blood was gone. What happened had upset her, too, although she wouldn't say so. The stomach cramps were gone by the time she and her brother passed by the bridge. They could see their house from there. Kensey liked walking through the silent town as the parents slept. During these quiet hours the children ruled Mussel Cove. The ghost girl had explained that fact one of the times she appeared to them. Now the children were beginning to understand the full extent of their power and they liked how it felt to control the world around them. They could do what they wanted and no one would stop them.

"Don't drag your feet, Robert. Lift them," whispered Kensey.

"Aw, be quiet for frig sakes," Robert growled. Robert was six years old, the physical opposite of Kensey, his hair almost white and his body short and heavy. He had always found exertion a difficult thing and his mother always told him he ate too much and too fast. "I'm lifting them as high as I can. I'm just glad I don't feel sick any more."

"It's okay, Robbie. I felt sick at first. We got to do what she says, all right? The ghost girl told us what happened to Eppie's parents will happen to other parents if kids disobey. Shhh! We're almost home. Don't wake Mom and Dad. As long as they don't know anything they're safe."

She glared into Robbie's frightened eyes. She wanted him to be afraid. If he stayed afraid he wouldn't tell anyone.

They climbed the tall willow beside the garage, the way they always did, feeling the familiar, gross crush of aphids under their hands. They scampered like squirrels across the garage roof and dropped through the small window into the darkness of their bedroom.

"Put on your pajamas and get into bed. I'll put our clothes in the washing machine." Kensey slipped out of her clothes and pulled on her pajamas.

"Don't wake them," whispered Robert.

She smiled. "I'll say I have to go to the bathroom. They hate when I wet the bed." She glanced through her parents' open bedroom door. They were asleep, their breathing noisy and reassuring.

"They don't have a clue," she whispered softly as she re-entered the bedroom. Robbie didn't answer. She climbed under her covers and closed her eyes. They had earned a good night's sleep.

CHAPTER SEVEN

7

"She's not really planning to look after that brat." Philip yawned and tried to stretch the tension from all six feet of his lean frame. He looked in the mirror and rubbed the stubble on his cheeks. He would have to trim them soon so they would have just the right amount of whiskers. He was aware that his blond beard looked good for a day or so without trimming but not so good beyond two days. He was also aware that he was blessed with a metabolism that kept him trim, as he wasn't much interested in any sort of exercise. It bothered him, though, that for some reason women didn't seem all that attracted to him. He was talking to Bertha about Sara.

"She and I both agreed to it, Philip. Eppie will be staying with Sara at the house. Sara told them she would be returning to Halifax soon. Children's Aid said that was okay, they really needed help on the short term to calm Eppie down. Something more permanent would come along later. They said they wouldn't have asked us except their foster homes are full, and the child was so pesky. And, of course they know me and how I brought you up and all."

"I don't get it. Why give up her freedom?"

"What's it to you?" Bertha continued ironing Philip's trousers as she talked. She'd been around him long enough to know what was on his mind. She had done her best to substitute for his parents, after the car accident that took his mother's life just months after the boy's father died of leukemia. He was a good boy, although he had never quite gotten over the insecurity that followed the sudden loss of his parents. Bertha figured he must have been thinking of asking the reporter to go out with him and he saw Eppie's appearance on the scene as a complication.

"I thought you'd sworn off women."

"Come on, Aunt Bertha. Don't bug me. Women around here can't talk about anything but the weather, their hair and their clothes."

"Maybe you spent too much time talking."

"No. I don't think so. But it didn't matter. The talk always got around to weddings and babies. I couldn't imagine marrying a woman who considered spring house-cleaning the high point of the year. I don't want to live in a house that smells of Lysol with the radio tuned permanently to the country music station. I hate fiddle music."

"Too bad ... So you must have met Sara Miles."

"No, I didn't. I had a glimpse of her the night of the last fire. She was talking to Carney Moffett and a friend of his. I saw her down at the village yesterday, too. She's hot."

"You planning to ask her out?"

"Not likely."

"How come?"

"Where would I take her? Besides, she wouldn't be interested."

"You could drive up to Sydney and take in a movie. Or go bowling or maybe invite her over for beer and pizza."

"Crawford's pizza would poison a billy goat. She'd be used to decent food. I'm not ready to make a fool of myself over someone who's only here for a few days."

"Jeepers Christmas. You complain about women wanting some - thing permanent and now you avoid Sara because she isn't going to be permanent. I could put in a good word for you."

"Please, Aunt Bertha ..."

"Don't get your drawers in a knot. I only meant I'd mention your name."

"Forget it." He tried to change the subject. "So, what brought her up here?"

"Her job. But there's more to it than that. I don't have it all figured out. It's pretty complicated. She quit teaching and dumped her fiancé and then her father up and died of a heart attack. She says she feels guilty, thinks that one might have had something to do with the other. Anyway her editor sent her to check out the mess of fires we've been having. But it's supposed to be a holiday, too, she said."

"So how come she dumped her boyfriend and quit teaching?"

"Don't know. Something she preferred not to mention."

"So word about the fires got all the way to Halifax."

"She said someone wrote a letter to *The Loyalist*, typed and unsigned. She asked me some questions about the children. The letter to the paper claimed the kids here were out of control, running wild."

"That's ridiculous! Some of the kids are out after dark, I know. But burning down houses? Hardly."

"Yes. Pretty far-fetched, I suppose. So, why not ask her out? Take her mind off the craziness. Think about it. It'd do you both good."

"I'm thinking." He lumbered up to his room. Five major fires and at least one death in each. Who would be next? Fires always happened in Mussel Cove, but usually in the winter. Most involved wood stoves and faulty flues. None of the recent tragedies involved stoves or flues. All were under investigation. But kids?

He had seen lots of the brats late at night when he'd been walking off the booze. Neither Bertha nor anyone else knew how much he drank. He preferred to drink alone in his room, a private thing. The only time it became a problem was when there was a fire alarm.

Once in a while, his drunkenness shook him up—like the morning he found himself in a shallow hole along the shore covered in gravel and sand. He awoke with no idea of how he got there. He had been on a date with a cousin of a woman who worked part-time stocking shelves at the pharmacy; he could no longer remember his date's name. He had been drinking, as usual, but no more than the other guys had that Friday night. He had lost track of several hours and was left with no memory, only an enormous sense of having done something shameful. His body the following morning was bruised, battered and bloody, as if he had been in a murderous struggle with someone or something.

Later, when he called the girl's apartment, she wouldn't even come to the phone. Next day she left Mussel Cove for good. Her cousin, Mary something, didn't know what happened either. She said her cousin just wanted "to get as far away as possible."

After much mulling over of the events, he called Jackie Cole, the village cop. The two men visited the beach below Safe Haven, where the incident occurred, but the tide had partly obliterated the hole in the sand and gravel where Philip said he had been "buried." Cole spent most of the time out there joking about how drunk Philip must have been to bury himself alive. Jackie wasn't the world's swiftest cop and Philip wasn't surprised that he found out nothing at all.

After that Philip stopped drinking for a month and a few days. But little by little he'd resumed the old habit, though he hadn't ventured out on a date since. He wasn't sure what he was afraid of. Not knowing was the most frightening. When would he black out again? Would he ever remember what happened that night below the old orphanage?

He had a niggling memory, if that was what it was, a day-dream fragment that kept recurring. What did he do to this girl, if anything? He wished he knew. And then there was the nightmare that haunted him every now and then. It didn't always begin in exactly the same way, but he always ended up trapped somewhere, surrounded by dwarfs in rubber masks, and there was always pain. They always hit him with sticks of driftwood, rocks and canoe paddles.

What about the many mornings he had woken with a fuzzy memory of the night before, with a nagging feeling that he'd been on the prowl? He planned to quit the booze a million times, but there wasn't much else to do in Mussel Cove. His life definitely lacked direction, but he couldn't seem to change it. Aunt Bertha was probably right. He did need someone to give some stability to his existence.

Sara Miles wasn't the one, though. He had a bad feeling about her, although she was beautiful. From his first glance at her the night of the fire, she had set his lean body astir. He hadn't been able to get her out of his mind. Not only that, he could feel trouble looming like an iceberg in the fog. Perhaps he could approach her that way. She would need his help, his protection. He could offer to be her bodyguard—and hers was a body worthy of guarding.

CHAPTER EIGHT

8

"Don't go!" Eppie said with clenched fists, and a determined scowl.

Sara shrugged. "I have to go. It's my job. If I don't do it, I don't get paid. If I don't get paid, we don't eat."

Eppie's brown eyes narrowed to slits and her knuckles whitened.

"They pay you for foster children. You don't need to work."

"Nobody's paying me for this. Bertha and I are doing it to help you. You're in Bertha's custody. I help when Bertha isn't here, which will probably be most of the time. Bertha can't be here most of the day. But she is right now and I have to take advantage of it. You'll have to be patient, okay?"

Sara stretched and yawned and looked around the kitchen. She pointed to the nearest chair. "Sit."

Eppie instead chose the chair beside Bertha, in front of two fat molasses cookies. Eppie's eyes, dark as the cookies, glared as Sara headed out the door. "I'll be back soon," she promised.

As she unlocked her car, Sara glanced back toward the house and spotted Eppie's freckled face pressed against the window of the parlor, looking out. Sara withdrew the key, stepping away from the car for a moment into the long grass. It frustrated her that she felt so bad about refusing Eppie. She had done the right thing again by saying "no" and walking away, but she still felt guilty. She needed more practice at saying "no." That was all.

The early summer sunshine warmed Sara's skull and her headache eventually evaporated like morning mist. She wondered how the village would look in daylight. She had heard part of a news item on her clock radio concerning a small house fire that had occurred in Mussel Cove while she was sleeping. She didn't catch where the fire had taken place. Not serious this time, the announcer had said, but it could have been tragic had the owner not awakened in time to put it out. She planned to investigate it.

The grass around Safe Haven seemed taller in the sunshine. Bertha said one of the local farmers had been engaged to cut it. The owner would pay. After all, the house was for sale.

She turned back to her car and her foot struck something solid in the tangle of grass. She bent down and pulled up a man's boot with a metal buckle shaped like a cowboy hat. Where had she seen one like it before? She tried to remember but couldn't immediately recall. She bent and raised it up to get a better look at it. She almost retched from the odor. It was disgusting. It was covered in slime that looked like spoiled gravy.

How did it get here in the grass? No one but Bertha and the child and herself had been on the property, as far as she knew. If there had been anyone else she would have noticed, wouldn't she? The candy wrappers she had found among the trees by the shore came to mind. They didn't get there by themselves. She started toward the house, holding the boot in front of her like something dead. Bertha might know something about it.

As she approached the building, her eyes took in the partly shuttered storm windows of the parlor. She would ask Bertha if there were summer screens. She waved her free hand at the flies swarming around the boot.

"It sure stinks," said Bertha. "There's some kind of fungus on it."

"I'm sure I've seen a boot just like this one somewhere before," said Sara. "Where's Eppie? I noticed her in the parlor window when I was outside." She paused, breathing in the stale, motionless air, which reminded her: "Could we get someone to put screens on the lower floor windows? It's so stuffy in here."

Bertha turned away. "Someone will take care of the screens. And Eppie knows where we're at if she needs us." She held the boot in front of Sara's face. "What do I do with this thing? It smells like rotten meat."

"I'm positive I saw this boot or one like it in the last day or so. But I can't quite place it since so much has happened. I want to know whose it is, and how it got here. What could have happened to cause someone to lose a boot out here? And why would it smell like rotten meat? It's fairly new and it doesn't seem to have been outside that long. I have a feeling that something strange is going on around here."

"I'm sure it's nothing, Sara. But if you want, I'll call Jackie Cole. He's the village cop. I'll see to the boot. You run along."

"All right. Thanks. See you when I get back."

Disturbed, Sara left the kitchen and strolled up the main hall past oak tables and paneled walls, dark, unsigned portraits and landscapes, and out the front door. Why had this wonderful house not sold? Why had no one grabbed it up from the realtors? Was it just too expensive, with all the land?

Her mind returned to the boot. Whose was it? What else might be hidden in the long grass? Was the owner of the boot still out there somewhere? Was the slime the residue of the owner's blood? That was ridiculous, wasn't it? Perhaps she had walked past his mutilated corpse already, or parts of it. She shuddered at the ghoulish thought and struggled to stop her mind from racing like that. Still, she wished she had never found the boot. It was dreadfully creepy. If the cop came, strangers could soon be prowling all over the property.

As Sara headed out, she saw that Eppie was now watching her from a room on the second floor. She couldn't make out the expression on the child's face. Once outside the gate the young American felt some of the weight lift from her shoulders and she looked forward to visiting the village of Mussel Cove.

To her left she saw the stone bridge she crossed on her way into the village. She turned to the right and passed a well-maintained sign, much in contrast to the smaller one she'd seen up closer to the highway the night she arrived. This one read: Mussel Cove, pop. 403—Visitors welcome—Lion's meetings second Thursday of the month at 8 p.m. Mussel Cove Consolidated School. It didn't take long to determine that the bulk of the village was spread out along opposite sides of Mussel Cove Road like a double string of rough pearls. There was another residential side street, called Safe Haven Road, School Street, Granite Bridge Road, which she had taken on the way into the village, and a small subdivision, which sat along the south bank of the narrow Mussel River.

A few businesses eked out a living serving the village and the surrounding rural area: Crawford's Pizza and Subs; Bell's Funeral Home, Monuments, Office Supplies and Real Estate; Mussel Drugs; MacKinnon's IGA grocery; the Soup's On Restaurant; MacDonald's Video and Newsroom and Clem's Hardware, whose window display appeared not to have been dusted in a decade. A small sign that read "Mussel Cove Consolidated School" pointed up School Street, a narrow paved road that disappeared behind the restaurant. The Royal Canadian Legion was just before the Soup's On restaurant and across the street an Ultramar Service Station between two houses badly in need of paint. Sara counted four churches: Mussel Cove United Baptist, The Free Church of Scotland, St. Dunstan's Roman Catholic, and St. Andrew's Presbyterian. There was also a large metal building that served as the Town Hall, Police and Fire Station, and the Mussel Cove Credit Union.

Sara pulled into a parking space in front of the Town Hall. She walked toward the door marked Police and knocked at the door. She waited a minute or two but there was no response. She tried the door and it was open. She stepped inside. She was in a small tidy room with a desk and a filing cabinet. A computer sat running on a small metal table next to the desk. There was another door that led somewhere else. There were no windows. The room was lit by a large flourescent unit, which hung in the center of the ceiling.

"Hello," she said, loudly enough to be heard beyond the interior door. There was no answer. On the wall behind the desk hung an oil painting of a small island in the middle of a lake or a large pond. The scene was shrouded in fog, and the artistry was quite skilled. The desk was neat and a file sat in full view beside the office chair. The folder had a tag on the front that said, "Safe Haven." She lifted the cover. There were several sheets of scrap paper with notes written in some sort of shorthand. At first she thought it was bad writing but decided it had to be shorthand because she could not make out a word. She had never learned shorthand. There were also copies of reports from various government authorities relating to Safe Haven's past. She wished she could take the folder home and study it.

She stepped away from the desk toward the closed door. She guessed it led to a corridor somewhere in another part of the building. She knocked again and waited, then tried the door. It turned out to be a washroom with a toilet and a sink. It, too, was clean and smelled of disinfectant and Old Spice, the latter smell reminding her of her father. She closed the door and decided to come back later. Near the exterior door a newspaper clipping was pinned to a small bulletin board. There was a photo of a clean-shaven man, in his thirties, she guessed, who was holding a child's bike while a tiny girl found her pedals. The headline read, "Sheriff Cole teaches bicycle safety." He looks very handsome, she thought.

Where to next? She wasn't all that hungry but her car's tank was full of gas and she had to start somewhere. The sign inside the door of the Soup's On Restaurant said, "Please DON'T wait to be seated." There were several customers eating, and others waiting to be served, and they all paused to watch her as she entered. She headed to the only available table, a table for two, one side of which hadn't been cleared from the last customer. She sat in front of the clean place-setting and waited for someone to come and clean up the mess. She tried to eavesdrop as she waited. What she heard was disappointing. No one mentioned fires, which she thought surprising given recent events, and for some reason the restaurant itself reeked of wood smoke. The customers around her talked about many things: the tsunami in Southeast Asia, the possibility of opening some Cape Breton coal mines, problems in the fishery, the violence in Iraq—one couple thought that the USA should withdraw and the couple opposite them disagreed—late unemployment checks and local and national politics. If the rash of house fires was on anybody's mind, it wasn't showing up in these conversations. She jumped when a thin, lanky man suddenly appeared and placed his hand on the chair opposite her.

"Sorry I startled you," he said. "But I had been sitting here. I was called to the phone."

Sara stood up quickly. "I'm sorry. I ..."

"Please sit down. I was just going to have a coffee before heading over to the school. I'd be pleased if you would join me. I'm Marcel Vertu."

Sara looked at him. He seemed harmless enough and almost handsome. She guessed him to be in his early fifties with neatly trimmed dark hair and a touch of gray at the temples. He had pale eyes that were almost as blue as the Maritime sky. He had a charming smile but the skin on his face was red and his right cheek blistered. Obviously he had been recently injured. He winced as they shook hands. His right hand was partially wrapped in gauze.

"Thank you," Sara said and sat. "I'm Sara Miles. I'm on holidays. Are you a teacher?"

"I'm the principal and the guidance counselor. I also teach science and history to the sixth and seventh grades. It's a small school. I own this little restaurant, too. I have a manager because I'm away so much. The restaurant gives me something to help pass the summer months."

"Is the food any good?"

"Better than you might expect. Especially in the summer."

"Why is that?"

"Sometimes I get the urge to cook. Cooking is one of the many things I tried before I took up teaching."

"So ... are you a good cook?"

"Yes. Are you hungry? Of course you are ... or else you wouldn't be here."

"I'm not terribly hungry. I just wanted something light ... and a coffee."

"I don't recommend this coffee. If you want an excellent coffee and some wonderful baklava I can brew you a cup. But of course you couldn't since you don't know me. But I'm a schoolteacher and therefore harmless. How daring do you feel?"

"Just what are you saying?"

"My apartment is out back. I have some good coffee beans and freshly baked pastry. You'll be perfectly safe, although my place is a bit messy. There was a small fire." He waved his bandaged hand past his burned cheek.

"I heard something about the fire on the radio when I woke up. You are offering me coffee and dessert? That's all, right?"

"That's all."

"Sounds good." This is a bit of good luck, she thought. Here was someone who had just had a fire and who worked with the kids of the village. "Tell me about the fire," she said.

"There's not much to tell." He turned toward the open kitchen. "Bernadette," he called out to the waitress inside, "I'm leaving for the day. Sara and I will be having coffee and then I'm off to the school." He glanced back at Sara and gestured for her to follow. They passed through a door marked "private," and followed a short, musty corridor to his apartment. An odor like damp campfire was everywhere.

"Pardon the stink," he said as they entered. "It bothers me more than my burns." He opened the windows and the door to the outside. "I don't dare leave anything open when I'm not here because of those vandals. Authority figures become the targets of every disgruntled kid in the community. I understand why but it still hurts."

The furnishings in the rooms were unique, much of the furniture apparently homemade, the walls covered in various masks and curious *objets d'art*. A pair of ornate cast-iron candleholders that looked like props from some medieval movie stood at either end of a large dining room table. Across an open hatchway into the kitchen hung an array of pots and pans in shimmering stainless steel and burnished copper. A wide shelf displayed an assortment of local pottery and a small toolbox with some small pieces of stained glass and an electric soldering gun sitting on top. Despite the burnt-wood stink, Sara smelled herbs and spices and recent baking, along with vanilla and garlic. Under a glass dome on the counter was the baklava that Marcel had promised. So he seemed on the up and up.

Sara watched as he filled a kettle and placed it on the burner of a large gas range. She turned away and looked around the cluttered living room. Through the wide picture window she could make out the roof and upper storeys of Safe Haven in the distance above the top of the dense grove of pines. It gave her a strange feeling to pick out her bedroom window from up here in the village. She noted that the sill of Marcel's window was charred black. The outside wall must be burned like that, too.

Long shelves lined the walls beside the door through which she'd entered moments ago. Several objects had been carefully arranged about the room to appear casually placed there: a violin and its bow, a brass bugle, a German Luger, and several ornate Asian daggers. A teacher with a taste for weaponry?

A bundle of envelopes leaned casually against the wall. The top letter was addressed to Bertha Morris, Mussel Cove, Cape Breton, Nova Scotia. The return address stated it was from Milligan Realty, the firm run by the present publisher of *The Halifax Loyalist*. Odd, Sara thought.

Marcel came into the room carrying two dessert plates of baklava. "I'll get our coffee in a moment," he said. He looked toward the envelopes in front of Sara. "How are you and Bertha getting along? She's quite the lady, isn't she?"

Sara looked puzzled. "How do you know I know Bertha?"

"It's a very small place." He pointed at the top envelope. "That letter is the one telling Bertha you would be using the house. She was here for a visit the day it arrived. She left the letters behind by accident. Bertha, besides being an old friend, does part-time secretarial work at my school. There aren't many hours, and the job doesn't pay much, but she does wonderful work for the pittance we pay her. We were discussing the old days. Bertha called me last night and filled me in on all the news. She's pretty impressed with

'the little reporter from Halifax.' And she's grateful for the help
with the child ... I'll get that coffee." He walked out to the kitchen
and returned with two large mugs. He handed one to Sara.

"Tell me about the fires," she said.

"I don't know much about fires, except this one. And I don't
know all that much about it. Something woke me up and I saw
the flames outside the window. I had several fire extinguishers in
the restaurant because of provincial government restaurant regula-
tions. The one here in my kitchen was due for refill. But I used it
and it was fresh enough to put the fire out before there was too
much damage. It could have been much worse. I didn't notice
most of my little burns, or the smell, until this morning. That's
about it."

"Do you think kids started this fire?"

He arched an eyebrow. "Possibly. As I told you, I'm an authority figure." He sipped his coffee and suddenly began to recite:
"Tiger, tiger burning bright/In the forests of the night..."

Sara interjected: "William Blake, probably his best-known
poem. I'm a teacher, too. Until recently I taught English in a high
school in Portland, Maine. So I know about Blake. I thought you
taught science and history."

He laughed. "I do. But that doesn't mean I have to be ignorant
of literature. Especially a poem as well known as 'The Tiger.' Mr.
Blake knew about children. He knew about how experience miti-
gates innocence. Innocence is the most precious gift. The willful
destruction of that innocence is the most heinous of crimes. Once
it is gone it can be replaced by something savage, like the Tiger
that burns in the night."

"What are you telling me?" Sara was baffled.

"I'm not sure. I tend to ramble." He chuckled. "Let me freshen
your coffee."

"I had better get going. The baklava was delicious." She
handed him her mug.

"Thank you. I hope that means you'll be back. Don't mind my
ramblings. I'm here if you need a friend. Small towns can be lonely

for outsiders." He paused and scratched his chin before speaking again. "Would you be interested in some substitute teaching?"

She hadn't expected this question. She had never considered teaching in such a remote community. She looked at him and smiled. "Perhaps. I am looking for full-time work as a teacher."

"I'll keep that in mind," he said. "You never know." He turned, opened the door and stepped along the corridor. She had other questions but they were back inside the restaurant already and had become the object of everyone's attention again, so she decided to wait. She wasn't sure if she agreed with Marcel's interpretation of Blake's poem, but he intrigued her. He was not the typical teacher, indeed. It might be fun to substitute at a rural school and it would give her the chance to meet and observe some of the local kids. She hoped she would be seeing him again.

CHAPTER NINE

9

"Saint John is the capital of New Brunswick, not St. John's. St. John's is the capital of Newfoundland and Labrador. I wish you would listen. We've been over this a hundred times already. I suppose you think St. John's is the capital of everywhere in the world. There'll be no recess today, children, and you have Josie Boone to thank for it."

Mrs. Stitch stood not quite five feet tall and yet she seemed to the children like a very large person. She didn't look overly fat but she was wide and solid. Her face came to a point in the middle, like a heavy wedge axe designed for chopping wood. She was pale—almost green—and always seemed to be angry and about to lunge and attack, especially when she was smiling. She was the oldest teacher in the school by far, well past the expected age of retirement. And she told anyone who would listen that she had no intentions of retiring soon.

A low growl rose in the children's throats that reminded Mrs. Stitch of the hungry wolves, and other members of the wild kingdom, that she and her late husband Ogden had liked to watch on the nature channels on television. A few students acceded to Mrs. Stitch's wish and glared at Josie but the majority continued the low snarl and stared at their feet. Most of them had, at one time, been made to feel just like Josie did at this moment and they were fed up. This was nothing new. Mrs. Stitch's class seldom had recess. The parents of Mussel Cove had warned their children that Mrs. Stitch hated to go outside. She always looked for an excuse to stay inside and some unpopular kid to blame it on.

Josie slumped in her seat, blood roaring in her ears like Niagara Falls. She picked up her freshly sharpened lead pencil and drove the point first into one palm and then the other. She stared, somehow enjoying the pain while the dark blood oozed out, forming two small pools in the center of her palms. She moaned, relishing the looks of fear appearing in the eyes of all the children who had heard this sound before. They knew just what it might mean.

You will pay for this, thought Josie. You will wish you'd never been born. She raised her right hand above her head and staggered toward the door at the front of the room. Rivulets of blood crisscrossed her arms, staining the front of her white dress.

"Where do you think you're going, Miss Boone?"

"I have to leave the room."

"You will do no such thing. How can you expect privileges after you've ruined recess for everyone by not paying attention in class? Everyone pays attention in my class. Return to your seat at once!" Mrs. Stitch moved to confront Josie.

"But I ... I ..."

"At once!" screamed the teacher, who was now directly in Josie's face. The teacher's hair appeared to stand on end, her outrage adding velocity to her anger. But Josie stood her ground. The cramps increased and her tight young stomach began to heave. The wounds in her hands stung as the blood seeped past fisted fingers and dripped onto the floor. She had stabbed herself too deeply. She fought to keep her mouth clenched, but could not. The vomit seared her throat as it blasted from her churning gut. The bulk of the outflow landed at the top of Mrs. Stitch's wide chest before crawling like steaming lava down her mountainous bosom, tumbling to the floor in viscous blobs.

The class was momentarily spellbound but soon recovered and, as a release, broke into violent and appreciative laughter. An embarrassed Josie fled from the room and hid herself in the washroom stall nearest the window where she sat angry and humiliated.

After what seemed a lifetime, the door squeaked open and a tiny voice spoke tentatively, "Josie, are you in here?"

"Who is it?"

"Amanda."

"I hate her," said Josie.

"We do, too. You got her good with your barf. She went home to change. Mrs. Haverstock is in the room now. She sent me to see if you were all right. She said not to worry. Everyone thinks what you did was neat. They want to know how you did it."

"I didn't try. She made me so mad that I just got sick. But I want to do more. I will ask the ghost girl to help us. I know she will because Mrs. Stitch was one of the people who hurt the children of Safe Haven. Tonight at the island barn we'll tell the others. They will all want to help. Everyone knows what she's like. My mommy said Mrs. Stitch has always been cruel. She is going to be so sorry. But by then it will be too late."

CHAPTER TEN

10

Something looks different, Sara thought as she pulled to a stop beside Safe Haven. The lawn! The grass had been cut.

Bertha's agitation showed on her face as she met Sara at the door.

"Eppie's teacher, Mrs. Stitch, wants you to phone right away. She said it's important."

"I will call her ... in a bit. I see the lawn was mowed. I thought the cop might want to have a look around before letting anyone do that."

"He didn't say anything about that."

"What did he think of the boot?"

"Nothing. He didn't see it. When I went to the kitchen to get it, it was gone. I thought maybe you changed your mind and took it with you."

"Of course I didn't take it with me. It's disgusting. You were going to show it to him."

"Like I said, when I went to get it to do just that, it was gone. Maybe Eppie chucked it into the stove. I wouldn't blame her ... stinky old thing." Bertha bit at her bottom lip and rubbed her forehead with her good hand. "I was out of the room a spell. I went down to the cellar to fetch wine and pickles for supper. You'll be having supper, won't you?"

"I don't think so. I hope you didn't go to a lot of trouble." Sara gritted her teeth. "What happened, exactly?"

"Well, like I told you, I stepped down to the cellar for vegetables and pickles and wine for your supper—which is in the fridge, if you get hungry later—and when I got back to the kitchen there was an odd smell, like burnt hair or something. Anyway, I didn't give it more than a passing thought. At my age strange smells aren't all that strange, if you know what I mean—hot flashes and all. Then my Philip popped in with my pills from the pharmacy. We had a short visit and I just forgot all about that old boot until Jackie, the cop, came.

"But later on, after I couldn't find it for Jackie Cole, I recalled the smell. I realized it could have been burnt leather, not hair at all. I remember looking in the firebox of the stove but there was nothing to see. I was putting in lots of wood all afternoon and a scoop of hard coal for the oven because I was baking bread and rolls and all, and by the time I thought of looking, there was nothing left in there but ashes and clinkers."

They sat down at the table. Eppie's head appeared in the entry to the pantry. As usual, her impish face was smudged with dirt.

"Hi, Eppie," Sara said. "Did you toss anything into the stove today?"

"No," Eppie said, her eyes worried. "I wasn't near any old stove. The heat makes my burns ache. Where were you all afternoon?"

"I drove down to the village," Sara replied.

"I wish you were here with me."

"I wanted to look around Mussel Cove. I hadn't seen it before in the daylight."

"I wish you wouldn't leave me alone. I get scared. And you better be careful around Mussel Cove. It's not safe for you here."

Sara sighed. "Tomorrow I want you back in school. It isn't good to be stuck out here with nothing to do but imagine trouble. You need to be busy to keep your mind off things. And you don't want to get behind in your schoolwork."

"Who cares. I hate school. I especially hate my teacher."

"Why?" Sara remembered Bertha telling her to call the teacher.

"Because she hates us. She never lets us have fun and I always get a pain in my belly. Besides, I'd rather stay here with you."

"That's sweet. I'm glad you like me, and I like you, but I can't do my job sitting around the house. I have to get out and ask questions. I have to do my work. You understand that, don't you?"

"I could go with you."

"You have to go to school."

"I don't want to!"

"Come with me while I freshen up. We'll spend some quality time together." She turned to Bertha. "We'll be down in a few minutes. I'm not hungry but that glass of wine you mentioned sounds mighty good."

The bathroom off Sara's bedroom was cavernous enough to produce a ringing echo after every sound that was made inside. Their nervous breathing was drowned in the gush of water filling the marble sink.

"Bertha's a big fat liar," said Eppie out of the blue. "She did bad stuff when she was little."

"Why is she a liar?"

"Because she burned the boot. She wants to get me in trouble."

"What bad things did Bertha do?"

"I don't know. My mommy said she did bad things when she was little. She said that's why her hand got chopped off. She said I'd get my hand chopped off too if I did bad things. My mother lived in Mussel Cove when she was a girl. She knew all about Mussel Cove."

Sara was shocked at the picture of Bertha's hand having been chopped off. Could it be true, or was Eppie making it up? Kids could, after all, be cruel. Or was this some tale concocted just to scare the child into obedience? She watched in the mirror as Eppie's face turned sour and angry. "Brush my hair," the child demanded, handing the brush to Sara.

Sara sighed and rolled her eyes, then put on a smile and set the brush to the tangled mass, gently tugging the bristles through. Eppie sat silently, wincing each time the brush found knots in the hair, but soon the brush slid easily down the brown curls and her face relaxed. Eppie's hair was soft and much longer than Sara's short-cropped strawberry-blond cut.

Later that evening, after Bertha had left and Eppie was tucked into her bed to get some sleep before her return to school, Sara decided to head up to bed. She was sipping from a large pewter goblet of chilled Chablis as she glanced out one of the tall front windows. Just then a battered half-ton truck swung into the yard and stopped beside the kitchen entrance. Her first reaction was apprehension. A second glimpse assured her it wasn't Tony. That was some relief. Who then? She set her drink on a table on her way to the kitchen door. She stopped there and waited for the bell to ring.

Once it had, she paused another moment before opening the door. A tall man, who looked like he stepped off the cover of the L. L. Bean Catalogue—with broad shoulders and narrow waist—stood on the doorstep. She recognized his wide forehead and his kind eyes from the picture she'd seen on his bulletin board. Those sleepy blue eyes enticed her as he held out a large hand and firmly shook hers as he stepped inside.

"We don't want to let the flies in, do we?" he said. "I'm ..."

"Jackie Cole," Sara interrupted. "I saw your picture."

He looked intrigued by the idea that she had seen his picture somewhere. "You did?" he said. "Where?"

"I was looking for you and went into your office today ... It wasn't locked. How come?"

"I don't know. I was likely in a hurry. No one goes in there anyway. There's nothing to steal."

"What about your files?"

"I left a file folder on my desk, didn't I?" He paused. "Yeah. You're right. I ought to lock up. Did you like the picture?"

"Picture?"

"On the bulletin board," he grinned.

She laughed. He was a saucy brat. She liked him.

"And you're the reporter. Sara ...?"

"Yes," she said. "Sara Miles. I expected you before this."

"Sorry. I got held up. Very busy. Some people wanted into the school. I'm the janitor over there and I also drive a school bus. It's a small village. Policeman, janitor, bus driver, put the three jobs together and I earn almost enough to live on." He paused and looked into her face. His eyes were lovely and laughing. Sara had to force herself to look away. He grinned and continued, "Bertha said you found some kind of a shoe and were concerned about it. Was there actually blood on it? Bertha wasn't sure but she thought you mentioned blood as a possibility. 'Slime' was how she described what she saw." He shrugged. "She couldn't seem to find it when I asked to have a gander at it."

"It's a long story, Mr. Cole. There was a boot and there was a mess like old gravy on it. It smelled like rotten meat and I thought it might be spoiled blood. It smelled like meat that hadn't been refrigerated. But, of course, I can't be sure. And I'm convinced this boot was intentionally thrown into the stove, but I can't prove that either. And I don't know by whom or why. For all I know a cold-blooded murder took place right out there on the lawn. I think I even have a picture in my mind of the guy who was killed: one of the two guys parked near that fire at Eppie's the night I arrived."

"I was at Eppie's house the night of the fire," Jackie responded. "I'd say you're talking about Jake Abbott and Carney Moffat, two ne'er-do-wells. Bums almost. I saw them parked out front. Now that you mention it, I haven't seen them make their daily loitering run today." He turned serious. "What makes you think one of them was murdered?"

"While I was tucking Eppie into bed last night I remembered where I'd seen the boot I found on the lawn. It looked exactly like what Abbott, or Moffat, had on his feet the night I arrived. One of them had his dirty feet planted on the dash of the truck. I can't recall who was who. I have nothing to go on but that, the memory of those messy boots, and a creepy feeling." She glanced at Cole, who looked like he was trying to be sympathetic.

"I'm pretty tired," she said with a yawn. "I was on my way up to bed when you drove in."

He opened the door and stepped outside, speaking through the narrow gap. "I'll not let the flies in. Get some rest. A boot that appears and disappears isn't much to go on, but I'll ask around. And I'll try to corner Abbott and Moffat. I'll be in touch. Call if you remember anything else. I have to run along. I have to lock up the school after the parents' meeting. I can't be late. The boss doesn't like me much. Lovely to have met you."

She watched him spring into his truck and rattle out of the yard. I wish I felt he believed me, she thought. He'd be a great ally. He's so cute. Plus I need to ask him about the arson investigation. She closed the door and turned the lock.

Once in bed drowsiness seeped through her like she had been sedated. She tried to focus on the ceiling as some buried thought nagged at her from deep inside. But nothing surfaced. As she was about to doze off, she remembered: the metal Stetson buckle wouldn't have burned if the boot had indeed been tossed into the stove here at Safe Haven. She could check the ashes in the firebox. If the buckle was there, she could show it to Jackie Cole. He would have to believe her then.

She had better do it now. If she waited until morning, Bertha would have another fire going. And there was still Eppie's teacher who had wanted her to call—no doubt to complain about Eppie's absence. But it was too late to call anyone now. Sara tried to drag herself up out of bed but an incredible lethargy prevented it.

Some time later she woke up. The hypnotic stupor had dissipated somewhat. She swung her legs out of bed. She would go down to the kitchen now. She would find the buckle in the ashes. The bloody boot would have meant more, but the buckle would be better than nothing.

She inched down the stairs and along the dark hall to the kitchen using the wall as a guide. As she entered, a break appeared in the thick cloud and lemony moonlight flowed through several tall, multi-paned windows.

She picked up the cast-iron stove lid, using the wire-wound lifter, and carefully placed the weighty circle beside the open hole. The moonlight wasn't sufficient to light the sooty interior of the firebox. The harsh incandescent overhead lights blinded her at first, but as her eyes slowly adjusted she dug around in the feathery wood ashes and the clinkers from the coal with the curved end of the chromed steel poker. She could now see well enough to be certain that there was no buckle in there. Someone could have taken it out. Who? Or perhaps the boot was never put in this stove at all.

If the guy who wore it was murdered on the property while she slept one night, then someone could be lurking out there now, perhaps even Tony. She hoped he hadn't discovered she was here in Mussel Cove, but he wasn't supposed to have known she was in Halifax either and he had somehow followed her from home in Portland across the Canadian border to the Nova Scotia capital.

She tried the kitchen door ... still locked. The key hung on a nail nearby. She ran to the switch and shut off the lights. She had better return to bed. Perhaps things would look more positive in the morning.

As she moved out of the kitchen, she sensed movement outside the window to her left and glanced in that direction. Her heart leapt into her throat and she fought to control her breathing. Faces. Young faces staring in at her. Children ... Impossible! Such small children wouldn't be lurking about in the dead of the night, would they? One of them seemed to have something in his hand. Was he showing it to her? She couldn't see the object clearly, but the thought entered her mind that it might be the buckle. It could be anything at all.

She strode to the window in time to hear a scurry of running feet, but then could see nothing. She summoned up courage and dashed to the door, unlocking it as quickly as possible, flinging it open and running outside. The frosty air pinched the lining of her nose as she breathed it in. There was nothing to see but the silent landscape as the light of the moon dimly backlit thick, overhead cloud. The children, if there were children, had disappeared. If they had taken the buckle, how had they gotten inside? The door had been locked. And why would they take it? They must have known it was there to begin with ... Sara shivered, returned to the kitchen and relocked the door. She dropped the key into her pocket.

She plugged in the electric kettle. She didn't want to sleep now. Better make a pot of strong coffee.

CHAPTER ELEVEN

11

Irma Stitch was finally asleep. A glass tumbler sat empty on her bedside table. On warm evenings, when sleep seemed far away, the determined elderly teacher pampered herself with warm milk flavored with a few ounces of rum. She loved the way the dark rum frothed and foamed up the sides of the glass as she poured in the steaming milk. She also loved how the scent of the rum reminded her of Ogden.

Her late husband had been haunted by the sins of their impetuous youth; sins committed under the supervision and influence of the Cobans. Irma felt occasional pangs of remorse for what they had done, but had always been able to cope better than had her dear disturbed husband. What is done, is done, she always told herself. While Ogden was living she pitied his mental anguish and abstained from the booze in a futile attempt to keep him sober, certain her small sacrifice would help prolong his life. Irma had dreaded losing her only friend, fearing loneliness above all things. Since Ogden's tragic death, she had added a dollop of rum to most of the drinks she consumed after school hours—just for comfort. Ironically, Ogden didn't die of "the drink," as Irma had expected, but was crushed because a school bus filled with screaming brats had missed a turn. The distracted driver had backed into their driveway in order to get back on course and inadvertently knocked Ogden's 1989 Buick from its jack. The driver didn't notice that the Buick had fallen on Ogden, who worked underneath while his radio blared out country music in the background. Irma found him there hours later, the radio still yodeling away, when she returned from school, her arms overburdened with homework.

The bus driver was fired, of course, even after he tried to blame the incident on the school children. He even claimed one of the children had stepped on the accelerator, causing him to miss his turn. But no one had listened. A few months later he was found dead in his garage where he had apparently done himself in by carbon monoxide poisoning.

Irma's drinking had started small, but had escalated over the years. She had recently taken to buying 151 proof rum along with her regular Old Sam, complaining to the woman at the liquor store checkout that all the lighter-proofed rums were watered down. Ogden made that claim for years, but it was only lately that she had begun to understand how right he had been all along. When she mixed it half-and-half with Old Sam, the 151 proof bit into the throat and the tongue just the way she liked it.

Tonight the indefinable fear had honeycombed her mind so thoroughly that it took several nightcaps to induce a heavily drugged sleep. Earlier, because of feelings she had been having lately that something terrible was about to happen to her, she had called the woman at Safe Haven, whom all the other teachers claimed was a reporter. But the woman hadn't called back as Irma had so hoped.

At eye level all around the compact bungalow, on shelves that she and Ogden had constructed of sweet-smelling local pine, were ranged a multitude of bone china figurines collected over the course of their marriage. She had never told anyone how precious these hand-painted dolls were to her. In her line of work, human-kind seldom approached the ideal she sought, and these wonderful china figurines were, by contrast, perfect. They were everything the children ought to be and weren't. Real children were never this lovely, never this quiet and respectful.

The horrible nightmares had returned. She was used to them. She had survived several thousand nights of fiery demons, monsters with runny eyes and sulphurous breath and razor-sharp claws, bad dreams begun in a childhood she had trouble remembering. Sometimes she was with her parents in a strange room filled with candles, and she was terrified. She recalled the waxy soot of candle smoke and the burn of shame but nothing more. She had managed to block most of it from her conscious mind, something Ogden could never do. Yet, her dream life was completely outside of her control.

Tonight's dream was new and frighteningly real. In her dream she was enjoying a deep and untroubled sleep and was disturbed by small animals creeping around her bed. In the dream she woke up to discover that the animals were, in fact, miniature monsters with ridiculous faces. One looked like Saddam Hussein, another two like Osama Bin Laden and George Bush, and there were several cartoon characters she had seen on television. Then she realized that these were masks, only masks. The dream was going completely out of control.

Then she began to feel pressure on her ankles and wrists. The monsters were tying ropes to her extremities and binding her to the brass bed. She tried to struggle but there were too many. At least a dozen of the little demons pulled at the ropes and tied her tightly and painfully to the bedposts, laughing merrily at her helpless screams as she thrashed about on the metal bed.

When the terrible truth broke through the alcoholic haze, she became suddenly and nauseatingly sober. This was not a dream. THIS WAS NOT A DREAM! She watched as several of the beasts climbed up on her bed and one after another peed on her. They had the bodies of children, little boys and girls. Although she'd never had children of her own, she knew all there was to know about the little monsters. She wrenched from side to side, fighting the ropes that bound her as the warm urine drenched her legs and belly and worked its way up to her flopping breasts, soaking finally into her face and hair. The acid vapors of their piss assailed her nostrils and she began to whimper, unable to control the bilious substances that rose in her and flowed from her mouth in continuous spasms, saturating the front of her nightdress. She threw her head from side to side in an attempt to clear her throat of the lumpy filth. She wouldn't allow herself to choke on her own vomit.

As she struggled with renewed vigor against her bonds, she gradually became aware of another smell. Into her consciousness crept images of their '59 Studebaker parked in front of the Mussel Cove Texaco while Ogden filled the tank.

Gasoline! That's what she smelled. Her fear now rose to new heights. Her heart wouldn't stand much more of this torture. One monster spilled gas from a red metal container, tossing it here and there around the room. The brat wore a Bart Simpson mask and laughed hysterically as he splashed the liquid onto the bedroom carpet. He hopped effortlessly onto the bed and poured more of the fuel over the bed and across her body. She remembered the boy by his mask. He was one of the ones who pissed on her face. She recalled the insolent way he had aimed directly at her. Now her mind exploded in horror as she realized that her life had been reduced to its last horrible moments.

A searing pain began in her left arm and moved upward to the center of her chest. She could feel her heart bursting. Her last memory was a crushing pain in her chest as she watched her precious china figurines smashed one by one against the satin wallpaper. "My children, my children," she tried to scream. Then, mercifully, everything cut to blackness.

CHAPTER TWELVE

12

When the pager jolted Philip awake, he missed what Stella said about the location of the fire—the chief's wife talked way too fast. The moderately intoxicated volunteer firefighter swayed awkwardly to the window. Then, as the world stopped spinning, he glanced outside. Because Aunt Bertha's house perched like an awkward wooden bird on the side of a gravelly hill, the discarded baggage of a retreating glacier, his bedroom overlooked much of Mussel Cove from outside looking east. Once in a while, if the night was dark enough and the fire serious, he could locate it without the embarrassment of calling Stella back. Tonight, it was a cinch.

What had the beeper said? Oh yes. Now the jumble of half-remembered sounds came unscrambled. "Stitch house on River Road." He remembered hearing something like "which mouse on river rowed." Then came the rhyme from school days, "Old Mrs. Stitch, the filthy old witch." He repeated the words aloud as he hurried into his clothes, realizing, though, that with the intensity of the flames he had just witnessed, there was no real need for haste. There would be little remaining of the bungalow by the time he arrived on the scene.

He snatched his boots from under the bed and tiptoed rapidly down the stairs; it was better not to wake Aunt Bertha. He passed her room, door ajar as usual. He had tried to teach her to keep it shut in case of fire but to her a closed room was just too claustro-phobic. He glanced inside and saw she was sleeping soundly. She rolled over as he passed but didn't wake. She was accustomed to his night travels.

The digital clock in his Jimmy read 4:25. The radio was kept permanently tuned to a rock-and-roll station in Sydney. He sang along with Sting as he arrived at the fire station. If someone later had asked him which song he sang, he couldn't have answered. Two trucks had left already, so he jumped into the cab of the one remaining pumper.

Several other firefighters finished scrambling into their gear as they hustled aboard. The truck accelerated rapidly from the station house and along the highway, taking the first left, down into the so-called "new" part of Mussel Cove.

The Stitches had been the only long-term residents of the cove who chose to buy a house in the subdivision of bungalows usually reserved for come-from-aways and occupied for the most part by public sector employees—teachers and nurses, social workers and technicians.

Since most residents of the subdivision would be asleep, Philip tried to limit the use of the siren. It was so painfully loud. He wouldn't engage it unless he spotted something in his path that might slow him down. Thankfully, nothing materialized.

As he had expected, the Stitch house was a mess by the time they pulled up in front. It had the look and feel of death. If that teacher were inside, she wouldn't need cremation. The house was gutted. He remembered when it was being built. He and a friend from school played tag between the parallel studs in the unfinished interior walls. He recalled having a pocket full of nails when his mother took them for pizza and fries to Myrna's Restaurant later that day.

Even after all these years Philip had difficulty dealing with memories of his mother and the accident that killed her. The car had hit a guardrail and gone up and over, tumbling end over end into the Bras D'Or Lakes. He could still see his mother's face in the coffin at Buell's Funeral Home. She was pretty, he recalled, and serious-looking, like she might wake up and tell him to get at his homework.

Aunt Bertha was at his grandmother's house taking care of the old woman when word came to them of the accident. First he had run to his grandmother's arms but she was too frail to hold him. He had then been gathered in Aunt Bertha's palatial lap where he cried on her shoulder for what seemed like hours and hours.

His mind returned to the present. He hopped down from the truck. Leon MacKinnon looked weary from wrestling the heavy fire hose. "Another bad one," Philip muttered, part question, part statement.

"Bad enough," Leon agreed.

Jackie Cole, the cop, materialized out of the darkness. "You guys smell anything?"

Philip sniffed. "Gasoline," he said.

"Right. The stink's not as obvious as it was. There's no doubt about this one. The Fire Marshall ought to be making a public statement before long. It's ridiculous that nothing's been said. You'd think someone'd put the lid on."

"Anywhere else they'd be protecting the tourist trade, but Mussel Cove doesn't have many tourists. Why would anyone want to kill old Stitch?"

"Who didn't want to kill her at one time or another? I've considered it myself," said Cole. "Don't tell me it never crossed your mind. It's just that seeing it now, the real thing, makes me sick to my stomach. Someone out there is in love with death. Death and flames."

"The old witch is inside for sure?"

"For sure. It looks like she was tied to her bed, arms and legs spread wide. It's still too hot to get close, but she's in there and it looks mighty suspicious. Scratch that: I'll eat my hat if it's not murder. We could make out what's left of her quite clearly with the spotlight."

"Clues?" said Philip.

"The smell of gas, of course. The door to the garden shed was open wide and the burned-out metal fuel can was just inside the back door of the house. The likelihood she was almost certainly tied down, for another. The only other thing we found was a Halloween mask. Half-burnt."

"A Halloween mask?"

"On the ground near the door," said Cole.

"Oh. What do you figure that means?"

"I got an anonymous letter a week or so ago. I was talking to your Bertha in the school office recently. She said the woman reporter from Halifax told her someone had sent a similar letter to her newspaper. My letter spoke about kids roaming around wearing Halloween masks."

"Where is the mask?" asked Philip.

"The fire chief tossed it into the rescue truck. We were too busy to study it at the time. I'll send it along to the forensic lab in Halifax if the village budget can handle it."

"Could it have been there since Halloween?"

"No siree. The elastic was broken. Other than that, and the burns, it was clean as a whistle. If it had been there since Halloween, it would have been moldy and crawling with grubs. No, someone was wearing that mask in the last few hours. They could even have been here when the place was torched. Likely they lit it," said Cole.

"Weird, eh?"

"Damn right it's weird. But it's a weird community, isn't it Phil?"

Philip bristled, but before he could answer, a red Honda pulled up beside the pumper and Sara stepped out. Someone else remained seated in the car. Another car drove up and slowed at the curb and after a brief glance at the Honda and the group in the driveway, hastened away.

"Excuse me, Ma'am," Jackie Cole called out, stepping past Philip and holding up his hand, palm turned to Sara's face. Instinctively she stepped back. "I'm going to have to ask you not to come too close. It's not entirely safe here and I'm afraid there's a fatality inside."

"Oh dear," Sara said and turned to Philip. "Eppie woke me up. She's in the car. She was sleeping with me."

"Lucky kid," Cole muttered, with a grin.

Sara acted like she hadn't heard him and turned back to Philip.

"I felt her stirring in the dark and when I opened my eyes I saw the reflection of flames dancing on my bedroom window. I jumped up, afraid at first that the fire was at our place. It was so bizarre because I had been dreaming about fire. It was so real I could even smell burnt wood."

"You must have gotten quite a fright," said Philip, drawing her away from Cole toward the shell of the burnt-out house. "You're Sara, aren't you? Bertha is my sort-of-aunt. She brought me up."

"Then you must be Philip, the pharmacist she brags about. Eppie wanted to go see the fire. She kept repeating, 'I want to see what it looks like now, I want to see what it looks like now.' I told her how late it was and that she could see it tomorrow but she kept saying that she wanted to see what it looked like now before the fire was all gone. I didn't know what to do. I found her request strange considering what happened to her family. But maybe that was the attraction. I'll never understand how a child's mind works." She glanced back at Cole who had taken a step closer. She started toward the house.

As she approached, its rank pungency caused her to sneeze. Both men followed. A mixture of smoke and steam rose from the charred ruins. She turned toward the window. Cole hurried past Philip and caught her by the arm. His grip was firm but gentle.

"Please don't," he said, his voice quiet and concerned, but Sara looked anyway.

"My God!" she said. "Jesus!" She paused, finding herself in his comforting embrace. For a moment the only sounds were soft wind and the occasional crackle of the cooling embers. Then, slightly embarrassed, she pulled away and spoke again, "She phoned me, you know. She told Bertha she had something to tell me. I wish I had returned her call. Perhaps this wouldn't have happened."

"Good Lord!" She shook her head and moved away from

Cole toward Philip, "tell me this wasn't done on purpose." Philip shrugged helplessly. She didn't wait for an answer.

"I must get back to Eppie." She turned away, brushing up against Jackie Cole in the narrow opening between the house and the truck. He had moved soundlessly up beside them. He smelled of smoke and clean sweat. "Excuse me," she said, slipping past, her heart pounding.

Philip followed her. "This was likely arson." He told her about the gasoline smell and the Halloween mask. When their eyes met he looked away.

She hesitated a moment before speaking. "Look, how long are you planning to hang around here tonight? Why don't you and Bertha come for breakfast? You're already up and about."

At that moment an elderly man in black appeared at the end of the driveway and stopped. He wore a Roman collar. "Is he a priest?" Sara whispered. For the first time she noted Philip's boozy breath.

"Yes ... Father Doyle," Philip answered quietly. "He walks the streets at all hours. He told me he never sleeps." Then Philip cleared his throat nervously and looked at his watch, which had a luminous dial. "I'll be out of here in an hour or so. One of the boys will relieve me. Even when the fire is out, we can't leave the place until things cool enough for the Bells—our undertakers—to pick up Stitch's remains."

"So you're coming over? ... If the gate is locked, ring the bell."

He nodded as she told him, "I really ought to get going."

She opened the car door and peered inside. "You still awake, Eppie? You know Philip, don't you?"

Eppie eyed him coldly without answering. The firefighter reeked of sour smoke and booze. Eppie liked the smell of smoke but not the alcohol. She hated what booze had done to her family. She turned her head to smell the shoulder of her blouse. It, too, bore the sharp smell of burning. But now she was tired and her head ached.

Sara watched Philip walk back toward the house then turned the key. Someone knocked firmly on the passenger window. At first she thought Eppie had knocked but the child was staring at something outside. She looked frightened. Jackie Cole's smiling face moved close to the glass. Sara felt the color rush into her face again as she pressed the armrest window control button and the glass dropped an inch or two.

"Can you give me a lift?" asked the policeman. "You go right past my place."

Sara looked at Eppie who had moved as far back from the side window as possible.

"I guess so. I have something to tell you anyway."

She unlocked the doors and Cole slipped into the back seat. Eppie glared at him. Sara told him about the search for the buckle and about the children who'd been outside her house. He said nothing.

"Still don't believe me?"

"I can believe whatever I want but what I need is evidence. Besides, if I had that boot or even the buckle, what would I do with it? Forensics could tell me I had a boot with human blood on it but without a body I can't use DNA to confirm whose blood it was, let alone how the blood got on the boot. Anyway, what possible motive could there be for murder? We've had murders here, but these have been by an arsonist. How would a murder on this property tie in with the fires?"

"You're the policeman. Someone must know what's going on. What about that old priest? There must be someone you suspect."

"Lots. If the fires and now a murder have some connection to Safe Haven, everyone is a suspect. Father Doyle is out all night, an insomniac. He's been in Mussel Cove on and off forever. I expect he's aware of much more than he'll ever tell. Ed, who owns the drugstore where Philip works, has a long history in the drug business. His father supplied the old orphanage. Everyone in the village has a family connection to Safe Haven. I assume you know about the orphanage?"

"I know a little."

"And then there's those kids who were roaming around your house the other night. That doesn't surprise me one bit. I've come across them late at night, packs of them. It used to give me the creeps although I've never caught them doing anything against the law. I used to drive a few of them home when I caught them out too late, but there were too many to deal with and I eventually gave it up. I phoned a few parents after that, but they denied that their kids were causing trouble. A few of them even told me their kids hadn't been outside the house. I insisted that I saw them, talked to them, but the parents just shut me out.

"One of the brats is the Baptist Minister's son, Ira, Ira Black. 'Bad News Black', they should have named him." He looked at Eppie, who scowled at him. He put his pointer finger on her nose and wiggled it as he spoke directly into her face. "I truly believe that if I put that kid away for a while things would improve around here." He removed his finger and sat back, joining his hands behind his head. Sara watched his shadowy movements in the rearview mirror. "But I can't do it, so I can't prove that either.

"You know what those brats told me they were doing at two in the morning?"

"No, what?"

"They said they were looking for night crawlers."

"What?"

"Night crawlers. Some people call them dew worms. They're slippery and they come out at night. They're used as bait for trout fishing. So that's what I call them now."

"Who?"

"The kids. I call the brats night crawlers. They're out fishing for something, but I don't know what that something is yet. But I'll find out. Maybe they do drugs, for example, though they seem awfully young.

"By the way ... what's his name? ..." He took off his ball cap and scratched his head. "Oh yeah, Jake Abbott. He and his friend Carney Moffat ... all that business about the boot. I've been looking around for them and that pickup truck. I can't find even a smell of them. Neither of them have family connections here any longer.

I reported the truck stolen to see if anything came up. So far nothing." He yawned and stretched. "Here's my place now."

They stopped beside a tiny, white clapboard house a few hundred meters from the bridge. "We're practically neighbors," said Sara.

"From two different worlds," said Cole. "Thanks for the lift, though. I'll see you around."

After Cole stepped out, Eppie moved back against the passenger door.

"I hate him," Eppie hissed. As they drove away the child relaxed and yawned. Sara thought of how comfortably Cole had sat in the back seat. There was something about him she liked. She didn't know what. She had made so many bad decisions about men already and no longer trusted her judgement. Eppie gave her an angry look as if she knew what she was thinking.

CHAPTER THIRTEEN

13

A local public service message interrupted Debussy's *La Mer* on CBC Radio to announce that, due to the tragic death of a teacher, Mrs. Phoebe Stitch, Mussel Cove Elementary School would be closed for the day. Sara had been glad, although she realized she would now get little done on her research and writing assignment with Eppie at home. But it would give the child a chance to catch up on her sleep. After a night of chasing fire engines, Eppie probably would have been too tired to attend school anyway.

The bell at Safe Haven's front gate rang moments after the small girl settled into her big bed. That would be Philip arriving for breakfast. Sara had tossed their smoky clothing into the washing machine and taken a quick bath. Then she had buttoned up the front of the smart summer dress she'd bought on the way out of Halifax. She had spent an hour shopping, watching constantly to be sure no one was following her. The dress was a faded blue cotton, cut low in front, and short. It might be a bit too sexy, showing too much breast and legs, but she had been in a hurry. She wondered if Philip would even notice. She realized she didn't really care, her mind was on someone else.

The firefighter had dropped his gear at the station and had showered. His face no longer bore the streaks of soot she had seen earlier. But the biting odor of smoke still oozed from him like garlic. He was startlingly attractive by daylight, with dark brown eyes that were almost pretty. He wore a clean, freshly ironed white dress shirt and blue jeans with a wide leather belt and a western buckle shaped like a cowboy hat. A bit too country for her taste, but still a hunk. "A hunk a hunk of burning love," she sang to herself. His buckle, however, looked a bit too much like the Stetson decoration on the missing boot.

For some reason, Philip had terrible self-confidence. He asked to use the phone to call his Aunt Bertha, apologizing over and over to the woman for missing the breakfast she had planned for him. From overhearing only this end of the conversation, it sounded like Bertha was annoyed at first but quickly got over it as Philip explained how "the American girl" had invited both of them for breakfast at Safe Haven.

Philip hung up and insisted on helping. He was no cook. Nonetheless she had fun. He seemed to enjoy his mistakes and learned quickly. He was smart and a good listener, if a bit too apologetic. Time passed easily and pleasantly.

By the time Bertha arrived they were ready. Philip met her at the door. He took Bertha's cape and together they escorted her to the big table. She giggled in embarrassment and delight, teasing them as they stuffed her full of French toast and sausage. She refused the tea, asking instead for a cup of hot water.

"I've been a bit fidgety," she explained. "I was wondering if it was the caffeine."

When Sara started to clear the dishes, Bertha would have none of it.

"Feeding me is one thing but you'll not take the dishes away from me. Besides, this here is a big kitchen and if you fellas put everything away I'd likely waste a lot of time finding things the next time I need them." She tied her apron in a half-bow with the fingers of her one good hand, and as Sara stared in amazement at the agility of her fingers, she frowned and waddled to the sink.

"You'd best be heading off to work, Philip," she said curtly. "By the time you get into town it will be 9 o'clock. Eddie Harding likes you well enough, but you know he won't be pleased if his druggist arrives late."

"How does someone get to be both a pharmacist and a fire-fighter?" Sara asked.

"Most fire departments outside of cities are purely voluntary.

So I volunteered. It's quite an honor, you know. I didn't expect to be accepted. There's a natural suspicion of university-educated people in small towns and villages.

"Anyway, when I'm down at the station I'm careful not to flaunt my education. I enjoy their conversation, guy-talk mostly. It's quite interesting. I had a very protected childhood. Aunt Bertha kept a pretty close eye on me until I left for university, making sure she knew where I was and who I was with at all times. But the fire department has helped make up for my missed education around 'the guys.' There's a lot of bragging and lies about women, you know the sort of stuff I mean. Pretty stupid, I guess, but at least it's a change from my usual conversations." He gestured toward Bertha's back where she stood at the sink.

Bertha chuckled. "Gives me a break from all his chatter," she said, "thank goodness."

Philip laughed and picked his jacket from the back of the chair where he'd been sitting. "I'd better get going. Thanks, Sara."

She frowned and nodded before pushing her chair under the table and following Philip to the front door. "Some day I'd really like to hear what those firefighters have been saying about the fires."

"Not much to tell," he said, opening the door. They moved out slowly. "If anything, the guys say less these days than they ever did. It's like they're afraid that whoever is behind it will turn on them. They have homes and families, too. I expect you've heard about the kids who have been wandering around after dark?"

"Yes, there was a letter. There's nothing unusual about kids roaming around late at night. It happens everywhere."

"I know that. But we're not talking about teenagers, you know," he said, lowering his voice. "Some of these kids are pretty young. The point is that when some of the guys started talking about the kids, things got real quiet. There were funny looks all around. I tried to bring the subject up again later and everyone just walked away from the bar and went downstairs. They spent the rest of the night polishing engines and fretting about the Blue Jays. You know about the Blue Jays?"

"Of course. I'm a Red Sox fan. We're number one."

"This year." He paused and looked down toward the Atlantic. "Something strange is going on around here. It's definitely arson and I do believe the kids are somehow involved. I don't know why the cops aren't more on top of it." He turned and put one foot on the bottom of the step, leaning across his knee. He looked up at her.

"Have you explored this place? It has an interesting history. If you want background information for the story you should ask Aunt Bertha to tell you about this house."

"Why?" Sara said. "What should I ask her?"

"She knows what it was like for an orphan in this place. You should visit the old priest at St. Dunstan's. You saw him last night at the fire. He hasn't missed a fire for years. People say he's crazy like a fox. But maybe he knows way more than people might think. And talk to Marcel Vertu."

"I met him."

"The priest?"

"No, Marcel. I saw him the day after the fire at his apartment—the one attached to the restaurant.

"I heard you were in there for quite a spell."

She creased her brow.

"It's a small village. People talk." He was blushing. He turned away. "I'm not snooping on you if that's what you think. It wasn't much of a fire at Marcel's. He put it out before the first truck got there. They didn't even call me in for that one."

"I see. So how did you know about the fire?"

"I heard them on my pager."

"Oh ... Well yes, I was in to talk to Marcel. He seems like a nice guy. Quirky. Unfortunately, I didn't learn much that will be of any use to my story."

"Too bad. Maybe you didn't ask the right questions."

"Maybe. He did warn me to be careful ... So you figure he might know what's going on around here."

"Maybe not so much what's going on now, maybe nothing. But Aunt Bertha claims he knows more about Mussel Cove than anyone." He hesitated. "Another thing. I've seen those kids in the middle of the night, but I've never seen them do anything wrong." He looked up the steps toward Sara, his mind far away. He was thinking about all those nights walking the streets, half-drunk. At the top of the steps, Sara flattened the front of her skirt. Philip realized that she probably thought he had been looking up her skirt. He had caught a fleeting glimpse of beige panties, but it was an accident. Yet he couldn't come out and say that. Guiltily he turned away and blushed, all the while filing the image of the thighs and panties away in his memory. She stepped down closer to him as Bertha appeared in the doorway.

"Are you still here, Philip?" the older woman said with a grin, noticing Philip's red cheeks. "Get yourself over to the drugstore, for heaven's sakes, and don't be wearing out your welcome. Let the young lady tend to her affairs."

"All right, Aunt Bertie. So long, Sara. Thanks again."

Sara watched until the firefighter disappeared behind the trees. She closed the door and strolled to the kitchen. Bertha was wiping the counter.

"I'm going upstairs should anyone call. I've been thinking about Safe Haven and its past. Maybe we could talk about it sometime. But I thought I'd look around the old house. I likely won't find anything pertinent to the story but it might make interesting background. Do you suppose anyone would mind if I explored a bit?"

"I don't see the harm. Are you looking for anything in particular? You won't find nothing new. Why, we've looked in so many nooks and crannies of this house, me and Marcel and a whole bunch of others, that we've worn tracks in the hardwood. We never found a thing that was the least bit useful. Marcel didn't miss a trick. He looked everywhere, poking around in places where you couldn't hide a deck of cards."

"What was he looking for?"

"I couldn't say for certain. For me it was clues to the past, things that would explain all the stuff that makes no sense to me." She paused to rub her artificial hand as if it were aching, as if to soothe it. Then her good hand shifted over to the wash cloth, kneading it absent-mindedly as if she were shaping a small loaf of bread. "Most of what I remember about this place is foggy-like. I was real young then. I've told a bit to Philip, but not the horrible things. I'm not even sure if they're things that happened or just nightmares I've had since them times."

"What did you tell him?"

"I told him I used to have a twin sister. That's definitely true and not a dream. I can't remember her face. In the dreams she never has a face. Isn't that terrible? But Marcel says he remembers her. He says she was comely. Says that my childhood was a real nightmare and that's why I can't remember much. I won't allow myself." She brushed a few crumbs from the table with the bunched-up cloth, catching them in her plastic hand.

"After the owners—the Cobans—left town and deserted Safe Haven, some local people moved in to care for the few kids who still lived there. Over the next few weeks all the kids but Marcel and I were put in foster care. The others still weren't home, but at least they were living with a normal family. He and I escaped to the woods for a while and then moved back into the house. The bank foreclosed and put the residence and property up for bankruptcy sale. The new owner, whose son owns the place now, found us here. My hand was long gone by then, Marcel says. My memory of those days is sparse. But I recall that the new owners were kind to me and arranged for a decent home for me and paid for my first prosthesis." She held up her plastic hand with its dusting of crumbs.

"Ugly, isn't it? But it's better than the first and I have no reason to get a prettier one now. When I started school all the children either treated me bad or avoided me altogether. I liked the ones who treated me bad better than the others. At least they didn't pretend I wasn't there. I used to cry myself to sleep at night but it didn't matter after a while. Marcel was smart and eventually went away to finish his studies. He got to see a lot of the world but I wasn't much good in school so I stayed around here." She rose and returned to the sink. "This is the only place where I belong.

"When I was old enough, people who felt sorry for me hired me to clean their houses and cook for them. I found that if I worked hard no one cared about my hand. I never had a fella—likely also because of the hand— but that was all right because I don't think I wanted anyone." She chuckled. "I can hardly remember now.

"Things have a funny way of working out. You can't imagine how surprised I was the day Philip's grandmother asked me if I would look after her grandson. The boy had lost his parents and was alone. I could raise him like a son. She would help me out financially when she could—although she was almost broke by then. Suddenly my life changed. I didn't see how I could do it. I didn't think I was fit to be someone's mother. But something told me to try it, and I did.

"There wasn't much money and finally the old lady died and left nothing but bills. I got some help from the welfare for awhile." She rinsed her cloth, wrung it out with her good hand and draped it over the spout of the sink. Returning to her chair, she sat, wiped that hand across her skirt, then dabbed at some soap suds on the artificial hand with the corner of her apron.

"We came out of this orphanage with nothing but our names. Most records had gone with the owners. But the people around here knew what had been going on. Marcel remembers a whole lot more than me. The couple who ran the orphanage brought in girls from all over and their babies were sold like livestock to the highest bidders, usually families down in The States or up in Ontario. People who couldn't or wouldn't have babies of their own." Bertha's voice dropped to a whisper.

"Now that part isn't so bad. At least the babies were getting decent homes and people were getting the babies they wanted. But there were weird things going on. Marcel told this to me and I believe it's true because it's so like my dreams. My dead sister is part of my dreams, too. She talks to me sometimes. I can't ever see what her face looks like in the dream and yet her eyes glare at me from that dark hole where her face should be and I wake up cold and alone and I can't ever get back to sleep."

Sara's skin turned cold as polished granite. "What does she say to you?"

"She warns me. She says everything will soon be over. Something is coming that will change Mussel Cove. Vengeance is coming. The Angel of Retribution is sharpening his sword. When she told me, I could feel her pain. I've felt it before but I don't remember when. After she goes I feel desperate and afraid, like I did something terrible I can't remember."

"Did your sister look like you?"

Bertha didn't answer right away. It was as if she had entered one of those disjointed dreams.

"Just her hand," she finally answered in a cramped whisper. "She lost a hand just like me. Otherwise nothing is the same. Marcel says I was fat. My sister was petite and lovely. Yet I was the lucky one. Beauty attracts the demons. I was just as beautiful and innocent on the inside, but my outside mostly kept the evil away. But not always." She lifted her artificial hand in front of Sara's face. Sara fought the urge to look away.

"Tell me about it," she said.

"My childhood is gone except for what Marcel told me. And there are those terrible dreams."

"Can you remember any of them? What do you dream about?"

"I suppose it won't hurt to tell you. As long as you don't tell anyone or write about them."

"I won't do anything without your permission."

"Okay. Well ... in one dream my sister and I are lying on a table. It looks like that altar up in your room—that table gives me the creeps—with people all around like in a church. They're singing songs that are ugly and pretty at the same time. Candles flicker and shadows dance across the ceiling. Somebody comes into the room. He's tall and handsome, with a beautiful, half-dressed woman beside him who calls the people to gather in a circle. Now I notice the people are naked and kissing and touching and they touch us. The tall man takes a big knife with a curved blade and cuts off my sister's hand. He picks it up, dripping blood, and holds it out in front of him. The people cheer, drowning out my sister's screams. The man bends down and kisses her on the mouth until she's silent. The woman with him starts kissing me and I can't stop her. I'm strapped to the table and she has my hair in her fist. The dream stops there and I never dream about them cutting off my hand. Marcel says it happened the same night but he wasn't actually there. That's one dream. There are lots of others."

"Oh my god. Were the monsters who ran this place ever punished?"

"They died long ago. May they rot in Hell." Bertha fell silent.

"What about the other people?"

"Other people?"

"There were all those others who took part and watched."

"I don't know. Remember it's only a dream. Or at least that's how I see it. I don't know who any of these people are, or if there were actual people there, or if that is what really happened. What Marcel tells me goes in one ear and out the other. I can't, or don't want to, remember. Lord, but that man can talk. Marcel tells me the dreams are real and that most of the people in them or their descendents still live around here. If so, I don't know how they could have known about Safe Haven and not helped us." She began to whimper and break down.

Sara felt a rush of sympathy. She could hardly believe all the suffering implied by the stories. She stepped forward and put her arms around Bertha. The woman pulled violently away.

"Don't! Please," she pleaded; folding her arms tightly across her chest she leaned, alone, against the wall.

"I'm so sorry," said Sara. "You were so sweet with Eppie when she first came here. You held her when she needed a hug. I was only ... "

"I know you meant well. It's not that I don't want your affection. It's just a horrible feeling I get when an adult touches me. I can hold a child, although it took me a while to get comfort from it. Raising Philip taught me that. Kids don't threaten me, I guess.

I trust them. But Eppie won't let me near her. That hurts my feelings so I can imagine how you must feel now. Maybe I'll get over it someday, but probably not. I'm not getting any younger.

"I think I'll head for home. I've said too many painful things. The dishes are done and put away. I got them done while you and Philip were jawing at the doorstep. I'm sorry I can't look after Eppie for a while. I have some paperwork I have to do for the school and a few things to take care of around home. Good luck with your looking around."

CHAPTER FOURTEEN

14

How different this house must have been when filled with children's voices, Sara thought as she climbed the stairs. She looked in on Eppie—head propped on a plump pillow, facing away from the rain-streaked windows. In sleep, the child looked angelic. Sara closed the door softly and decided to begin her search at the top.

The third-floor landing was a large rectangle, accessible through a decorated cast-iron gate in an oak railing that surrounded the stair opening. There were several pieces of heavy Victorian furniture, including worn velour settees and embroidered armchairs. Beside them sat lamp tables and in front a few low tables covered in bric-a-brac. Around the perimeter, Sara counted eight doors, five of which opened into what must have once been dormitories of various sizes. Each room had a series of shelves spaced approximately a bed-width apart, and below each, slightly off to the side, a small bedside table with shelves. Each table was equipped with a small King James Version of the New Testament. Each of the dorms had a large bathroom with several individual stalls. Along one wall sat a series of cast-iron bathtubs with no provision for privacy. Sara thought about how hateful that would have been for a shy child like herself. The sixth door opened on a large, lavishly furnished bedroom containing a huge canopied bed, which appeared, oddly, to have recently been occupied by someone. On the walls hung paintings draped with black cotton cloth, for preservation. On the way out of the room, Sara raised one cloth and discovered an oil painting of satyrs fleeing sword-wielding angels. What's with these creepy paintings? Could they have been here since Safe Haven days? These are bizarre decorations for an orphanage, she thought, frowning.

The seventh door led into a large linen closet. She wasn't surprised that the final door was the one she sought.

This door was solid and swollen from summer humidity. Or had a leak in the old roof been the source of the moisture? She gathered all her strength and the stubborn door opened with a shriek. Above her head she heard a shuffling scurry. She wasn't overly afraid of rodents, if that's what they were. She simply didn't enjoy the way they darted about.

She stood absolutely still and waited. A minute or two should do. Was Eppie still asleep? Sara gazed long and hard up the stairs into the near darkness. After a few moments, perhaps a minute or two, she stepped up onto the first tread. It was so dusty, a claustrophobic nightmare, barely three feet wide, and spanned by massive cobwebs. She fumbled for the light-switch and found none. As her eyes adjusted to the dim light, she slowly crept toward the top, noting heavy rafters overhead. Halfway up she set her teeth and dashed the rest of the way, slashing frantically at spider webs and the brittle bodies of dead flies attaching themselves to her face and the fabric of her good cotton dress.

Once her breathing and heart rate returned to normal she began to appreciate the immensity of this unfinished space above the dorms on the third floor. Whatever had scurried here moments ago was gone. From floor level on her left and right, the roof sloped to a peak. All around sat discarded wooden cribs and changing tables, playpens, even a couple of rocking horses with grotesque faces, and other toys, layered in thick gray dust. Bertha and Marcel may have played with these very items when they lived here as kids.

Deep dust that showed signs of considerable foot traffic covered the floor, and empty junk food bags and wrappers were everywhere, much like those she had found on the paths near the sea. All of this gave her the creeps. Who had been up here and when? To her left was a tall candle holder that reminded her of the pair she had seen at either end of Marcel's table and whose decoration resembled the grotesque faces on the altar-piece in her bedroom two floors below.

Her main reaction was disappointment. She had been expecting the sort of thing found in most grandparents' lofts. In her mind had been photo albums and bundles of old letters tied in ribbons that would paint a picture of old times. This was not someone's house. It was a business, an orphanage. But there were also no record books, no files, and no jewelry. There was nothing that gave any evidence of the lives that had once been lived in this building.

There was one small steamer trunk, empty except for a few waxy red sticks. She didn't know what they were, although her first reaction had been that it was dynamite. But it couldn't be dynamite. As she closed the lid she wondered why this trunk was not layered in dust like everything else in here. Odd. She should give Jackie Cole a call and have him take a look at the sticks, though she wasn't sure he'd know any more than she did. But having a cop around, especially a cute one, was a comforting thought indeed.

Off in one corner Sara discovered another small cardboard box devoid of dust. This one contained small electric motors like the one mounted on her family's boat trailer to winch the ski boat up out of the lake. Beside this box was the remains of a large coil of electrical wire and a box of electrician's solder. Someone must have been doing recent repairs to the old building.

She walked along cautiously, checking every square inch of the large attic. Nervously, she peered around and behind furnishings and other objects, moving them aside as she went, not wanting to overlook anything that might hide the tiniest clue, all the while half-expecting to uncover a darting mouse or a squirrel that would make her heart leap into her mouth. In another corner, well covered in thick, gray dust sat a large pile of empty wooden boxes about thirteen by sixteen inches with wooden lids. Next to them were a few larger unmarked wooden crates. On the sides of the smaller boxes were printed the words, "Clover Meadow Creamery." These boxes had probably held the blocks of butter that Bertha and Marcel and all their housemates spread across their bread every day. The butter boxes were made of good-quality hardwood. Sara wondered what secondary use the empty boxes had been put to by the obviously frugal managers of the home. Otherwise there was nothing that provided a single clue. Bertha had warned her to expect nothing, but she had still hoped. She brushed at her clothing one more time, hating how the dust felt on her hands.

As Sara left the dark attic by the stairs and re-entered the brightness of the upper-floor landing, she was momentarily blinded. She stepped out into the hallway, and was startled that she was not alone. Eppie jumped, too, pupils dilated, eyes wild with fright.

"I had a scary dream," the young girl said. "They were trying to hurt you. I made them go away. They listened to me because they were afraid of me. It's all right now. She promised me it would be all right."

Sara felt suddenly overwhelmed with fear. "Who promised?"

"She did. The girl in my dreams ... Today she came to me in my daydream and said it was going to be all right. Some people are going to get hurt real bad but you and I are safe." Eppie paused. "Can we go down to the ocean today and over to the island?"

"It's raining. We ought to wait for a decent day."

"It's not raining," Eppie said. "It stopped while you were up there." She pointed up the stairs as Sara closed the door. "It's perfect now. Can we, please?"

Sara looked at her watch. "It's after 10 o'clock. All right, we'll get you cleaned up and dressed. You'll want a bite of breakfast. Then we'll pack up a lunch and go down for another look at the beach. Let's make good use of this 'perfect' day of yours. Tomorrow you'll be back to school. We'll make hay while the sun shines." She forced herself to be cheerful for the child's sake, ruffed up Eppie's hair, and together they skipped down the stairs with smiles just a bit too wide.

CHAPTER FIFTEEN

15

"He was in the middle aisle puffing on a cigarette. I asked him to please put it out and he ignored me." Shirley Black's face glowed red with suppressed anger. There were signs that she had once been quite pretty. But now Shirley looked tired and under great stress. She stood about five feet tall and retained her excellent, shapely figure, although she had grown a bit heavy in the hips and thighs as she approached middle age. Her hair was thick and red, her complexion freckled, her face prone to a moist redness when she was agitated, which was often. Stanley placed a hand on her right shoulder and hoped his calm demeanor would relax his aggrieved wife. When he touched her he felt a vestige of the excitement he had felt in her arms last night. But he knew she was out of reach in this present moment.

"Ira defied you? Obviously something is troubling the lad. Where did he get to, Hon?" Stanley was tall and gaunt, his hair dark and well-oiled, balding at the front. He dressed as clergy used to dress several decades ago: formally. No one had ever seen him in jeans or a T-shirt because he had not owned either since he was a child in his parents' house.

"I don't know. I expect he's still in there. It breaks my heart seeing him desecrate his body with those filthy cigarettes. After I asked him, I begged and pleaded. When that didn't work I ordered him to stop. He looked at me like I was a speck of manure or a blackfly that was bothering him. You can imagine how humiliated I felt, and not because he's my stepson. You know that's true, don't you? I have always done my best—and still he resents me."

Reverend Black sighed as he put on the jacket of his black suit
and headed out for the church. He actually hoped Ira had run off.
Why must that wayward boy undergo yet another confrontation
with Shirley? It would be better to deal with this when the anger
had passed. Stanley knew about making allowances, allowing time
for thought and repentance. It almost always worked. Be patient
and allow time for healing.

Ira was contrary enough, but still a mere boy. Shirley had been
raised up in a family of girls and knew nothing about boys. She
wanted hard and fast rules for every eventuality, and was always
inventing fresh dogma: rules that were guaranteed to drive young
Ira wild. Shirley was much better at devising rules than enforcing
them. Stanley ended up Grand Inquisitor for a regime with which
he seldom agreed. He was getting tired of speeches about love
and understanding when she found it much easier to criticize and
belittle. His was a privileged perspective to understand the frustra-
tions that drove his son to act out.

Stanley Black firmly believed that "boys will be boys." This fit
well with all of his religious training and with all that he had read,
which was mostly the Bible and selected works of theological
commentary on that book. It was simple logic: God created Adam,
and from his rib, the woman Eve. God didn't make errors. He
created the species in His own image and He designed them to
function well. And they had. Mankind had prospered and filled the
earth and done so because of the perfection of His design.

Stanley was proud of his manliness. He'd had enough of that
demonic phrase "political correctness." Man had fallen on hard
times. The materialism that had driven Eve toward the apple had
always been at the root of man's misplaced aggression. Man's need
to satisfy the material yearnings of women had driven men from
their leisurely pursuits of games and the joy of the hunt to raid the
property of neighboring tribes. Men had mothers and lovers who
helped shape their behavior and send them off to war.

Now, since western women lived in wealthy and powerful
countries, which had cornered the world's wealth, they wanted
men to act and think and communicate like women. They had

already convinced most young males that manhood was an ugly thing. Men were aggressive monsters. Why would a boy ever want to mature into a man? Women forget that the world outside their luxury apartments, and especially outside their well-guarded borders, is still a dangerous place. The entire world goes mad every few generations, it seems, and when it boils over, women are only too glad to have a man around to take the bullets for them.

Yet Ira did remain a mystery to his father. Stanley also believed that bad things don't usually happen to the righteous, with the exception of Job, of course—but God had had plans for Job. Stanley had an idea that the situation with his only child had something to do with his having married Shirley with her Catholic background, and having done so too close to his first wife's death. Shirley had been Angela's private nurse during those terrible months when the cancer was eating up Angela's lovely body and her wonderful Christian mind. Stanley had remained physically true to his Angel to the bitter end. But in spite of his best efforts he had to admit that he had begun to experience feelings of love for the nurse before God finally took Angela home. Yet they had done nothing wrong. At Stanley's insistence, they had waited almost a year before they married and returned to his home village to serve the Lord.

Shirley turned out to be better at caring for the dying than for looking after babies. Right from the start she was convinced Ira was a manipulating scoundrel who was trying to destroy the new marriage. She felt that too much cuddling would turn the boy into a sissy and ruin him for a normal life.

She had done her best, acting against her natural prejudices. It hadn't been easy. She clearly found the boy repulsive, with his enormous head and the deep black bags under his large bulging green eyes—"ex-ophthalmic" the doctor had called them. But Shirley was determined to make the marriage work and Ira was part of the bargain she had made. She would be a decent mother to her step-son even if it killed her.

If Ira was bothered by his personal appearance, he never let on to anyone. In fact, his persona of superiority was part of what turned people against him, Shirley thought. Far more intelligent

than most of those around him—his peers, his uneducated neighbors, and even his Bible-college educated father and his dad's new
wife—he took pleasure in heaping scorn on anyone or anything
that did not measure up to his scrupulous standards.

Stanley's heart swelled with pride, as it always did, when he
approached his new church. It had been built based on drawings he
had made from photographs he had taken on the short honeymoon
trip he and Shirley had made to New England. Several Colonial
Revival Churches there had taken his breath away with their red
brick and tall pillars. It had taken several years to convince his
flock and now they worshipped God in the most beautiful building
in Mussel Cove. The Catholics might have a bigger structure—for
their larger brood, he thought—but it didn't have the solid beauty
of Stanley's church.

Stanley quietly entered by the side door and peered nervously
inside. The church seemed empty. He stepped inside, the hard soles
of his shiny black shoes tapping the gleaming hardwood floor and
echoing past the colored glass images illustrating the life of Christ.
He took a few tentative steps toward the pulpit, half-expecting Ira
to jump out of the shadows and shout "Boo!" He was relieved at
not finding his son. He could return to the manse. Thank God. He
could use a strong cup of tea. Where could the boy have gone?

...

Ira watched his father scurry out of the sanctuary. He
imagined how the old man would react to being surrounded by
shovel-wielding kids in rubber masks. Would he pray to God, or
simply whimper and beg for mercy like all the others? No matter.
It was interesting to watch people when they didn't know they
were under observation—you can learn such interesting things.
His father wouldn't try too hard to find him. He was like that. He
didn't do anything unless it would have a pleasant outcome, if he
had any choice in the matter. He hated visiting the sick and the
dying as much as he loved weddings and baptisms. The old man
wasn't so bad—a bit of a coward but always trying to lead people
to better lives. Too bad he couldn't recognize when his help wasn't

appreciated. Ira wondered if his father knew how naive and stupid most of his congregation thought he was—not too likely.

He stood up and stretched, peering through the stained glass of the door panel as his multi-colored father crossed the blood-red lawn and entered the dark blue house. Those two will sit and wait, as usual. This time it might be a long wait. Perhaps he'd return tomorrow or the next day. Maybe this time he would stay away forever. They would probably be thankful to see him gone, if they were capable of being honest about their feelings. Obviously they didn't like him very much. They spent a lot of time talking about love—she especially, lots of fancy words. Love to them meant "taking responsibility for commitments" they had made and they were real good at being responsible. All it took to be responsible was to run around scared shitless all the time, loaded down with guilt and just waiting for the God-beast to find some instant when they were in a sinful state and pounce on them. Ira believed it was the devil who ran their lives. It was the devil who put the fear of the Lord into their hearts. They would do what they were supposed to because they feared the fires and the pestilence of Hell. That kind of love was easy for them. But loving a boy the way he needed to be loved was not. He knew how they felt—and in spite of himself it hurt.

They never got passionate about anything but The Word. They took no pleasure in anything except themselves. The only time Ira ever heard them laugh was in their bedroom when they were being gross together. Everything else about their lives was plain: no cream or sugar in their coffee or tea, no drink other than water or unsweetened fruit juice. Neither one had ever smoked or bought a lottery ticket. They never went to a movie or a party unless it was church-related. They were the only family in the village without a television.

Ira didn't care about those things. But it made him furious that they scorned him, because they were nothing to brag about as parents. He wouldn't have picked either one of them if he'd been given a choice.

He struggled to shift gears. Tonight all the others would be back out there looking for those dead babies. The ghost girl had said it was time to bring them home. This was the only hateful part of all the fun they'd been having lately. It always seemed to be raining when they went out. The girl told them they had to avoid digging under the light of the moon. There was too great a danger of them being seen. They had to be careful that no one found out because what had happened to the children so long ago could happen again. There were still empty boxes in the house where the woman from Halifax lived with Eppie. Eppie had seen them there.

This could not be over until all of the forgotten ones were freed from their secret graves. The digging had to continue until all of the children could be free forever.

Ira reached behind the framed photo of the first pastor of the Mussel Cove congregation. His mask was there where he had left it. It was the only safe place he could find in the new church to hide things. The photos of former pastors had been transferred from the walls of the old church and no one ever went near them except when his stepmother cleaned, and she did that on Mondays. On Mondays he moved the mask into his room for the day. She never came into his room without permission. He had won that fight.

He would slip out the basement door in case his red-haired bitch of a stepmother sent the foolish old man back to look for him. They had better stay home. Being nosy in Mussel Cove was becoming very dangerous.

CHAPTER SIXTEEN

16

"Who owns these?" asked Sara, pointing to the line of red canoes.

"The people who let you use the house."

"How do you know that, Eppie?"

Eppie's hesitation was enough to make Sara want to continue her probing questions. "Bertha said."

"Said what? ... When?"

"Not to me ... exactly." Another pause. "On the phone." Eppie's eyes brightened as she grew more confident. "I think she was talking to Philip, but I'm not sure. Let's go. It'll soon be time to get back. You promised me we could go over to the island."

"Sort of. It's just that I'm uncomfortable using these canoes without permission."

"That's silly. You have permission to stay at the house—and the boats belong to the house! So you're allowed to use them. Let's take this one."

Eppie's logic made perfect sense and the small girl had already raised one end of a plastic canoe, flipped it right side up, and was dragging it towards the water. The rattling staccato of its passage over the rolling gravel prompted Sara to cease her protest and lift the trailing end. The weight surprised her since Eppie managed her end with ease. In a few moments the canoe was afloat in the light surf that licked the course sand at the ocean's edge. Eppie sauntered casually back to where they picked up the canoe, took a few steps beyond, bent over and returned with two birch paddles.

"How did you know where to find the paddles?"

"There's a huge pile back there by the canoes."

Sara held the canoe steady as Eppie bent low and scrambled to the bow where she sat facing the island. Sara stepped into the stern with one foot, placing her paddle athwart the gunwales, and with the other leg pushed the wobbly craft away from the shore. The skies had clouded over once more. Sara was all too aware she had a job she ought to be doing, but Bertha was tied up with paperwork and housework and couldn't stay with Eppie, so why not try and enjoy the outing. It would probably do the child good to have some special attention.

"It's farther than it looks," said Eppie.

"We're doing great. We'll be there before you know it. Keep paddling on one side of the canoe. I'll look after the steering and I'm counting on you to keep us moving forward. Did your folks have a canoe?"

"No. We had nothing but our clothes. And most of those were second-hand."

"I'm amazed how comfortable you are with canoeing. You knew to stay low and you know how to paddle correctly."

"Red Cross summer camps. Paid for by the government. What about you?"

"We had canoes at our summer home in Maine."

"Were you rich? You look rich and you act rich."

"No, not rich. The Kennedys and the Rockefellers were rich. We were comfortable. My dad owned a chain of small-town business supply stores in New England. I guess we had plenty because I can't remember a discussion about money at our house."

"It got discussed a lot at our house. Mostly where it disappeared to. Sometimes over home in Carbonear—that's in Newfoundland—we ran out of food. I guess you didn't know that my old man drank like a fish. Most people around here knew that." Eppie paused and, while Sara waited, she listened to the splash of the oars and the cries of the seagulls overhead. "It must be nice having money," Eppie continued. "I want to be rich someday. I'll buy a big house with a wall around it to keep bad people away. I'll get some big dogs and lots of friends will come to live with me in my house."

Sara laughed. "It doesn't matter about money, as long as you're happy. That's all that counts."

"That's not true. Poor people never say stuff like that. How can you be happy with a pain in your belly from nothing to eat? Then your mother yells at your father and he gets mad and sorry for himself and starts drinking."

"How could he drink without money?"

"Drunks have friends. They need one another. And Daddy used to hide booze when he had money and save it for when he didn't. He spent all his paycheck sometimes. If there was no booze he stole Lysol from the corner store and vanilla or lemon extract and stuff like that."

In silence they dragged the canoe up to the rolling pebbles on the shore and stood a moment to catch their breath. The beach air was a rich mixture of clean salt, stale seaweed and kelp. For Sara it conjured up the taste of raw oysters. Above the gritty sand sat mounds of pebbles shaped by the oft-times violent action of the sea. Still farther up, uneven fragments of granite and shale protruded below the grassy bank.

"Is the canoe pulled up high enough?"

"It should be okay," Eppie replied matter-of-factly.

Sara was certain that the child had been to the island several times. What had she been doing?

"Are you certain? I bet the tide rises quite high sometimes."

"Yes."

"I wouldn't want to get stranded out here."

"I'm positive. Come on."

"What makes you so sure? How often have you been out here?"

Eppie stopped in her tracks. Sara read something close to a threat in the anger she recognized in Eppie's face and the iciness of her tone.

Eppie tried to smile. "A shore's a shore, and a tide is a tide. I was born on The Rock! When you grow up in Newfoundland, you know about the sea. The only time the water goes past where this canoe is—up there on the piled pebble—is in a big blow with high tides and there ain't no blow or big tides today. The sky is cloudy but the air is still. Trust me, Sara, this canoe is high enough." She climbed up the bank and onto the grass above. Sara took a deep breath and followed.

"I'm sorry. Obviously you know what you're talking about."

As she pushed herself up the steep grassy bank she looked back on the sand behind her and noticed for the first time slightly weathered tracks running parallel to the fresh line they'd drawn in the pebble and hard sand by pulling up their canoe. All of those canoes must have been here recently. The entire area was stamped with what must have been small footprints. Children, Sara thought. She heard Eppie's voice up ahead urging her to hurry. Ahead of her a well-worn footpath wound through stunted, interwoven evergreens.

She quickly caught up to Eppie and asked about the dense mat of shrunken trees along the shore.

"Tuckamore, we call that in Newfoundland," said the child. "The cold ocean wind in winter stunts them. Where do you want to go?"

"You lead the way. Show me around. I'll follow."

"I'll go where you want."

"Go ahead. I'm right behind you. Let's follow the path."

"Whatever you say," answered Eppie.

The path swayed through the tuckamore and came to an abrupt end in a wide grassy clearing in which grew tangles of wild rose and other bushes covered in pink blossoms unfamiliar to Sara. The center of the clearing was marked by a great rectangular depression with rhubarb growing wild at one end and a tangled, neglected apple orchard whose trees consisted mostly of weathered, barkless limbs on the opposite side. This must have been the site of the farmhouse. She looked into the pit from which protruded the weathered ends of a few charred timbers.

The barn, by contrast, seemed in excellent repair. The shingles were weathered and dry but still fit snugly together. The line along the horizon of the roof was straight and level, and the entire structure was nestled into the side of a hill next to a raised roadway leading to a set of double doors on the second level. Beside the road was a second, smaller stone-lined hole in the earth, perhaps the cistern that once fed water into a stable on a lower level.

They climbed cautiously down beside the roadway, Sara taking the lead with Eppie at her heels. They stepped away from the front of the barn (Sara calculating its width) and scampered down another steep bank and along the side of the barn, where they found the entrance to a stable that might once have served as a milking room for a small dairy herd. Its outer door was ajar.

"Let's go inside," said Sara, stepping through the wide opening.

"I don't want to." Eppie sounded afraid.

"Why not?"

"Someone might come."

"Come on, Eppie. You said it was all right about the boats. If that was okay, then surely it will be okay to explore an abandoned barn. Come on in, please."

Jaw firmly set, Eppie reluctantly crossed the straw-laden threshold. "It might not be safe."

"Don't worry. We'll be careful." Sara looked jerkily around, noting the heavy beams, joists and studs that ran across the ceiling and up and down the walls. This structure must have sat on the island for more than a century. Timbers like these came from old-growth forest. Such trees no longer existed along the eastern seaboard. Old buildings had been her father's passion. He had taught her about wide boards, peg construction and Common Rosehead nails. God how she missed him. She tugged at one nail in a bit of dry-rotted wood near the doorframe and it pulled away easily. She could find no cast mark so it was likely hand-forged. She showed it to Eppie, who wasn't interested and tugged impatiently at her sleeve.

Eppie pressed close as they neared the far end of the stable. Another two doors led somewhere into the lower guts of the barn.

There couldn't be much space back there because, by her reckoning, they mustn't be far from the rock of the hillside. She tried the solid maple doors but found them locked firmly shut. She yanked at first one and then the other for a few seconds while Eppie pulled at the back of her blouse and whispered, "Come on. Let's go!" Then the tugging of the blouse stopped and Sara turned around in time to catch a glimpse of Eppie's back as the child fled through the door.

Eppie was hovering in the long grass well away from the barn when Sara exited the stable. The reporter decided to circle the barn and see if there were other ways to get inside. Eppie followed at a safe distance. Halfway up the hill on the back side of the barn she discovered another set of sturdy doors that were locked as tightly as the ones inside the stable. Each had heavy cast-iron hinges bolted through the wood. Three old-time padlocks made certain she would not be getting inside today. She wondered where she might find a key. Her father would know about these locks: who made them and when. They were well-preserved, she thought, as she wiped grease from her fingers onto an old bit of discarded chamois she found in the long grass near where she was standing. It reminded her of the chamois she had used to scrub chalkboards in the school back home in Portland. She sighed.

Tony, her former fiancé, might not be far away. She hoped he had returned to Maine. She missed her home and her city and how she and Tony used to be. Thank God she had found out what he was like before the wedding and before there were children. Still, it hadn't been easy. She had been happy in her undergraduate years working on the university newspaper with her friend, Laura, and she wanted to feel happy again. Laura's offer of a temporary job in Canada until she found new work teaching was all it took.

She enjoyed Halifax. In many ways it was like being home. If she stayed here, and she had lots of time to think about that, health care would be free even though there were longer line-ups and longer waits than she was accustomed to at home. Canadians were lucky to live where they did, next to the richest and most powerful nation on the planet. They enjoyed prosperity and security second only to that of Americans, and didn't have to pay for it.

It was hard to take the arrogance of Canadians when they started their anti-American complaining. Whenever people heard she was American they began to list all that was wrong with America, especially foreign policy. Sara didn't always agree with what her government did but she knew it wasn't as easy as some Canadians thought.

"What's wrong, Sara?" Eppie asked, stepping up beside her. "Why do you look so sad? I'm glad we can't get in there. You should be glad, too."

"Why, Eppie?"

"Because I'm scared. I want to go now."

Sara put her hand on Eppie's thin shoulder. She decided not to ask Eppie why she was scared. "I'm not sad because we can't get inside. I was remembering some things that happened to me before and just thinking about other things. That's all. Do you ever feel sad?"

"Sometimes. I used to feel sad all the time, but now I feel happy sometimes. I still get scared, though, and I get lonely, too."

"You must miss your family."

"I miss the way they were when I was little and there was lots of work for Daddy. He used to bring us candy and he would play the accordion and sing about the green sea and about fishing. But that was a long time ago, before we moved over here. When I got a bit older he wasn't working so much and he was drinking real hard. My folks started fighting all the time. After we moved over here there was nobody my father knew and people made fun of his accent and his ways and things got much worse. But the ghost girl promised to take care of me and not to ever let anything bad happen to me."

"There's no such thing as ghosts, Eppie. They're not real. You know that, don't you?"

"The ghost girl is real. I've seen her lots of times. Everybody has."

"I see," said Sara. "If she's real, Eppie, who is she?"

Eppie hesitated. "You wouldn't know her. She's one of our friends. She knows everything about us. She helps us and protects us. She says that if we do what she wants, nobody will hurt us any more. She says the bad people will be punished and everything is going to be all right again."

Sara suddenly felt weary. It was difficult to listen to this nonsense from Eppie. What was going on in her childish mind, anyway?

"When will I meet your little friend?"

"I don't know."

"Perhaps you can invite her over some day after school."

"I can't."

"Why not?"

"I've never seen her at school."

"Is she in a different grade?"

"I don't know. I don't think she goes to school."

"Where did you meet her, then?"

Eppie looked at the ground.

"I want to go now. I'm scared out here." She turned and headed down to the shore. Sara watched her go. She too felt fear, but not of the island or the barn. She had a sudden vision of a burning house and Eppie's parents lost inside. Was this a fire of retribution for some crime, real or imagined, in the minds of children? Surely Eppie had nothing to do with these fires. And what about that teacher, Mrs. Stitch, who was turned into charcoal on top of her brass bed?

"Eppie, wait!" Sara called. The girl stopped and turned around. Slowly she returned and stopped a few meters away.

"Does this mysterious little girl have anything to do with the fires?"

Eppie's nostrils flared. She stepped past Sara and started up the ramp at the back end of the barn. "Don't ask!" she snapped and continued walking, head down.

"Does she?" Sara waited but Eppie didn't answer. Eppie had shut her out.

Sara climbed to the wide double doors at the top of the ramp. She tried the hasp and one door swung easily past the second. She stepped inside. She was in a huge, open hayloft with a solid spruce floor. She sensed a mild, steady vibration as if the building were alive. Running along a metal railing on the ceiling was a fork mechanism once used to lift large mounds of hay from the backs of open wagons. Below the fork the empty space rang with a lively echo as she called out, encouraging Eppie to step inside. The air smelled of the animals, which at some time in the past had inhabited parts of this building. There was something else, a faint trace of the smell she usually associated with electronic equipment. Like when a TV or computer monitor is on for a while. But there was no electricity here, not even a light bulb, and she had seen no sign of poles or wires carrying electricity to the island. This seems odd, she thought.

She walked to the far side where one wall was finished, in contrast to the open studs on the others. The boards seemed new, and flimsy, like cheap wall paneling. She reached out and touched the wall, which moved easily under her fingers. A recent addition. Next she checked where it connected to the side walls. It appeared to be built into a metal track like the pull-down front of a desk-secretary. Oddity number two.

Suddenly she remembered Eppie. Where was she? Sara turned. Where had she gone? Sara hurried outside, closed the door behind her and fastened the hasp. She glanced right and left. After a quick look around the remainder of the exterior she was satisfied that she had seen everything she could without a set of keys. She hurried down the curved path to the shore. The child stood next to the canoe, tossing pebbles into the sea. She turned at Sara's approach.

"I told you the canoe was all right," she said.

"You frightened me," said Sara. "I didn't know where you'd gone."

"I got bored."

"It's getting late. Let's head back."

"Yes, real late. We better get. I don't want to be here after dark."

Sara felt the cold chill return. She thought of asking Eppie what there was to be afraid of after dark, but she saw in the child's face that it would be a waste of breath. And she didn't wish to be out on the island after nightfall either.

CHAPTER SEVENTEEN

17

"What kind of gutless wonder are you, anyway?" muttered Philip aloud. He was by himself, quite drunk and parked just outside the cast-iron gate at Safe Haven. "If you had any balls you would have telephoned her, or dropped in on her, or something.

"But what do you do? You sit in your car and get half in the bag to muster up the courage to cower in front of her gate. You haven't even the guts to ring her frigging doorbell ... well, okay, her gate bell.

"Oh yeah? I'll show you!" he answered himself, threw open the door of his silver Crown Victoria, staggered to the gate and pressed the button for the bell. He laughed quietly at himself as he waited ... no answer. He rang again ... again no answer. Hovering between disappointment and relief, he turned toward his car.

He was almost there when he heard a clicking sound followed by a small, sleepy voice carried on the night breeze. "Is someone there?" Sara said through the tinny gate speaker. He turned and swayed back toward the gate uncertain as to whether he should answer or not.

"Who's there?" she repeated. Her voice had now developed a nervous edge. Oh shit, he had scared her. He hadn't meant that. Why had he come? "Is someone there?" This time she sounded angry.

He had to answer now. He moved close enough to the gate so the microphone could pick up his voice. "S'me," he mumbled, his speech mangled by excess of liquor.

"Who the hell is this? Is this some kind of a joke? Go away or I'll call the police!"

"Sara! S'me, s'Philip. I only wanna talk to you. I'm sorry. I didn't mean to scare you."

"Philip? What's the matter with you? Have you been drinking or something?"

"A li'le," he slurred. "Can I come in?"

"Not tonight, Philip. I'm in my pajamas. It's been a long, nasty day and I don't want to see anyone. I just want to sleep. Some other time, okay?"

"You mean that?"

"Sure, but not if you're drunk."

"Yeah, sorry ... stupid, so stupid ... Not thinking so straight. I don't suppose you'd want to go to a movie sometime, and get something to eat?"

"Sure ... I'd like that. Bertha could watch Eppie?"

"I ... I'll ask her."

"When?"

"T'morrow?"

"No ... I mean the movie."

"How about Friday night?"

"That sounds fine."

"I'll pick you up at 7:30."

"I'll be waiting."

On the drive home, Philip tried to whistle. His lips wouldn't co-operate, so the result was less than satisfactory. He didn't mind; he was happy, and she had said yes. When he pulled into his driveway, he took his daily planner from his hip pocket and scribbled down the details of his Friday date. He likely wouldn't forget something like this but he had blacked out before and didn't want this memory erased.

...

Sara, too, thought Philip might forget. From the sound of his voice he was completely soused. Perhaps it would be just as well if he did forget. She was pretty sure she didn't want to get involved with him. Oh well, she yawned, I'll give the poor guy a chance—for Bertha's sake. It could have been worse. It might have been Tony ringing the bell.

She drifted easily into sleep. It was as if this were an enchanted house. It was beautiful, except for the dreams she'd been having, which were often too graphic and horrible. Tonight she would try to dream about Philip—or Jackie Cole.

Down the hall, Eppie wasn't sleeping. The young girl stood on her window seat and gazed hypnotically into the darkness. The scudding clouds allowed only brief teasings of moonlight and it was difficult to focus on what was happening outside. If she kept very still she could detect movement. Knowing they were there made it easier. They would expect her to arrive soon and do her share. She stayed where she was and pulled her nightdress up and over her head in a single movement and wondered if anyone could see her. It didn't matter much, though, because she wasn't beautiful yet. That would happen soon, she could feel it; she might be just as beautiful as Sara.

She picked up the nightdress and folded it on the bed before putting on the clothes she had earlier laid out on the top of the bedside table. Then, as lightly as a kitten, she scurried downstairs and into the dark night. Her steps lengthened as her eyes accommodated themselves to the available light until she was hurrying along the path.

"You shouldn't ever do that," snapped a familiar voice from the long grass to her left. By now she had walked beyond the area recently mowed by the farmer.

"What do you mean, Ira?" she asked. She stared at the ugly boy with the large, moist eyes. Ira Black lived with his parents in a church manse and he always seemed to be hanging around her but he was so weird, bossy and ugly that she still hadn't decided whether she liked him or not.

"You shouldn't stand in the window the way you did earlier. If some bad people saw you they might do nasty things to you. Just because you don't have titties yet doesn't mean you're safe, you should know that. Two weirdoes were looking in the windows the other night and that woman from Halifax was standing in front of

the window without a top on. You should have heard what they
were saying about her. We got them good, but you better be careful. We might not be around the next time."

"The boot!" said Eppie, remembering what Sara had found.

"What?"

"Sara—that woman—found a man's boot in the long grass,"
she pointed to the lawn, "before it got mowed. It was all covered
in slime and she said she thought it was blood."

"So what?" he grabbed Eppie's arm tightly enough that it
hurt.

"She called the cop."

"What did he say about it?" his voice was not so brash. She
could hear fear in it.

"He said nothing. Old Bertha threw the boot in the stove. I
knew the buckle on it wouldn't burn so I dug it out of the ashes
and left it on the doorstep for one of the others. I watched Kensey
Mahoney throw it into the goldfish pond. You can get it back if
you want. She had that fat little Robert hanging around her like
always. You guys have got to be more careful or the ghost girl is
gonna be some mad." She walked toward the pond. Ira followed.

"Are you gonna tell on us?" asked Ira.

"Should I?"

"You better not. We'll be more careful. But you got to admit
it's hard to notice a boot falling off in long grass at night. Anyway
... How come you and the woman went over to the island? What
were you doing there? What if she finds out what goes on in the
barn?"

"She won't. It was the ghost girl's idea to take her out there.
She left me a message in the usual place, under the kitchen doorstep. It said to bring the woman over to the barn. She was supposed
to see it the way it is now. It is part of the plan."

"I wonder what she means by 'the way it is now.' Are we going
to torch the barn next? Did the woman notice anything out there
she shouldn't have?" asked Ira. He watched Eppie stoop and dig
about in the mud at the edge of the pond. In less than a minute she
found what she was seeking, rinsed it off in the pond water and

handed it to him. "I'll put this somewhere it'll never be found," he said.

"Good ... I don't think she noticed anything she shouldn't have on the island. I don't understand how Sara is important to the plan. I'm not even sure what the plan is, except to find those bones. Most of the barn is locked up. I was with her almost all the time. I don't want her to get hurt."

"So she didn't see anything?"

"She saw where we have our meetings. There was nothing to see. The Gingerbread Man must have cleaned it up. There wasn't even litter on the floor. It sure looked different in daylight. It gave me the creeps." She paused a moment before continuing, "Did you find any more of them?"

"Not since you were out last, but we haven't stopped looking. It takes a long time because we have to use so many kids as lookouts all the time. We don't want to get caught at it. Can you stay out and help tonight?"

"For a little while. Sara might wake up and go looking for me. I have to watch over her. I'm her guardian angel."

CHAPTER EIGHTEEN

18

While Shirley Black was waiting for the boy Ira to come out of the church, there wasn't much to do but think. She sometimes wondered what kept her here in Mussel Cove with Stanley and Ira. But, it wasn't all that complicated. It all came down to the way Stanley treated her. Never in her life had she been treated as well by anyone. And she knew what made Stanley tick better than anyone ever had, or ever would.

Take last night for instance. Shirley's mind drifted back pleasantly and replayed the event. She had known the instant Stanley entered the bedroom and turned the lock on the door what was on his mind. There was a certain goofy look he got in his eyes when his brain descended. She waited ... Stanley stood at the foot of the bed, formally dressed in his suit and collar. He didn't speak for a moment and then he cleared his throat.

"Can we do it tonight—the special way? Would you mind very much? I know it's a bit late," he said.

"Okay, Stanley," she told him, sighing and getting up out of bed. "Are you not feeling well? Poor dear. Why don't you get off your feet for a few minutes while I change?"

Stanley climbed up on the bed and closed his eyes, while Shirley disappeared into their large walk-in closet. When she emerged she was wearing her white nurse's uniform, complete with the small starched cap, one of the same uniforms she'd worn when she nursed Stanley's first wife through her long painful illness. It fit her reasonably well, although it was a bit tight around the hips.

Shirley walked slowly over to Stanley and stood beside where he lay. She placed her hand on his forehead and he sighed, smiling from ear to ear. He reached up inside her skirt and pretended to be surprised that she was wearing nothing underneath; she rewarded him with a soft moaning sound, then bent and kissed him wetly and passionately. And then with her tongue.

Stanley lifted her up onto the bed beside him and opened the top buttons of her uniform. He unfastened the snap of her bra and, reaching up her short sleeves, slipped her bra straps off of her shoulders, sliding one side down under her elbow, and off her arm, before pulling the bra out the other sleeve. He told her how he loved the way her plump breasts with their huge nipples looked, floating free inside the fabric of her uniform top. He undid another button of her top and lifted the right breast, taking the warm brown nipple into his mouth. He pulled at it slightly with his tongue and teeth, causing her to exclaim with delight.

By then Shirley had opened Stanley's belt and unzipped his fly. She was always reminded of the first time. She had never had a more wonderful surprise in her life. Stanley wasn't a big man in most ways, but the Lord God had made up for Stanley's stature when he created his penis. Stanley's peter was the most amazing thing Shirley had ever handled, and that included the many penises she'd encountered during her nursing career. She called it the Reverend Mr. Big.

Stanley's "special way" never failed to get him intensely excited, so these encounters didn't often last as long as Shirley would like. But Stanley's excitement, and being back in the uniform, was usually enough for Shirley to enjoy the experience to a certain extent.

Last night, though, had been one of the better ones. She had taken Stanley's penis into her mouth, loving how it expanded and firmed until her jaws ached. He had been inspired in the way he touched her; so, by the time she had hiked up her skirt and worked him inside of her she was more than ready. She hadn't been able to hold back her cries, all of her accumulated stress washing away in seconds. She continued to move as she watched Stanley's green eyes. That was the only way she could ever tell that her tightly wound husband had come. The eyes always rolled back in his head and his body underwent a small, almost imperceptible shudder. Then they had held one another, he in his suit and collar, his trousers down around his knees, and she in her nurse's uniform, buttons all undone. They had fallen asleep like that and had later woke up and dressed properly for bed. It hadn't been until later that she had wondered if Ira had still been awake.

Ira, the very thought jolted her back to the present, where she stood watching for him. The little twerp thought he was smart, brazenly smoking cigarettes in front of his mother and then successfully hiding from his father before sneaking away from the church. He must figure I'm stupid, she thought. And the Reverend Stanley. She shook her head, rolled her blue-green eyes and smiled. She had told her dear husband that their son Ira was still inside the church. If you wanted something done, you had to do it yourself.

Shirley watched Ira slip out the basement door of the church, bold as brass, fresh cigarette dangling from his lips. She had made up her mind to follow. He was her son, too. Maybe she didn't give birth to him, but neither had Stanley; she'd done everything else for the little brat. Nobody in the world changed his dirty bottom more times than she had. Who could deny he was as much her child as anyone else's?

She was acutely aware that Ira had been prowling around Mussel Cove at night like an alley cat. He knew his territory. It would be tough to spend an entire night following him, but she knew it was her Christian duty to get to the bottom of whatever shenanigans were leading him astray.

Once she knew what the boy was up to she could devise a plan. Ira was in some sort of trouble. Mothers had a way of knowing things like that, even stepmothers. Someone or something was having an evil influence on him. There had been too abrupt a change in his behavior for any other explanation. Was it drugs? Or something worse?

Ira's first stop, after a long, meandering walk Shirley thought would never end, was the site of the latest fire in Mussel Cove: the burnt-out shell of the former home of that unfortunate Mrs. Stitch. Everyone said that kids learned how to hate school in Mrs. Stitch's class. The gossip was that the old girl had taken to the drink, and lately had been heard massacring hymns in a drunken off-key soprano from her back doorstep.

Shirley knew about drinking. Her childhood had been a time of hardship and neglect. Her parents loved to party. After Sunday Mass and days of obligation, parties took priority over everything, including children. The dominant memory of her childhood was of crawling into an unmade bed in dirty clothes after a supper of potato chips and seven-up. Her parents weren't intentionally cruel or unloving. Most likely they never knew what they were doing to her. She never was one to complain about her lot in life. But she never forgot, either. As a result, Ira had never gone without a proper meal, and there hadn't been a single party in this house since her arrival.

Shirley worked hard to keep Ira from relationships with children who had destructive attitudes toward the solid Christian values she and Stanley provided. Many of the children in Mussel Cove belonged to families who seldom attended church. She couldn't understand what attraction scalawags and ne'er-do-wells had for decent children. Ira seemed to be intrigued by the most unchurched children in the community.

Parenting was tough these days. Children seemed to be running the parents! Shirley wouldn't let that happen in her house. She watched from behind the scorched metal garden shed in the Stitch back garden. Ira wandered around the burnt-out house, tossing chunks of rock at the smoky glass shards in the blackened window openings.

It was almost dark before he stopped puttering and veered away from the ruins back toward the village proper. When he came to the bridge he decided not to use it and instead marched through the shallow water below and then kept to the shelter of the trees while Shirley waited and crossed the bridge as it should be crossed. It seemed to take forever to walk past the wall around Safe Haven, and by the time they were well inside the built-up portion of the village of Mussel Cove, Shirley was freezing. They passed Crawford's Pizza, where Shirley paused to watch Ira stop in front of Mussel Drugs, look up and down the street, and then, satisfied that no one had seen him, run up the stairs and in.

Shirley snorted aloud. Old Man Harding and his cursed pinball machines, she grumbled to herself, not to mention those addictive video lottery machines. Too many toughs used his establishment as a hangout. It had become the local den of iniquity.

Every instinct told her to rush inside and drag Ira out by the scruff of his neck, just like Jesus as he cast out the thieves from the Temple. Two things stopped her. First, he was much too strong for her to drag anywhere—especially if his "friends" were inside—but mostly she was aware that she still had no clue what he was up to. She would have to be patient. A cup of tea and a sweater would be nice, but she couldn't risk going home to get them. If Ira left the drugstore while she was gone, her efforts would all be for nothing.

An eerie blue light illuminated the front of Bell's Real Estate, Office Supplies and Funeral Home. The Bells regularly attended Mussel Cove Baptist Church and Amy always had a pot of coffee on the go. A hot cup would help solve Shirley's problems. Perhaps she could even borrow a sweater.

She found Amy Bell, the undertaker's wife, seated behind the counter, smelling strongly of lilacs. Her gray hair was neatly arranged in a bun and her large, tall body was covered in one of the large, billowing dresses she favored. She wore heavy dark plastic glasses with thick lenses that distorted her dark blue eyes. Behind her were rows of shelves containing business envelopes, boxes of staples, pencils, pens and numerous other office supply essentials. Beside her was a photo album opened to the picture of a farmhouse with a large veranda. Below the photo were typed the words: New Reduced Price. Amy was surprised to see Shirley out this late in the evening away from the church and without her husband.

"Shirley Black, is that you? Is something wrong?"

Shirley had stopped just inside the door, nose twitching from the perfume and flowers. The next few days her sinuses would punish her for this visit. "No, Amy, I was just stretching my legs and I thought I would visit. This isn't a bad time for you, is it? That coffee sure smells good."

"Colombian beans from the Super Store up in Sydney River. Here, sit down and I'll pour you a cup. Cream or sugar?"

"No, thanks. I'll take it black. That's kind of you," Shirley said. "I'll park here next to the window." She moved a bundle of headstone brochures and a dish of candy and advertising pens from the windowsill to the coffee table and sat on the edge of the sill, looking out. She had a perfect view of the entrance to Mussel Drugs.

After a few minutes Amy returned. "Here's your coffee. Enjoy, dear."

Shirley sipped at her cup but hardly tasted it. Her eyes were riveted on the front entrance of the drug store across the street. Amy had watched Ira enter the store just before his mother arrived for her uncharacteristic visit. There was nothing odd or unusual about Ira being in Mussel Drugs; he spent lots of time in there. So what? It's normal for kids to seek out other youngsters their own age. What did Shirley expect? The drugstore had become a major hangout for the younger set ever since Harding installed those quarter machines inside. She'd heard that the druggist, Bertha Morris' stepson Philip, argued against it but, as you would expect, Old Man Harding won. He was the boss. It was obvious Shirley wasn't happy about her little boy being in there, not happy at all.

That boy was no prize. Every time Amy heard rumors—and there were plenty these days—about the frightening events taking place in the Cove, Ira's name was the first to come up in speculation about who was setting the fires. Perhaps it was those watery, bulging eyes or the massive head that bothered people and made them instantly uncomfortable around him, eyes that looked right through a person. Looking odd made you odd in a place like this—maybe everywhere. There was a kind of logic in that thought that pleased Amy. She wondered how Shirley felt about the boy. Did she love the boy, or was she just as afraid of him as everyone else?

Shirley jumped up and handed the cup to Amy. "Sorry, but I have to run," she said. "Great coffee, thanks." She dashed out the door and sped back in the direction she had come. Amy was not surprised that the cup was still full of lukewarm coffee. She emptied it into the big split-leaf philodendron near the door.

Shirley first felt and then heard the deep pedal notes of the church organ as she passed in front of the open door of the Catholic Church. She stopped for a moment and caught her breath. She had to give her out-of-condition body time to adjust to the rapid change of position and pace.

"Ira almost got away," she panted aloud in the deepening darkness.

She watched as Ira marched on past the Baptist Church and the manse that was his home, then stepped by the front wall at Safe Haven, turned left and trotted down toward the Atlantic between the wall and the narrow Mussel River. She followed as close as she dared, tracking Ira's progress until he dissolved without warning into sudden blackness.

Her breath caught in her throat. She ran up along the wall to where a section had succumbed to gravity and fallen, allowing easy passage to the inside. Ira had hopped through like Alice's white rabbit and disappeared into the grounds of Safe Haven.

She stood motionless and listened. Nothing. She took a few tentative steps, stopped, took a few more and found herself on a narrow path in long grass inside the wall. Despite the darkness, she felt exposed and decided to take refuge in an orchard of twisted and rough-barked apple trees. There were muffled voices in the near distance and the adjacent house seemed to cast a forlorn spell through the eerie blackness. As Shirley pressed her small body against the arthritic trunk of the closest tree and shivered, a long-forgotten prayer, learned on the knee of her Irish grandmother, unearthed itself from the gray folds of her brain. It did nothing to exorcise the fear that locked her feet to the ground below her.

Little Jesus make a spark
I'm so scared and it's so dark
Stay with me all through this night
With you I'll need no other light.

She couldn't be sure how many there were. But by now her eyes had adjusted to the lack of light enough to see their general shapes as they moved around the property. Some carried shovels like Snow White's dwarfs and moved through the dark like it was daylight. Ira joined a group and they moved with a single mind toward the house. They gazed at a window whose shape she could barely make out. She tiptoed closer. They were oblivious to her presence. Several children dug excitedly at a spot in the lawn while others looked on with great interest. A small child, a girl she thought, emerged from the house and joined easily with the onlookers. Ira began to scold her, sounding just like his father.

Then his voice rose above the others who turned and swept like a receding tide in the direction of the ocean, carrying their shovels across their shoulders like marching soldiers with their rifles. Shirley felt desperately tired, but she was determined to follow, whatever the consequences.

The narrow path led into dense trees. She crashed heavily into low-hanging abrasive limbs of gnarled spruce, sometimes tumbling to the earth in her haste. In the morning she would be a mass of huge welts. She breathed a sigh of relief when she emerged from the trees and she found herself standing beside the lapping ocean. Ahead of her the children pushed off from the shore in five canoes. She looked to her left and saw a single canoe pulled up on the pebbles. She could follow if she dared.

She feared the water. Like so many of her neighbors, even fishermen and their children who depend on the ocean for their livelihood, she had never learned to swim.

She held back a few moments in heart-pounding indecision until the children had paddled out of sight, and finally she forced her legs to move forward. She had come this far and this was her only chance to find out. She knew in her heart that she would never find the courage to do this again; it was now or never. She lifted the bow of the remaining canoe and dragged it to the water's edge. Someone had left a single paddle inside, as if they knew someone was still to come.

Shirley took a deep breath, pushed the unstable craft out into the water and climbed aboard. Her stomach churned as the canoe lurched about before righting itself. She lowered the blade of the paddle into the water and pulled. To her surprise and delight, the tiny craft surged through the water in the direction of the island. Phosphorescence sparkled all around her. More light danced with each dip of the paddle blade into the dark water. She found herself giggling. This wasn't so bad. Though she remained quite aware of the deepening water, her confidence grew and her fear was pushed well to the background. Perhaps it had been the prayer she had whispered back in the orchard garden.

She raised her head and gazed toward the island expecting to see children swarm up the shore at any moment. She saw nothing. They ought to be there by now.

Then in a moment of mind-numbing horror, she knew why.

They came at her out of the shadows from four sides, one canoe to a side. She looked for the one carrying Ira but it never appeared. Swift as spectres they glided toward her, stirring up glistening spray as they moved.

Shirley's voice was lost in their youthful exuberance as they rammed and pulled at her canoe, dumping her out. She reached hopelessly for a handhold in the splashing water, creating a light show of flying droplets before slipping finally into the chilling blackness of the Atlantic.

She struggled in blind terror under the icy water until panic and fatigue sapped all her will to continue. She breathed the water into her lungs, feeling the suffocating burn of it, the intolerable pain, and the reality of impending death. She realized she would never have been what her husband and son needed her to be and God was releasing her from the burden of this difficult life. First she felt a suffocating pain and then a warmth filled her like the healing breath of a thousand angels. The briny fluid filling her lungs was like the waters of the womb. Another birth was coming. This time she would be reborn into the arms of her Savior. She opened her eyes to sudden moonlight filtered through a thin layer of the dark green Atlantic. Her cares drifted away and she began to pray silently as she approached the light: Our Father, which art ...

CHAPTER NINETEEN

19

"There are a few more people I'd like to talk to down in the village," said Sara into the telephone, "and then I'm off to Sydney to check out newspapers and archives ... Yes, sure and you never know until you check, right? Oh, would you mind contacting the RCMP and anyone else around here who has files going back fifty or sixty years, anything connected to this house, or with the orphans or orphanages or adoptions? Now remember, you asked me if there was anything you could do to help."

"Okay." Laura interrupted and paused. "This trip was intended for you to escape and get a bit of rest. Your research on this story was intended to pay for the holiday, as I recall. Not a big production, just a small story about a frightened community—with the potential for more if arson turns out to be involved. Have you been getting any rest?"

"Plenty. I sleep and I sleep and I sleep some more. Honestly, Laura, you'd swear I was working at hard labour. I've never slept like this before. I don't know what it is, the air perhaps. My head hits the pillow—you should see this room, by the way. It's unbelievable. And I already told you about Eppie—I'm practically a regular Mommy. Anyway, my head hits the pillow and I'm gone for the night."

"My god, Sara. You sound like you're on amphetamines. Are you really all right? I worry about you, my dear. Any sign of Tony? Are you still blaming yourself?"

"For what happened with Tony and with Dad's death? I don't think so. I know it wasn't my fault. Truth is I haven't had time to think about it. It's all such a blur, and I'm trying to focus on my job. There's no sign of Tony but it makes me nervous thinking he could appear at any moment. But, like I said, I've been too busy to do much thinking. There are certainly bizarre things happening as I'll explain later. I'd better hang up before I put *The Loyalist* into bankruptcy. Oh, and I met some cute guys, too."

"Watch out for those Cape Bretoners!" said Laura with a chuckle. Sara's editor had spent her childhood summers in a cabin near Glace Bay, where her mother had been born. She loved to tell stories about her teen adventures in Cape Breton. Fast times in a slow place.

"Hey, these guys aren't so bad. One fellow reminds me of my father in a way. His name is Marcel, Marcel Vertu. I investigated a small fire at his place. He owns a restaurant that's attached to his apartment. He also happens to be the principal of the elementary school. And he's got a weapons fetish, I think. I only talked to him a few minutes and I accepted an invitation for coffee. I like him. He has class. Of course, he's old enough to *be* my father. Maybe that's what I liked about him, hmmm ...

"Then there's this other creature, the local cop. Jackie Cole. Man, he's really cute. He smells like my father—Old Spice, I think, but more than that. I don't think he's much of a cop though. You'd think he'd be more on top of these fires. But there's something very hot about him. Ha ha—get it?" She chuckled and Laura responded with a good-natured groan.

"But the third one isn't like that," Sara continued. "Mr. Insecurity. Philip. He's maybe younger than I am, a volunteer firefighter and a pharmacist. Great buns. He was brought up by an aunt who really isn't his aunt—that's Aunt Bertha. He's tall, dark, brown-eyed and muscular. He may have a booze problem, but I've already agreed to a date with this guy—beggar for punishment that I am. I may see if he can come up to Sydney with me later today. I can see what I've got myself into. Besides, he knows his way around the area and I don't, and I could use some adult conversation.

"Listen Laura, I'm going to sign off. Sorry to blather about the boys. There's a story here—perhaps a big one. It might go national if I can tell it right."

"All right, girl. But don't forget to have some fun. Let me know how it goes with all that Cape Breton manhood. Story or no story, call me soon. I sure miss you around here. I had forgotten what great company you are. Just like the good old days on the college paper. Take care, eh."

"Okay, you're the editor. Bye, Laura."

"Ta, Sara." Laura hung up, but Sara thought she heard a second click. Was someone listening in, a wiretap, or just her imagination? But who would listen in? Police and governments did things like that, or huge corporations trying to get information, or perhaps a private detective. From what she had seen of local police enforcement, such sophistication wasn't likely and what corporation would be bothered with her? Was there even a large corporation around here? And a private detective? Chilled, her thoughts turned to Tony. Oh God, please no. Don't let him come after me.

Sara hurried down to the kitchen. Bertha was there, wiping off the table.

"Good morning, Bertha."

"Good morning. I just heard something on the radio."

"What?"

"A missing woman."

"That's too bad," Sara said. "But don't people go missing all the time? They usually get found wandering about in the bush." She pulled out a chair and sat down. Bertha went to the sink and turned on the tap. While the woman rinsed her cloth she continued to speak. "I can't see her wandering too far, although she was obviously out somewhere last night. I'm talkin' about the Baptist minister's wife, Shirley Black. She isn't the type to run out on her husband or to go anywheres by herself. She's more the type a husband might want to run away *from*. She's one of those timid, clingy women who hide in their houses. It's like she gets her strength from the house. At home she has power over her husband and kid."

Bertha began wiping the table again and Sara pushed back her chair and stood up. "No, no, you sit down here," Bertha said. "I'm all done of the table."

Sara sat. "Thank you," she said. "Tell me more about Shirley Black."

Bertha sat down and began to speak again. "Well, the radio said she was seen out walking last night. She visited the funeral home and someone from there told the reporter she was following her son around for some reason.

"Now you have to picture what sort of woman this is. Stanley—that's her husband the Baptist minister—always was the one who bought the groceries and supplies, cleaners, even her feminine things. He even went with her to buy her clothes. She accompanied him on a few home visits to the sick and the dying. But she must have really wanted to follow that boy—if that's what she was doing. She was a stubborn cuss. If she got the bit between her teeth she might stampede."

Bertha continued. "I phoned Philip at the drug store. Amy from the funeral home was in for her thyroid medication and told him she had called the police to tell them Shirley had visited her last night. She claims Shirley was definitely following that weird boy of hers around. Anyway, now the boy's home fretting about his mother. The cops have organized a search party and are out looking, but so far there's no sign of her. It gives me a funny feeling." She placed her artificial hand across her round abdomen. "I hope they find the poor creature alive." Bertha's voice sounded weary. She waddled to the window and gazed outside. Sara spoke to her back.

"I do, too. Listen, Bertha, you said that the people who ran the orphanage died. Are the present owners of the property connected to them in any way?"

"No, dear. If there was any connection, I wouldn't be here now. The family that owns the house now found Marcel and me here after the Cobans left. They came to look over their new property and discovered they had inherited two lost orphans along with it. Their intention was to retire here for the summer months, but when they learned some of the history of the place, they couldn't bring

themselves to stay here. Instead they bought themselves another
place in St. Andrews, New Brunswick. They write me regular and
ask questions, to which I don't know the answers. Sometimes I ask
Marcel. He keeps in touch with them through me because he's so
busy, what with the school and the restaurant.

"So that's why I started helping out here. Marcel and I were
in foster homes for a few years. When I was old enough to be on
my own they sent me a few dollars every now and then to keep an
eye on the place. They've had it on the market for years now, but
no one wants to buy it. I don't do it just for the money, though,
although the bit of cash helps. I make a small salary working for
Marcel as part-time secretary at the school. What I do here is my
way of thanking them for helping Marcel and me out after they
found us. They spent quite a bit of money on us for a while. The
people who lived in Mussel Cove weren't about to do anything for
us."

"Why not?"

"I don't know. But Marcel claims they all knew everything
that was going on at the orphanage and they still supported the
place."

"Why would they support an organization that sold babies and
maybe even did harmful things to children?"

"'Maybe,' love? Did, child. Did. Marcel says the kids were
getting good homes in Ontario and the States. But he also says
the orphanage was a big business. They spent a lot of money in
the village and supplied jobs." Bertha paused, her voice distant
and tight. "He says it was like a big hog operation. No one really
thought much about it. We were just another sort of livestock."
She stopped again, dropped her head and stared at her feet.

"I wish I had been brave enough to go away and travel like
Marcel did. But I never was. For a long while he lived in France.
He had several jobs. He's some smart—a genius, I bet. I seen
some posters he had, and some of his scrapbooks once, just after
he came back to The Cove."

"What sort of work did he do?"

"Circus work, and later he worked in theatres across Europe.

He worked building animated displays for a fancy theme park in France. I asked him about it again just the other day and he said he didn't feel like talking about it. Said all that was behind him now, like he was ashamed of it or something. You could ask him, though. He likes you. You're young and pretty." Bertha sighed. "The Cobans, the ones who ran the orphanage, were like that, too. They liked the pretty ones best. Maybe most men are like that, I don't know."

Bertha sat at the table, her face pale, tired. She gestured for Sara to sit. "You probably should head back to Halifax. I'm worried about you being out here by yourself."

"I'm not quite by myself."

"You'd be better by yourself. I'd be no use to you in a crisis and that child won't be a bit of help if something goes wrong. She might be worse than no help."

"What do you mean?"

"Just a feeling I get. There's something not right about her. Mostly, though, I'm worried about you being here in this big house. Why, anything could happen. All these fires ... and if something bad could happen to Shirley Black, the minister's wife, it could happen to anyone. She wasn't what you would call personable, but she didn't have enemies either. I don't think."

"We don't know something bad's happened. She's just missing."

"Something's happened. I know it in my bones. Did I ever tell you that sometimes I feel pain in the phantom bones where my hand used to be." She lifted the plastic hand in front of Sara's face. "Sometimes in dreams I feel my child fingers in that tiny hand touching my body, dancing across my tired old chest, or reaching across and taking hold of the dry and cracked fingers of my real hand. It's like the feeling a person gets holding the hand of a child. I feel happy for a bit. But other times my dreams terrify me. Sometimes when there's danger I hurt like when I lost my hand. Danger is coming to this house. That's why I think you should leave."

Sara shuddered, feeling a sudden chill in the air. Was Bertha threatening her, or looking out for her? "I can't," Sara replied. "Not yet. I have unfinished business. Besides, I feel relatively safe here. I had more to be afraid of in Halifax, actually. Out here I feel that there's some power watching over me."

"In some of my dreams," said Aunt Bertha, "I hear strange prayers and I feel afraid. I wake up soaking wet, and my wrist burns with pain. I always imagine I'm covered in blood so I get up and turn on the light to be sure I'm not."

"Life here must have been hell. And to think they called it Safe Haven," said Sara shaking her head.

"Yeah, I recall a Bible quote on the top part of some letters Marcel found in the office of the house, after the Cobans left. First I laughed and then I cried after he read it to me. Marcel said it was ironic. Ironic. I didn't understand the word 'ironic' back then but I looked it up. I don't know if the Cobans meant to be sarcastic or if they started out decent and then turned cruel. But I wouldn't be surprised by anything they did."

"What was the quote on the stationery?"

"Suffer the little children ... "

"Oh, Bertha." Sara winced.

"Awful isn't it, when you think about it? Them, taking a quote from Mark's gospel. Can you imagine? Them people must have been godless to do what they done and to use God's Word in that ironic way. Anyway, if you're sure you're not heading back to Halifax, I'd better let you get some work done. I'll finish what I'm doing here and run along home. I want to catch my breath, and I have things to do. You do what you have to do, and I'll look after things on this end."

"Are you all right?"

"Of course. Don't worry about me. If I survived this long, nothing can hurt me now. But thanks for caring. I really do appreciate that, Sara."

...

The sun was warm and the wind that tossed her hair, as she sped along with the windows down, felt refreshing. Five minutes later she pulled up in front of Mussel Drugs. Perhaps she could coax Philip to take some time off. It would be fun to have some company.

She hurried past a noisy crowd of smoking teenagers to the dispensary at the rear of the store, past aisles of baby supplies and a glassed-in perfume counter. A strikingly attractive young woman with platinum blonde hair sat entering a prescription into a computer in front of her.

"Can I help you?" the blonde asked without raising her blue eyes from the keyboard.

"Is the pharmacist in?"

"Huh," grunted the girl. "Who?"

"Philip. I'd like a word with him."

"Oh. Is this for a prescription? I can get it for you. He's on break."

"No. I would prefer to talk with him, if it's not too much trouble."

The woman wrinkled up her forehead and sighed. "He's having coffee with the old man. Can you give them a minute? He won't be long. It's been busy and he deserves a break."

"Could you get him for me. I'm sure he won't mind. Tell him it's Sara. I won't keep him long." The blonde was obviously intent on making things as difficult as possible.

"Sure, why not, I have nothing better to do," she said sarcastically, got up, stretched and yawned.

A moment later, in his awkward, lanky way, Philip bounded out to the counter, grinning broadly. Fragments of chocolate donut and icing clung to his teeth.

"Come on in, Sara. Meet my boss. How's about coffee and a donut?" He held up the mangled remains of the one he'd been eating. Sara avoided looking at his teeth.

"I had coffee before I left the house," she said to his disappearing back. The blonde barely paused in sliding pills from the blue plastic counting tray in front of her, and, without looking at Sara, lifted a section of counter. Sara followed Philip into the pharmacy office. The tiny room was smokier than an arcade. Philip's boss sat slumped in a battered recliner whose stuffing protruded here and there in stained tufts; his distended belly tugged at the buttons of a yellowed dress shirt, exposing a nauseating quantity of bulging hairy gut.

"Mr. Harding," said Philip. "May I introduce a new friend, Sara Miles. Sara, this is my employer, Mr. Ed Harding."

"How do you do, Miss Miles." Ed jumped up, stuck out a fat hand with nicotine-stained fingers and flopped back in his chair. Besides the nicotine and tar, Sara detected some strong aftershave that had a high alcohol content, or perhaps she smelled liquor. Were all the guys around here boozers?

"What's going on?" asked Philip.

"I hoped you'd have time to show me around Sydney. But I see you're busy."

There was a brief silence before Philip spoke. He looked over at Ed who remained passive. "We're not all that busy. What do you think, Ed?"

Ed looked out past them to where the blonde stood, probably eavesdropping, then at Sara and finally at Philip. He smiled, shrugged and scratched his balding head. "Well, I suppose Jane and I can hold down the fort until you get back. If the little lady needs your help, I won't see her stuck. Maybe you can give us a dingle later in case Jane runs into something she can't handle."

"Thanks, Mr. Harding," said Philip, looking pleased. "Give me a minute, Sara."

...

They were a few kilometers outside the village before either spoke. Some silences are born out of contentment. This silence was not like that. It was heavy and expectant, both of them uncertain who should speak first or what to say.

Sara finally gave in. "Do you enjoy working in that place?"

"It's okay, I guess," Philip answered after an awkward pause. He glanced toward Sara, puzzled by her tone of voice. "Is there something wrong with where I work? Old Ed's not too pretty, but he's decent to work with."

"Who's the rude blonde?"

"So that's it."

"What do you mean?"

"You don't like Jane. Jane doesn't bother to be friendly."

"She certainly doesn't."

"She used to be sweet to everyone. That's how she came by the two kids she's bringing up alone."

"Is she alone by choice?"

"I don't know. Maybe so. She's probably better off alone. Anyway, it doesn't matter. I don't care anymore."

"You did at one time?"

"For a while."

"She's pretty."

"Not as pretty as you."

"Or you," Sara countered, looking him in the face. Philip blushed and grinned. She noted he'd brushed his teeth.

...

Philip proved to be a real asset in getting around Sydney. At the public library, Sara found a few newspaper clippings—about Mussel Cove and the orphanage—which she photocopied from archival microfiche.

They celebrated their findings with a coffee from the local Lick-A-Chick, and headed back. They drove in silence, enjoying the beautiful day, the rugged, refreshing scenery enough to occupy Sara's mind. As they neared Mussel Cove, Philip broke the spell.

"Could you drop me at the drug store? A few things will need my signature before they shut down for the night."

"Are you picking up Bertha or would you like me to drive her home?"

"I'll pick her up. She often walks, you know. She should get more exercise. It's really not far to our place." He paused and remained silent until Sara glanced his way. "Is our date still on for Friday?" he finally asked, his voice quiet and uncertain.

"Of course, silly. I don't get a lot of offers up here."

She dropped Philip at the pharmacy and stopped at the Mini Mart for a can of frozen lobster meat. She craved a lobster burger like the one Bertha had prepared for her the day before. She hurried home, mouth watering. But before she had a chance to hand over the frosty can, Bertha hustled her into the kitchen and sat her down. The woman looked grim and pale.

"They found her," she said.

"Found whom?"

"The minister's wife. Shirley Black."

"Was she all right?"

"She sure wasn't. They found her face down in the Atlantic, drowned."

"My God!"

"You were no sooner out of the house when Jackie Cole and two Mounties rang the outside bell. They asked permission to look around. Finally, I thought at the time, the cops are starting to get serious. Jackie said people in a passing car had seen Shirley walking toward Safe Haven last night, not far from the bridge. I didn't know what I should rightly do, but I couldn't think of no good reason to keep them out, and I figured you wouldn't mind."

"It's all right. It's not my house. Where did they find her?"

"In the shallows offshore down below here, near Pox Island. You know where that is, don't you?"

Sara nodded and Bertha continued. "They found the canoe upside down. She wasn't far away. There wasn't a mark on her. Her husband said she couldn't swim. He even told the cops that he couldn't even get his wife to take off her shoes the only time they went to the beach."

"That doesn't make much sense. Living right here by the ocean all these years?"

"The world don't make much sense to me at any time. You really ought to get yourself out of here before it's too late."

Again with the pressure to leave, she thought. "I'll give it some thought, Bertha, I really will. Philip said he'll be over to pick you up. He has a few things to finish up at work. Oh, I bought this so you can make us all one of your famous lobster burgers." She handed Bertha the frost-encrusted can.

"Sure, dear." She stood without speaking a moment, then held Sara's gaze as she spoke. "Would you feel safer if we stayed the night here with you? There's lots of room and we have no pressing need to go home."

Sara's eyes dropped to the floor. "Not tonight. I'll be all right." She didn't want them to stay. She would feel uncomfortable with Philip sleeping in the house. "How did Eppie do in school today?"

"Well enough, I guess. She got right at her homework after she got home. I never had to say a word about it."

"Where is she?"

"Up in her room, I imagine."

"I'll have a word with her. Philip should be along soon." She touched Bertha's arm lightly and was pleased that the woman no longer showed signs of being repulsed by her touch. "Look, don't worry. Eppie and I will get along just fine."

"I hope so. You go up and see her now."

CHAPTER TWENTY

20

Sara fought against sleep—the enormous lethargy that descended upon her and seemed to turn her bedding into leaden blankets each night after she dragged herself upstairs. She had grown to look forward to Eppie's arrival in her bedroom. And not entirely because of her fears. The child was too small to offer any real assistance should some intruder threaten them, although Sara did feel more secure knowing she was not alone at night. She sighed contentedly when Eppie arrived and moments after the child hopped eagerly into the big bed they were both fast asleep.

In the morning, for the first time, Eppie didn't leave at the break of dawn. Sara rose quietly, pulled on her housecoat and drew the thick duvet up over the sleeping child, who stretched like a contented cat. Eppie seemed to be growing healthier and lovelier with each passing day.

When Sara got downstairs she found that Bertha wasn't in the kitchen, another first. Although repeatedly told that it wasn't necessary, Aunt Bertha had, until this morning, insisted on being there to prepare breakfast. "It's the most important meal of the day, you know."

Sara felt the pleasant buzz of contentment at the back of her neck. It would be grand to be the monarch of this huge kitchen, if only for one morning. The surface of the stove was icy cold, but she had no urge to cook another gut-stretching breakfast. Tea and toast would do just fine. She filled the electric kettle and plugged it in as the morning sun poured through the eastern window. She squinted and gazed at the distant evergreens, imagining the green ocean lapping the rocky shore just beyond.

A woman drowned down there. Why? And the woman had been seen near here the night of her death. Even in this brilliant stream of light, Sara's mood darkened and her mind formed a reproduction of the slimy Wellington boot she had found on her lawn. What had happened to the boot's owner? What had happened to those two young men she had met—whom the cop Jackie Cole said he'd look for? Sara shook her head, as if the action would erase her thoughts. It was all too much to absorb. Yet another part of her realized it could be, as they say, journalistic dynamite.

The breathy hissing of the boiling kettle took her back to the present moment and she rose to finish making the tea. She placed a single gauze bag of tea into the brown ceramic teapot as her mother would have done, filled it halfway up with water and added a second bag of Red Rose for good measure. She wanted it strong. She left the pot to steep under Bertha's colorful knitted cozy and dropped four slices of thick whole wheat bread into the toaster. Then she stepped out the kitchen door into the morning air. Beyond the shadow of the house the sun beckoned. Twenty steps brought her under the warming fingers of the light and she stood absorbing its therapeutic touch. She closed her eyes and breathed deeply.

She was startled out of her moment of peace by Eppie's panicked voice coming from just inside the kitchen door.

"Sara! Where are you? Where did you go?"

"I'm out here, Eppie." She waited until the child had run to her and stooped to meet her embrace. Eppie clung, burying her face in Sara's bosom. "What's the trouble, Sweetie?"

"I had a scary dream. When I woke up, you were gone and I thought I was all alone again."

Sara sighed. "It's all right. You're not alone anymore."

"I'm so scared. I don't want them to hurt you. Please don't ask too many questions. You aren't going to ask too many questions, are you?"

"Oh, Eppie. Aren't you being a little silly? What's wrong with questions? I work for a newspaper and that's what I do. No one will hurt me for asking questions." She separated herself from Eppie's grip and the two stood side by side in the sunshine.

"Oh, yes, they will. I had a dream and dreams are real. They come true. Don't ask too many questions. Promise!" She waved her finger in Sara's face like an old aunt.

"Okay, okay, I'll try not to ask any more than necessary." Eppie didn't look convinced so Sara decided to change the subject. "It looks like Bertha isn't coming over this morning. It'll be just you and me for breakfast. Won't that be lovely? You must be starving. I am." She draped her arm across Eppie's shoulders. Overhead, small clouds obscured the sun's warmth and light. She began to march the child toward the door. "Come back inside. I'm suddenly feeling a bit chilly. I'll make you a cup of tea just like my father made for me when I was your age." She was pleased that the idea seemed to brighten Eppie's face.

The sun had escaped from behind the clouds and the kitchen bloomed with light, which matched Sara's exuberant mood as she prepared breakfast, her maternal instincts ablaze. After their breakfast, Eppie took her plate and teacup to the sink and picked up her backpack. Sara saw Eppie safely aboard the yellow bus and, as it departed, did a spiraling dance across the graveled roadway, sending a flock of song sparrows fluttering boisterously from the willows that lined the road.

Inside her bedroom she let her housecoat drop and left it just where it landed. She could pick it up later. She walked naked to the dresser, feeling naughty, and set out a fresh outfit for the day, something soft and bright, she thought, something sexy. She decided on French vanilla cotton slacks and a red cashmere sweater. She slowly laid the clothes on the bed, drawing her cashmere sweater over her erect nipples, enjoying the gentle caress of the fabric, then turned the lock in the bedroom door, and slipped into the large bathroom, which adjoined her bedroom.

She placed the plug in the massive, free-standing tub, turned on the hot water and ran it a few minutes to warm the tub before adding cold from the other tap and walking out of the room while it filled.

Her eyes were drawn to the altar in her bedroom, which stood along the wall to the left of the huge bed. It had been several weeks now since Tony had left her, and almost as many on top of that since they had experienced decent sex together. There had, on occasion, been a kind of relenting, acquiescent sex that pleased neither of them before she finally resolved to put an end to their too violent relationship. What had once been magnificent had turned to something to be avoided, even dreaded. But she felt a longing to be with someone who cared for her and respected her and then passionately desired her. She would like to marry and have a child all her own. For some reason she could not comprehend, she felt intensely aroused as she approached the wooden altar—visions of erotic pleasure flitted through her mind as she pictured herself draped like a sacrificial virgin across its polished oaken surface, waiting to be ravished.

At that moment she passed before a tall mirror in a wide gilt frame and saw herself there, a lovely, nude stranger, looking incredibly sexy. Her fingers began to move across her golden body as if they belonged to someone else. They moved quickly and provocatively and her skin felt warm and alive. The nearby altar was decorated with carvings of grotesque cherubim with demonic faces and grossly disfigured bodies, which repulsed her. Yet the touch of her fingers excited her at the same time, in an exaggerated way, as if some innermost longings had taken possession of her arms and fingers and knew perfectly how to give her pleasure. She wanted to resist but she did not have the will to do so. She loosened her now reddened left breast and ran her fingers across the brilliant red oak surface of the altar, feeling the flesh-like warmth of the wood.

She moved her pelvis against the rounded corner of the altar, which seemed to have come alive, fitting itself to her, and gyrating against her, moving with her and filling her as she climbed to the top, her body exploding in spasms, collapsing in an immense screaming orgasm. She lay there; breath coming in rapid gasps, in a dream of bursting stars for what seemed only a few near-perfect moments.

...

Sara was startled awake by the obscene nagging of a telephone. She jumped up shivering and ran for the phone, picked it up and remembered that by now the water was likely overflowing the bathtub. She tossed the receiver onto the bed and picked up her housecoat from the floor, tying it around her as she ran into the bathroom. The overflow drain had handled the excess water. The tub was full and water continued to gush from the tap. She turned off the water and returned to the bedroom, trying to recall her dream. Oh, yes, the phone.

"Hello," she said.

"Good god, Sara. What's with you?

"Sorry, Laura. I was running a bath and I was afraid the tub was going to overflow."

"I've been calling you all day. Were you out?"

"I was right here. I must have dozed off."

"Dozed off! You must have passed out. This has to be the twentieth time I called. Did you have the phone unplugged or something?"

"No, I must have been asleep. I told you I was sleeping well. What time is it anyway?"

"Almost two o'clock."

"Holy shit!"

"What?" said Laura. "What's going on, Sara?"

"Nothing, don't worry. I just didn't hear the phone, that's all. It's a big house." Sara's head was spiraling. She felt breathless, alone, and out of control. It had been a few minutes past eight when she had come upstairs. She had been asleep nearly six hours. Six hours in the raw on top of that ugly old altar, perhaps the very altar that had been used to mutilate Bertha and the other children. What was happening to her? Why was she sleeping so much?

"Are you still there, Sara?"

"Yes, still here ... "

"Good. I've done some looking around. There isn't much out there, I'm afraid. I found a carbon copy of a certificate issued to a business called 'Safe Haven, Inc.' giving them the authority to operate a home for orphans and 'wayward girls'—funny to think how much our world has changed since those days, not so long ago, really—and the right to place 'the issue' of these girls in appropriate homes for their well-being and 'Christian welfare.'

"The certificate was made out to a Mr. Albert Coban. In another document, an act of incorporation, his wife was listed as Vice President and head nurse. He, of course, was President and a Mr. Calvin Coffin is listed as Secretary and Treasurer."

"Inabelle's husband."

"Pardon me?"

"I met that man's wife. Calvin Coffin was a victim of one of the house fires. He used to be the janitor at Safe Haven."

"I see. Well, there were the usual health and sanitation inspections—a clean bill of health each time. The operation ran about twenty years and then, suddenly, without explanation, it ceased. No more license applications, no more inspections, nothing. Not a single word anywhere about what happened. I tried to establish the whereabouts of Mr. and Mrs. Albert Coban, but no luck there, either. They seem to have disappeared without a trace."

"Keep trying, please. Don't give up."

"I won't. I am glad you are getting rested. I have to run. There are a couple of calls waiting on the other lines."

"Okay, thanks, I ... "

Laura had hung up.

The room came back into focus and with it a desire to get away from it. Yet she sat on the edge of the bed in a kind of daze. Slowly she pulled on her slippers. She had wasted the best part of the day and accomplished nothing—except a great orgasm. Eppie, though, should be pleased. Sara hadn't even been to the village, so she hadn't been able to ask too many questions.

The water in the bathtub was cold enough to make her teeth chatter. She reached into its icy depths, shivering as she pulled the rubber plug. When it was nearly empty, she replaced the stopper and turned on the hot. Good, she thought, the water heater had begun to catch up. This time she would put in just enough water to do the job. She lathered herself in soap, trying to scrub away the gloom that had descended on her following the phone call. After toweling herself dry, she threw on the clothes she had laid out earlier.

Something made her turn toward the altar. Its very presence made her angry. What had happened to her over those six hours on top of that piece of furniture? Why did she even have the urge to mount it in the first place? She felt foggy. She had the sense there had been a dream, or rather a nightmare so ugly her mind wouldn't let her recall what it was. She began to shiver, her attention once again drawn to the altar by something that seemed out of place.

A small drawer jutted from its side. With pounding heart, Sara approached the drawer and reached inside. Her fingers found and grasped something solid with the texture of dry skin. She held her breath and drew the object from its hiding place. In her grasp she held a small book, bound in tan suede. When she looked up from the book the drawer had disappeared as mysteriously as it had appeared. She set the book on the bed and tried to relocate the drawer and the mechanism that allowed it to open. The lines were there, barely discernible, but nothing she did would reopen it. What force had been behind the discovery of the book? Did she rock it open?

She struggled to recall something. And then a small door opened in her subconscious. She remembered the face of the girl she had seen in her dreams as she slept on the altar. The girl had spoken to her, pleaded with her, but Sara could not recall a word the child had spoken. But she was convinced to the depths of her being that the book that now lay on her bed was the reason for the dreams and it was extremely important.

CHAPTER TWENTY-ONE

21

Sara was jarred from her speculations by the distant blare of an automobile horn. Was Eppie home from school already? Sara looked at the clock. Yes, it was probably the school bus. She took the notebook she'd found in the secret drawer in the altar and placed it under her pillow, checked herself self-consciously in the mirror, blushing at the memory of her masturbation, and ran downstairs to meet the child.

Eppie was in a fury.

"What's the trouble?"

"They don't know nothing about nothing."

"Anything ... Who?"

"The kids. They say you think you're better than us. They say you're writing lies about Mussel Cove."

"Why would I write lies about Mussel Cove?"

"To punish us for what happened to the children."

"Do the kids know what happened at the Safe Haven orphan's home?"

"Everybody knows."

"Eppie, I'm going to ask an important question and I want you to answer honestly. You won't get into trouble, I promise."

Eppie waited, her face betraying her nervousness.

"Eppie, what happened to the minister's wife?"

No answer.

"Do any of your friends know how she died?"

Eppie stood like a pillar of salt. Sara didn't understand the danger. Eppie had lived here long enough to know that if Sara kept asking questions like these she would end up like the others.

"Are you going to tell me about the fires?" Sara asked.

Eppie sighed, relaxed her muscles and dashed toward the house.

"Bertha didn't show up today," Sara called after her. "Did she say anything about not coming over? I called her house and there was no answer."

Eppie stopped in her tracks and spun around. Color drained from her young face. "No," she blurted nervously. "She didn't say nothing ... I hope nothing bad happened."

"I'm sure it's all right. She's been coming here out of kindness. It wasn't a job and she wasn't paid. So I guess we shouldn't make a fuss about her missing a day."

Eppie interjected, "But she did promise we could make home-made pizza for supper today. It was going to be a surprise for you. I told her not to forget and she crossed her heart and promised she wouldn't."

Sara had a creepy sense of foreboding. "I'll call her," she said, trying to sound reassuring. I'm sure there's a simple explanation."

The phone rang sixteen times. There was no answering machine. Sara redialed the number carefully, checking it in the phone book in case she got it wrong the first time, but still no response. She gritted her teeth and called Mussel Drugs, hoping that blonde didn't answer. Luckily she heard Philip's sonorous baritone on the other end.

"Hi Philip, this is ..."

"Hi, Sara. I'd know your voice anywhere. And the call display says Milligan, the man who pays the bills at Safe Haven."

"I was wondering if Bertha mentioned that she wouldn't be coming here today. It seems she had a cooking project planned with Eppie and she hasn't shown up. I called and there was no answer at your place."

"That's strange. When I left for work she hadn't been in the kitchen. She usually starts the coffee and sets things up for me before she goes out. That concerned me but I just assumed she wasn't feeling well and was still in bed. She used to stay in bed for long spells when she was depressed. A few times in the past she just up and left for a few days without explanation. But that was years ago. I thought she was over all that."

"I'm sure it's nothing. But I could use a favor. If you could spare a few minutes to watch over Eppie, I'd love to run down into the village."

"Need a new sitter, eh?"

Instantly irritated, Sara's voice cooled. "Look, if it's a big deal, never mind. Eppie and I will manage. She can come along with me."

"Just kidding. I'll be over as soon as I finish here. If you need me before that, give me a call and Jane can come in. She doesn't mind. Her father loves to sit with her brats. See you in a while, all right?"

"All right."

As she hung up she noticed Eppie standing beside the window, staring out toward the woods.

"How long have you been there?"

"A while," said Eppie. "Do you think Bertha's dead?"

"Of course not," answered Sara, horrified. But her voice lacked conviction. "Why would you say that?" Eppie just stared at her. Sara didn't know which was worse: the ghoulish question or the blank stare. When it was obvious that no answer was forthcoming, Sara blurted out, "Let's get something to eat. We'll make what used to be my favorite meal when I was your age. My grandmother cooked it for me at our summer place. She called it: *Petti di pollo alle nocciole.*"

"What does that mean?"

"Bits of chicken with hazelnuts, I think. It has chicken breast and hazelnuts and other good stuff. I told Bertha about it and had her pick up the ingredients on her last shopping trip. It's so delicious and I'll bet you love it, too."

Eppie willingly helped cut up the vegetables. Sara worried about the child cutting herself with the kitchen knives but Eppie proved quite adept with the razor-sharp stainless steel Henckels. It turned out that Bertha hadn't bought any hazelnuts (Sara guessed they weren't available), so they used walnuts instead. The kitchen soon filled with delicious smells and good feelings, and yet both ate only to please one another.

Eppie was the first to break the silence as they worked together to clean up the table. "It was awful good, Sara, but all I can think of is that it's not the pizza we were going to make for you. I wonder what happened to Bertha."

"Me, too, Eppie. How about dessert?"

"No thanks. I got tummy cramps, and I'm scared I'll throw up. Can I go up to bed?"

"Of course, Eppie. Come here and let me feel your forehead." Eppie rose from her chair, dragged herself slowly and sadly around the table, stood next to Sara and waited patiently while Sara's warm hand measured the temperature of her forehead.

"My mother did that when I was sick. I like your hand on my head. It makes me feel safer."

"Well, you don't have a fever. You're as cool as iced tea."

"But I feel sick inside my belly."

"I hope you'll be better soon. There is something else I wanted to ask you." Eppie stiffened and Sara rose before speaking again. "You heard me talking to Philip so you may already know what I'm about to say ... Would you mind if he sat with you for an hour or so tonight? I have to run down into the village. You would really be helping me if you agree."

"You won't be asking too many questions, will you?"

"I stayed home all day today, so I wasn't able to ask a single one. I won't leave you alone with Philip if you're not comfortable with it."

"It's all right."

"If you fall asleep before I come back, I'll see you in the morning. I had agreed to go on a date with Philip tomorrow evening, but it looks like that's not in the cards unless Bertha shows up or I can stumble on another babysitter. And that's not likely considering I know hardly anybody in Mussel Cove. But it's not your worry. I won't leave you with anybody I don't trust."

"I know that. I'm going up now. I'm real tired. Please be careful. Good night."

"Good night, sweetie. Come here and let me hug you." They embraced a long minute before Eppie pulled away and raced upstairs. In spite of herself, Sara felt tears of maternal pleasure forming in the corner of her eyes. "Damn," she said quietly to the empty room.

...

A half-hour later, the doorbell rang. Philip was expected, but Sara hoped instead to find Bertha at the door, back from the doctor's appointment she hadn't wished to worry anyone about, or something simple like that. She opened the door a crack and peeked out. Philip stood on the doorstep, peering across the lawn in the direction of the ocean.

"Come in," she said, hurrying him along to the kitchen. "Have you heard anything from Bertha? You don't suppose she left for an appointment or a visit."

"No, I heard nothing. Aunt Bertha wouldn't do that without telling me—if she was well—and she's never been better than she's been feeling lately." He smiled at Sara and looked around the room. "Where's the kid?"

"Gone to bed. The poor little thing was exhausted. Did you have supper?"

"I got a pizza at Vito's."

"Any good?"

"Greasy and soggy and cold, but it half-filled the hole. Our date is off, I suppose?"

"Looks that way unless we can get a sitter."

"Maybe we could chat after you come back."

"Let's see how I get along. If I'm not too tired, we can have a cup of something and a bite to eat, but no promises. I'll try to find out if anybody saw Bertha. I might even find a babysitter, but don't hold your breath. Perhaps you can think of someone."

"Yeah, right. I haven't had much call for babysitters, but Jane might know someone who would come at short notice. She's always got sitters looking after her kids. I'll call her if you like."

"Perhaps. But I've just promised Eppie that I'd never leave her with anyone I don't trust. I'd hate to have her with someone she doesn't know."

"Will you be seeing anybody tonight while I'm here babysitting?"

"Am I going to see anyone? Of course I'll be seeing people, I'm a reporter! How can I be a reporter if I don't see people?"

"That's not what I meant."

"Do I detect a note of jealousy in your big, firefighter's voice? Look, Philip, if you don't want to do this for me you can buzz off. For Christ's sake, you sound like a jealous husband. You're not even a boyfriend and I've had enough of jealous men in my life."

"Touché," said Philip, blushing. "I'm being an asshole again. I don't know what's wrong with me lately. When I'm around you, my brain goes numb. The truth is I don't like Jackie Cole. In school he was a loser. He had lousy marks. He never took part in any after-school clubs and yet he made all the teams and he was always a hero in the games, even though he skipped practice. He didn't seem to care about girls and yet he could always get any girl he wanted. I didn't understand him then, and I don't understand him now. We had cops here who went to college and studied police techniques and they didn't last. Jackie never went anywhere or studied anything. He applied for a part-time policing job one summer a few years ago and he's still there. The village adores him and yet he rarely arrests anyone or does anything much else for that matter. We've had all this trouble lately and he doesn't seem to know what to do about it, or he doesn't care."

"No one seems to know what's going on. Not exactly a bunch of crackerjack experts."

"Yeah, you're right. And you're right about these feelings of mine. It's not your problem and what you do is none of my business. I'm sorry. You go along and do whatever you've got to do. Don't mind me. I'll look after things here." He stood up and walked to the sink, looking out the window. "I'll even do these dishes if you want."

She shrugged. "Did you call Marcel?"

"Marcel?"

"To ask if he's seen Bertha. You said you'd get in touch with him. I hope you're not jealous of him, too." She sat.

He turned and faced her. "Look, I said I was sorry, and, as a matter of fact I did call him right after I talked to you. In fact, I called him a number of times but he wasn't answering his phone. I'll try again later from here if you like."

She rose and walked past him to the window. He was standing at the edge of the table, his fingers spread, pressing firmly against the surface with his finger tips. He was contemplating his fingers and she watched them, too, as she spoke to him. "No, just leave him for now. If I come across him in the village, I'll ask."

"All right. I almost called the RCMP up in Sydney River, but I figured they'd just tell me to be patient. It was too soon. They told me the last time that people have to be missing 48 hours before they even listen to you. Or, they'd go digging around for information and start up that old unpleasantness about Aunt Bertha's nervous breakdowns. If she's just off somewhere doing her thing—whatever that is—she'll be madder than a wet hen if we get things all stirred up for nothing. Hey, what smells so good?"

"That was supper. I cooked tonight. There was lots left over. It's in the fridge. Help yourself, but don't eat what's on the pink plate. That's Eppie's, and she wants it later. There's cold beer in the fridge if you want, but you might want to go easy, since you have a big responsibility tonight. Remember that you're babysitting my little girl." She picked up her sweater.

"You sound like her mother or something. You're starting to take this domestic stuff pretty seriously." He stepped to the refrigerator and took out the platter of chicken. Sara slipped on the sweater, thinking it would likely get much cooler later, and misty. She crossed to the cupboard, handing him a plate and a knife, fork, and spoon.

"Don't hold your breath, darlin', though there'd be worse things than being that child's mother. I already like her a lot. I'm going to hate giving her up when this is over and I have to head back to Halifax."

"Maybe you won't go back to Halifax."

"Yeah, right. I might settle down and live out the rest of my natural days in this stimulating and enriching environment." She shook her head and rolled her large eyes. "No, I'll leave that to you."

"It wouldn't be so bad. You could keep the kid, and maybe find some dark, handsome professional to support you in a life of indolence. You could write a book or something." As he talked he loaded his plate and slipped it into the microwave. He tried several combinations of buttons with no success. The microwave beeped several times but refused to start.

Sara stepped over, touched two buttons and the appliance began to hum loudly. "Don't count on me being satisfied to be kept anywhere by anybody. I'm not a naive teenager who believes in fairytales."

"No, I suppose not. Thanks for the help. I wish they'd standardize the controls on microwaves." He shoveled food into his mouth and spoke before the mouthful was half-chewed. "Mmm, this is some good, Sara."

"I have to go," she said after a few moments passed in an awkward silence broken only by Philip's sounds of frenzied eating. "See you after a while. Keep a close watch on Eppie, okay?"

"I will, don't worry," he said, lifting another forkful into his open mouth.

CHAPTER TWENTY-TWO

22

St. Dunstan's Roman Catholic Church had been built with the intention that it would be the most substantial building in Mussel Cove. It was an outward sign of the deep devotion and enormous pride to have been found in this small parish when the building was built more than a century ago. It loomed above its squat neighbors like a fat mother hen in the midst of her brood. A wide, pillared portico spanned the full width of the massive stone structure and as Sara drove up an elderly priest sat smoking a cigarette on the limestone steps leading up to it. Sara guessed this was Father Doyle, the man who made a practice of wandering the streets and lanes of Mussel Cove night after night. She watched him watch her as she parked the Honda. He rose as she approached on foot.

"Can I be of assistance, my dear?" he asked. His blue eyes reflected the light from the lamps flooding the face of the church and seemed to be looking through her and beyond into some place in another time and space. Those eyes must have been compelling in the man's younger days, she thought. Now they were cloudy, bloodshot, puffed and tired, the eyes of someone who regularly struggled with insomnia. There was ample light to detail the heavy cigarette stains on his fingers. She wondered if there might be similar stains on his soul—stains that kept him from sleep.

"I don't know, Father. A woman disappeared last night. I was wondering if you noticed anything unusual when you were out walking."

He laughed. "I don't normally pay much attention to women," he said with a wink.

"I've seen you out walking. You must know what goes on around here. I thought you might have noticed something unusual last night."

"Who are we talking about? There was that unfortunate minister's wife who was found floating like a dead porpoise with a starfish dining on her face. And now my housekeeper tells me poor old Bertha Morris has gone missing. Are we talking about Bertha?"

"Yes."

"I haven't seen her for years—except passing by in the druggist's car. I know her from a long way back, an orphan in the house where you live. How are you able to stay there? I wouldn't sleep in that place—even if I could sleep—for all the Hail Marys in Cape Breton. And that's a lot of Hail Marys."

"So you know where I stay. Then you must know who I am?"

He snorted. "Everyone knows who you are. Aren't many faces like yours in this village."

"Faces like mine?"

"Pretty and unattached. The kind of face that usually means trouble for someone in a small place like this."

"I forgot that the clergy still used thought processes from the Middle Ages."

"I've been around a long time, but not since the Middle Ages," he chuckled. "Pretty faces have changed the world more than once. They're the stuff of great literature and the greatest stories in the history books. Cleopatra, Helen of Troy ... It's not your fault. God's, I guess. He miscalculated and made some of his children too beautiful, and others too damned evil. I've seen pretty faces come and go, and I've been here to witness the consequences. This village has seen more than its share of consequences."

"What about the children in church-run schools, the orphans and natives? Surely you can't blame women for that?"

"Who said anything about women? Women aren't the only ones with pretty faces. I'm not trying to make excuses for those leaders with whom I share the faith. Neither ordination nor a strong vocation ensures that evil will not enter a person. Perhaps the church is at fault for its policy on celibacy, I don't know. Are you a Catholic, by any chance?"

"Sort of."

"You can always tell, you know. Do I detect bitterness? The Christian faith is such a wonderful gift. But once it ebbs away, it's gone, perhaps forever. The eyes view the world in a completely different way, not permitting the simple joys and comforts of faith. An incalculable loss." He strode like a young man to the cemetery fence and leaned his elbows on the top rail. "Would you ever come to Mass on Sunday?"

"How long have you been serving here? I thought you guys moved around. I didn't think priests spent entire careers in one place." She moved over to the fence beside him.

He gazed across the graveyard, his eyes focusing on one stone after another as if recalling the lives of the persons lying beneath.

"I began here as an assistant to Father Campbell, who was also here a very long time. Then the Bishop moved me around to several other parishes in the diocese. I returned after Father Campbell passed away—that was around the time Safe Haven closed its doors for good. I was trained in counseling, and my talents were put to the test. I left again for a few years, to clear my mind, but by then I had witnessed too much to be fit to live anywhere else, so they let me retire here."

"Then you know all about Safe Haven."

"No one ever knows all about anything. But I knew enough about the Safe Haven operation from the beginning to want the heathen place shut down. When I was young I labored under the illusion that the devil was mere superstition. Safe Haven taught me how wrong I was. I learned that evil is manifested in the power the fallen angels exercise through the minds and hearts of susceptible human beings. Nowadays we choose to ignore evil. No one wants to be responsible for his or her own behavior. I saw the folks at Safe Haven encourage frightened young girls to drop their babies as if they were mere excrement and walk back to their meaningless lives. I didn't fully realize the extent of the evil, but I had a bad feeling that refused to go away. Now the curse of Safe Haven will be upon this village forever. And what you're doing will see that it sticks."

"Just doing my job, Father. What good did silence ever do?"

The old man shrugged and sighed. "Will I see you at Mass on Sunday? A few fragments of God's grace would do you no harm."

"I'll ask Eppie if she'll come with me—color for my story. No promises, though."

"Good." He lit a fresh cigarette from the butt of the last one and coughed several times. He returned to the church steps and sat, "Some of the babies were adopted and there were certain fees. That part was all very legitimate, if not totally ... ethical There weren't the government controls then that there are now. Rich Yankees paid big bucks for those pretty little Canadian bastards. And lots of my parishioners benefited financially from this baby farm, though all of them were eventually cursed by their prosperity." He coughed again and spit.

"Pardon my bad manners, dear," he said, wiping his mouth with a large cloth handkerchief. "I know many things which I can't ever repeat. Being a Catholic, you are aware of the implications of the Seal of Confession. I'm on shaky ground as it is. I can't do something that guarantees the loss of my soul. But there are others who know almost as much as I do. Keep on asking. Someone will probably have the answer.

"This town is full of folks whose parents were involved in shameful doings. Most of the elders are gone now. Keep your eyes open if you want to find the truth, and it won't hurt to stay up late—really late. Mussel Cove at night shows a different face, perhaps its true face. Be observant but be careful whom you trust. I have to go in now. I'm getting a chill."

"One more question," Sara insisted. "What happened to the woman who drowned in the ocean?"

"The Baptist. Shirley Black. Kind of funny if it wasn't so tragic. She died in the exact location where most of the Baptist christenings were done back in the good old days. There were Baptists involved in the very early days of Safe Haven, before

the Cobans bought into the operation. It was a fairly decent en-
terprise in the beginning, a bunch of people who only wanted to
do what was best for those unfortunate girls and their babies. But
those folks didn't last long after the Cobans arrived. It became a
business—and a cruel, calculated one at that. They dumped the
ordinary people from the board and brought in the suits—the
business types. The almighty dollar was the bottom line after that.
Ironic, isn't it, about her drowning? Total immersion, ha." The
priest's irreverent laughter brought on a coughing spasm and the
rank tobacco bitterness of his breath was almost enough to make
Sara retch along with him.

"If you want to know more you should ask the Baptists. There
is no seal to be broken there, especially by Mrs. Bell at the funeral
home. She'll be delighted to fill you in on all the gossip. Mind
you, that isn't primarily a Baptist trait. My own flock could match
her word for word. I expect most of the citizens wouldn't want to
talk to you, but I'm betting Mrs. Bell won't be able to resist an
attentive audience. There isn't much gets by our Mrs. Bell—especially at the very end of it all." The old priest began to chuckle
once more, and then to cough and retch. He obviously considered
himself quite the comedian. She turned to leave but he called after
her and she stopped and turned.

He was grinning. "I'll be watching for you at ten-thirty Sunday
morning, unless you're one of those Saturday evening types. Now
you be careful around those Baptists." He chuckled and managed
to restrain himself from coughing. "The dead woman was a loyal
and devoted wife—not such a rare thing as some folks think. Her
husband is a fine Christian gentleman, a credit to his own or to any
denomination, I might add. It wouldn't hurt to have a word with
him as well. He may know a thing or two about Safe Haven. His
folks worked in the kitchen up there—paid his way through Bible
school with the money they earned working for the Cobans." He
climbed the steps, flicking his cigarette butt into the middle of the
thick lawn, where it landed amid a shower of sparks before fading
and disappearing into the gloom.

"You ought to be more careful, Father. You could start a fire," she said under her breath, aware that he was out of earshot.

...

Sara left her car in the church parking lot and headed out on foot toward the funeral home that was only a short distance from the large church. She enjoyed the stroll, and the fresh Maritime air washed the remnants of cigarette smoke from her nostrils.

The plastic sign on the funeral home door read, "Come in, we're open." Sara opened the door carefully—funeral homes always made her nervous. A plump woman in a billowing dress covered outrageously in scarlet and orange flowers sailed in from an inner door.

"I'm sorry. We're closed, dear," she said.

"The sign said 'open,' and the door wasn't locked."

"That sign always says 'open'—and the door is never locked. People know when we open up and they know when we're closed," she said, as if anyone with a bit of sense would know it, too. "What can I do for you, dear?"

"I hoped we could talk."

"You're that newspaper woman who's been keeping the McNeil child over at the old orphanage, eh?"

"Yes. The priest suggested you were the person to talk to for good, solid information. He said you knew everybody and you got your facts straight."

"Did he now," she smiled, obviously pleased at the old priest's recommendation. "Odd that he'd say that. I hardly know him. We're Baptist, you see."

"Father Doyle mentioned that. But he said you were decent and reliable. I suppose he would have been involved in funeral arrangements and the like."

"That's right, we are an ecumenical business. Mussel Cove is too small for religious strife. I'm proud to say that all the churches deal with us."

"So you are reliable."

"I suppose so. Well, come on in. But first I got to get my bread out of the oven before it turns to charcoal. Wait a minute, and I'll cut us a fresh slice. I'll bring you coffee, too. You may as well have a bite while you ask me those questions. I won't be a minute."

Forty-five minutes later, Sara left. The bread was delicious and Amy related in minute detail all she could recall of Shirley Black's life and her penultimate visit to the funeral home.

Next, Sara reluctantly decided to visit the Baptist parsonage. She hated to bother the family of the deceased so close to the tragic event—and she was still hurting from her own father's recent funeral. But the truth was the truth.

There was no response to the doorbell, so she tried knocking. Either no one was home, or they had decided not to answer. Where to next? If anyone knew Bertha's whereabouts, it would be Marcel. Sara recalled the realtor's letters addressed to Bertha that she had seen in Marcel's apartment and how Bertha had spoken so often of her old friend from Safe Haven, Marcel Vertu, the school principal.

His restaurant was almost empty, and a waitress was wiping tables and setting them for the next morning's breakfast rush. The tall thin woman guessed why Sara was here. "He's in his apartment doing up some school work, I believe. I bet he'll be glad to see you. You made a real impression the other day. He hasn't been able to shut his yap about you since."

Sara hesitated.

"Go on in. Give his door a couple of kicks before you open it."

Sara approached the door, and just for the heck of it, kicked, but only once. Moments later it opened, and the lines on Marcel's usually pleasant face rearranged themselves from a scowl into a grin. "Ah," he sighed, "civilization has returned to my humble abode. Please come in, Sara. I was afraid you'd had enough of me. I'm sure you've been busy? I heard about the tragedy down below your place. You must find it all terribly disturbing. I thought this latest event might drive you out of Mussel Cove before I got a chance to see you again."

"I'm still here. May I come in?"

"Of course, you must. You will have a glass of wine. I have a treat for you. I found a decent French Bordeaux in Sydney yesterday, in anticipation of just such a visit. Come in. Come in."

Sara waited until she had almost finished her first glass, and Marcel had refilled it before she asked, "Have you been speaking with Bertha lately?" She watched his face.

"Not for a couple of days. Isn't she a marvel? How is the old girl?"

"I don't know. She seems to have disappeared."

Marcel's forehead became creased with lines. "Disappeared. Have you spoken with Philip? Surely he knows where she is."

"I spoke with him. As a matter of fact, he's sitting with Eppie right now so I could step out for a bit and make some inquiries. He has no idea where Bertha went, either."

Marcel stood up, stretching and groaning, muttering about how he must be getting old, as getting up from a chair was becoming a lot harder than it used to be. He stepped to the window and turned. He looked her in the eye, his face full of intensity. "This is upsetting. How long exactly since you've seen her?"

Sara reviewed the events of the past few days for him. She was feeling a fair buzz from the wine and her mind strayed to the book she had hidden under her pillow and the circumstances leading up to its discovery.

He tilted his head to peer at her, but something personal and private in her eyes made him turn away. She blushed, confused by her emotions, and pondered mentioning the book she'd found, but decided she wanted to have a thorough look at it before turning it over to anyone. He topped up her wineglass and sat beside her, closer than she might have expected. For some reason she trusted him. As she turned slightly toward him, their legs touched briefly and she could feel his warmth. He pulled away quickly; it was his turn to blush. Sara was surprised. She recalled how Bertha had reacted to intimacy and wondered if Marcel had been similarly damaged by his experiences at Safe Haven.

He stood and seemed to be distracted by something in the kitchen. She wondered what he saw in there of interest, but decided it was simply his way of not looking her in the eye. "So," he said nervously, "Philip is back at your place caring for the child. I envy his youth and vitality. I wouldn't let you out of my sight if I were him."

His eyes looked sad. Yet there was something quite attractive about him. But why had he pulled away? She had had enough experiences with men to realize she was attractive enough. Normally men responded positively and warmly to contact with her. She tried to recall whether she had said or done something to make him react negatively to her.

Marcel seemed to sense her unease. "There is so much about me you do not know," he said, trying to explain what had never been voiced. He continued, "Just understand that I would change places with Philip a hundred times over without a moment's hesitation. He has everything I don't. Some women find me interesting because of the charming manners I put on."

Sara reached out to touch his arm, trying to reassure him in some way. But Marcel winced and stepped back out of reach.

"What is it, Marcel? Did I do something wrong?" She wondered: What is happening here? She considered reassuring him that she had no interest in him in that way but decided it wouldn't help.

"Oh, poor Sara. More like, poor me ... you're not doing something wrong. I'm ... sorry ... you are the loveliest creature to have entered my life since ... " He stopped in mid-thought and stared up at the ceiling. "But it doesn't matter. I'm so sorry. My reputation is a huge joke. Around the restaurant, the girls make up stories about what happens when they visit me in my apartment. For some reason I attract beautiful young women the way cats are attracted to those allergic to their dander. That attraction has been both a boon and torture."

"Does any of this have to do with Safe Haven?"

"Everything here has to do with Safe Haven, Sara. Everything."

"You are such a weirdly interesting man, Marcel," said Sara, her eyes misting over in spite of her efforts to control her emotions. Too much wine, she thought.

Marcel took her shoulders in his strong fingers and held her firmly at arm's length. He appeared to be looking through her and past, into some invisible distance. "It's time to return to your young man. Then you ought to make plans to leave the village as soon as possible. I mean it: it would be wise to put as much distance between you and Mussel Cove as possible. It is no longer safe here."

Sara reflected. Again with the threats—or well-intentioned warnings. Just like Bertha, now missing. She spoke: "Perhaps, but I have things to do. I'm not walking away from Eppie just yet."

"Take her with you. I don't think it is too late for her, although it soon will be. There is no need to remain here. This place has nothing to do with your life and Eppie's leaving will change nothing. She is no safer here than you. Mussel Cove is not the place to define a life for someone like you. You can do more for Eppie's future by getting her out of here and giving her a new start. That I guarantee." His fingers tightened on her shoulders. She was suddenly frightened and could hardly bear the pain, but resolved not to let it show. "Please think hard about what I am saying to you, and then do what is wise. You must. Pack your bags. Tonight."

She could stand it no longer. "Let go, Marcel! You're hurting me! Do you have any idea how strong you are?"

His eyes widened in alarm. "I'm sorry." He released her. "But I insist you get away from here. For your own safety and for the child."

"Perhaps, but not for a few days." She rubbed her arms and no longer looked at him when she spoke. She had had enough of being bullied by men using force.

"You are being as foolhardy as that minister's wife," he said, his attempt at a smile now abandoned. "I'm so worried. With Bertha missing you are in more danger than before."

Sara didn't know what to think. "You may be right. I will consider what you've been telling me. I have a few promises to keep, though," she said. "Perhaps you could help me with just one of them?" She no sooner spoke than she wondered if she could trust this man to act rationally enough to deserve her trust. Then she told herself that he was, after all, the principal of Eppie's school. But she had just been given a glimpse of his private demons. She seemed to have a knack for discovering the flaws in the men she met.

She watched as he worked to get himself in check. The emotion seemed to drain from his face. It was replaced by a sort of cold dignity. He coughed and then spoke in a clear, controlled voice. "I would love to do something to make up for having hurt you."

"Philip asked me out tomorrow night. This was, of course, before the trouble with Bertha. She was going to babysit Eppie but now she's gone who knows where. I wonder if you might watch the child if Philip and I went out. We're trying to figure out what became of Bertha. We won't be awfully late."

He didn't hesitate. "I would be delighted to look after Eppie. Be as late as you like. In fact, the later the better. I don't sleep all that well at night and I have schoolwork to complete and there's the restaurant bookkeeping to check over. What time do you need me?"

"How about eight?"

"Eight it is. So long, Sara. Thank you for caring." He kissed her cheek lightly and fatherly as if she were a porcelain doll. "I still wish you would change your mind about leaving. But if not, promise me you will be very careful."

"You can be sure of that, Marcel," she said, rubbing her sore arms.

CHAPTER TWENTY-THREE

23

Philip checked his watch; time had slowed to a crawl. If Sara didn't get back soon he'd go nuts. They would have no time together. It wasn't fair.

He wondered if Eppie was asleep. If she wasn't, he could pass the time by talking with her. He was jumpy. Did all old wooden structures make sounds like this? Usually it didn't bother him to be alone in a building. He spent a great deal of time by himself at the pharmacy after hours, and at the fire hall. But something about the creaks, groans and rattles of this ancient relic kept his heart in his throat. Between wind gusts, the house fell silent, leaving Philip to listen to the thunder of his own heart.

He stretched and yawned, then stood up and began to whistle "The Old Gray Mare," hoping that a change of position and some noise of his own would ease the tightness he felt across his shoulders. He yearned for a television but knew there was none. He consciously avoided looking out the dark-faced windows, figuring if he didn't look out, no unexplained movement out there could alarm him. He wouldn't be scared if he was outside, he knew from experience. He wasn't afraid of the night, or darkness. It was this speculation on the unknown that spooked him. Some wayward child could just now be poised to toss a rock through the glass at him, or some nut with a high-powered rifle could be mistaking him for some imagined enemy and the bullet could blast through his face before he saw anything. Sara could return and find blood and brains, bone and guts splattered across the kitchen's fading wallpaper. He coughed and cleared his throat. He had to settle his churning mind, slow it down before he suffocated.

Perhaps I will check the kid, he thought. Standing idle allowed the mind too much scope for stupid, wasteful speculation.

The steps leading up the stairs were wide, solid, and highly polished, obviously Aunt Bertha's work. There was not so much as a creak beneath his stockinged feet. He had removed his shoes earlier so the noise they made on the hardwood floors would not wake Eppie up, but now he wished she were awake. So what if she was still up when Sara returned. He didn't care any more. He just wanted to get out of here and go home.

Not that being at home was any great joy. He was not accustomed to being alone in that house either. At university and graduate school he had shared accommodations with several other rural Nova Scotians. The relationships had always been cordial but he never developed the sort of strong lifetime friendships he witnessed all around him. It hadn't seemed appropriate somehow. He didn't have much in common with any of them and he likely wouldn't see any of them after school was over. For the most part he had spent his time in study, occasionally having the room to himself, but there were always the constant comings and goings expected in college residences.

He had only spent one night alone since Aunt Bertha had disappeared and already he had become aware of strange noises in her house. As a result he hadn't slept well and found he was actually a little nervous even in his own room. If it hadn't been for the liquor he probably wouldn't have slept a wink. Now he was alone in Safe Haven, a house of which he had always been very much afraid.

He arrived at the top of the stairs and found the first door ajar. He looked inside, noting a pile of Sara's clothing on the bed. So this was her bedroom. He wanted to step inside and explore, but thought better of it, until he at least knew whether Eppie was asleep or awake.

The next door was also open wide. So stupid, he thought. A

closed bedroom door could mean the difference between life and death. So many otherwise intelligent people died in their beds from smoke inhalation every year with the fire occurring dozens of feet away. Had the door been closed they might have had a chance to wake up and escape before they smothered or were consumed by flame. Philip glanced inside the room where moonlight streamed in through the window. Eppie lay contentedly on her side. He envied her. How could she sleep in this creepy, noisy house? He started back along the hall toward the stairs.

This time, when he came to Sara's door, he stopped and slipped inside. He knew there couldn't be anyone in there with him but, still, he felt as if he was being observed. His heart rate increased and his palms began to sweat. Yet he was excited by the fact that Sara couldn't possibly know he was in there. He looked around the room, up into the corners and at the light fixtures, expecting to find a camera, but saw nothing out of the ordinary.

His eyes took in the elegant oak furnishings and trim and the extravagant draperies. He glanced right, past the tall mirror, to where the door of the bath stood ajar. He tiptoed over and peered inside, his imagination creating images of her daily routine.

This is where Sara bathed. Here she peeled off her clothes and slipped naked into this very tub. Lucky tub, he thought, to contact her soft womanly flesh, flesh sparkling with shiny droplets of water and bath oil, clumps of fragrant bubbles clinging here and there or else gliding like a graceful skier down her glorious slopes.

He returned to her bedroom and sat on the end of the large bed, letting himself bounce gently and regularly as if testing the tension of the bedsprings. The clothes she had worn earlier lay beside him in a pile where she left them before going downstairs. He picked up her bra and looked at it, read 36C on the tiny label with the washing instructions. He felt himself hardening. The bra wasn't especially sexy; no lace, just beige material designed to support those glorious breasts. He set the bra approximately where he found it a few moments before. He bent down and pressed his face into the middle of her underwear, his nose inside her panties, and savored their mustiness. He lay down across the bed with his face in her clothes and ground his pelvis against the firm surface of the mattress. Smelling her sex while grinding his manhood, he came almost immediately in his briefs.

He quickly rose from the bed, eager to clean up any evidence of his having been there before Sara returned. As he returned from the washroom and did one final sweep of the room, he discovered the leather-bound book Sara had partially hidden under her pillow. He carefully removed the book, noting its exact location and orientation, so that when he finished looking it over, he could put it back exactly as it had been found.

The first few pages, written in ornate fountain pen ink, which had begun to fade, consisted of dates and numbers indicating the payment of substantial sums of money. In another section, there were pages of names and dates that had been crossed out by a single line of thick black ink. Each name had been assigned a circled number. Unlike the entries on the first few pages, no amount of money appeared following these entries. Philip continued to flip through the pages.

In the center of the book he found a small hand-drawn map of what he assumed to be the Safe Haven property and adjoining land, including Pox Island. Small circles appeared on the map at varying intervals all over the property, each containing a different number.

Philip suddenly heard a noise, the concussion of a door being firmly closed. He pushed the book under the pillow, and scurried out into the hall. Sara was nowhere in sight. Good. He heard a quiet rustle of fabric in Eppie's room. The child was likely shifting her position in the bed; no time to check on her now; he ought to hustle down to meet Sara before she had a chance to get upstairs. He was afraid she might read some guilty look on his face if she met him up here. Before he was halfway down, Sara arrived at the bottom step.

"Eppie's sound asleep," he said. "How did you get along in the village?"

"Okay, I guess." She turned and stepped back toward the kitchen. He hurried down the last few steps and followed close behind.

"I managed to speak with a few people," she continued. "I had hoped to have a word with Reverend Black and the boy, Ira, whom I've heard so much about, but they must have been out somewhere or decided not to answer when I rang. I stopped in on Marcel after that."

"Oh," said Philip. In spite of his best effort, he was only too aware of his mincing tone. Immediately he regretted the sound, but it was too late.

"Can't I even use Marcel's name in front of you? What have you got against him?"

"I don't like the man."

"Him, too. How come?"

"I don't know. He gives me the creeps; he always has. Besides, you seem to like him a lot. I can't help feeling a little jealous. It's nobody's fault that I have these feelings, is it?"

"I suppose not, although it's absurd."

"You're probably right. Maybe my dislike for him is another kind of jealousy. When I was a kid he moved back to Mussel Cove. I remember it like it was yesterday because it changed my life. Aunt Bertha started to go over to his place lots of times and left me with a sitter. I didn't like that one little bit. She was never the same after he came back here. She told me how he was helping her, but that wasn't how I saw it. Unless getting help automatically made you completely unhappy."

"So you have a vivid memory of that time. Do you remember what she said about him?"

"Of course. One day she came home and told me a guy she used to know as a kid had moved back to Mussel Cove. I remember she was all excited, like it was Christmas. Aunt Bertha kept saying she couldn't understand why he came back. I remember being afraid they'd get married and go away and leave me, but nothing of that sort ever happened. I don't quite know about their relationship, but there's certainly a close connection. Did he know anything about where she might be?"

"If he did, he didn't let on. He seemed genuinely surprised to hear she had disappeared. But it was strange. He said almost exactly the same thing Bertha said the last time we talked. Except he said it more forcefully." She rubbed her arms and sighed.

"What was that?"

"For me to pack my bags and get far away from here. Like Mussel Cove is the Pit of the Damned or something."

Philip swallowed and reddened, looking concerned. "And what did you say?"

She walked to the window without answering. Philip stood behind her, looking out. Without a word she slipped past and they sat at opposite ends of the long table. Several minutes passed in uncomfortable silence.

"I think it's time we called the cops in on this and firmly pressured them to give us results," Sara finally said, "Jackie Cole is entirely too absent from this whole sordid business."

...

Eppie had heard Sara's return. Shortly after Philip had gone downstairs to meet Sara, Eppie had followed them on tiptoe. She entered the den beside the kitchen, where she now squatted in the corner covered in darkness. She had heard Sara call Jackie Cole and leave a message on his machine about Bertha's being missing. She enjoyed the invisibility darkness gave you once you got used to moving around in it. She had heard Philip at her bedroom door a bit earlier and had faked being asleep. He was an adult, and like all adults, he assumed children were completely predictable. That was why adults were so easy to fool. She had decided to watch where he went and what he did. He was completely unaware of her eyes following his every move as he went sneaking around Sara's things in her bedroom.

Eppie wondered what he thought about the little book he'd discovered under the pillow. She'd found it earlier and had figured out what it was. It would mean they could finish digging earlier than planned and the cycle could finally end. Freedom could come for all of them, even the dead. The thought made her very happy. She had made a carefully drawn copy of the map in pencil and hid it in her shoe. It wasn't perfect but it would do. Now she hated Philip even more than before. It made her sick to remember how he had held Sara's underwear to his smirky face and rolled around like a nasty dog on her bed. She growled like a small animal, stretched and yawned, then settled down to listen to the voices in the kitchen.

"I told Marcel I couldn't leave just yet," Sara said with a sigh. "Because of Eppie. She's really sweet, you know. I let her come into my room at night and crawl up beside me."

"You mentioned that the night of the fire at the Stitch house."

"Did I?" She returned to the window. This time Philip stayed put.

"I like my privacy, but once I realized how frightened she was I didn't mind so much. Now, somehow I don't feel right until she comes in and settles down. It's really silly how we work at fooling one another sometimes, she and I. I wonder if she knows that I always wait for her. Sometimes she comes in when I'm awake. Other times she goes to bed in her room. Those nights I go to look in on her and she pretends to be asleep. Then I go to my bed and pretend I'm asleep until she comes."

"You're not actually considering raising her, are you?"

Sara picked up a soiled plate and its cutlery from the table and carried them to the sink. "I haven't planned that far ahead. I have thought about it a bit lately. I would love to have a child of my own. In fact ..." she trailed off. "Well," she said, snapping back, "I suppose reality will set in once I finish the story. It's easy to forget what life is really like while I'm living free up here in this mansion with a free housekeeper ... well, I used to have a free housekeeper." She dropped in the plug and began to fill the sink with hot water. She tossed a dish towel at Philip and turned to the sink. He caught it as it sailed like a magic carpet toward his knees. He rose, grimaced as he adjusted his undershorts, and stepped to the sink.

"I'm sorry," he said. "I meant to have those dishes done before you got back."

"It's all right. I appreciate your having been here. I'll wash. You dry. It'll just take a moment."

"Glad to," he said.

"I couldn't raise her by myself, I don't think. Back in Halifax I've got this tiny apartment that I just love because it's so cozy. Well, it was until ..."

"Until what?"

"It doesn't matter. Where was I?"

"You were talking about your apartment."

"Oh yes. My apartment is small and my lifestyle isn't family-oriented. I don't stay around the apartment except to sleep and maybe watch an occasional TV program or listen to music. I guess I'm selfish. When I quit my teaching job in the States I left behind a relationship reaching back to my childhood. Tony turned out to be a bit too prone to violence to suit me. It was likely for the best because I was already feeling like my life was ... on the point of devouring me, almost. My decision meant having to cope with loneliness for the first time in my life, but I had to make it. I had no real choice. The past few months were the only time in my life when I've been completely independent and I think I'm starting to really enjoy it. I want to keep exploring that path. Plus, to tell you the truth, I had a bad miscarriage in connection with Tony. So I'm not sure about becoming a mother and having a child—or taking care of a child—so soon after that."

In the adjoining room Eppie stiffened. Anger burned like fire within. She was shocked to discover she hadn't been thinking about the future either. Sara had arrived in her life precisely when she was needed. One set of parents had been consumed by forces Eppie couldn't control. It was like the war her father told her about, the war that had taken her grandfather out of the world before she ever got a chance to know him. Her father had told how the war marched across Europe and his father had gone across the ocean to stop it. But it was unstoppable until, like a forest fire, it had burned itself out. By then her grandfather and millions of others had died in its path.

What was happening in Mussel Cove was like that, she thought. She was like a soldier in danger of being burned and anyone who got in the way of the fire would die. Her parents were gone already, and Sara had taken their place. She was like Eppie's parent now, and parents shouldn't leave their children. Except for the fire her parents would never have left her behind. But Sara was planning to leave. Eppie had believed in her, and trusted her, and even begun to love her, and now Sara was ready to leave—to go away and forget, as if none of this had ever happened.

Eppie realized she was grinding her teeth. She stood up and prepared to return to her room. She was too angry. Tonight she wouldn't go to Sara's bed. She was trying to decide what to do. Should she call the others for help? They would punish Sara if she asked. They could change the plan. Someone else would come to tell the story. There might even be a bigger story to tell if something awful happened to the pretty woman from Halifax.

When she arrived at the base of the stairs the two voices were still audible although she was now trying not to listen.

"Oh, Philip, it looks like our date, which was off, is on again. Marcel agreed to look after Eppie tomorrow evening if we want to go out somewhere, if you don't find the arrangement with my 'friend' too offensive."

"Marcel agreed to babysit while we go out? That's great!" Philip grinned at her.

"You *are* looking forward to this aren't you?" She was chuckling, enjoying his enthusiasm. She was flattered but confused. "One thing bothers me. It doesn't feel right. It's almost like you don't care. Or is it that you don't want to think about it?"

"About Aunt Bertha?"

"Yeah."

"If you only knew how relaxed I'm NOT. She took off a few times before. I believe I mentioned this."

"Yes, you did."

"It was a mess. She was having a nervous breakdown a few months after Marcel came back from Europe. She simply up and left. Disappeared for two weeks and then returned without any explanation. It happened several times. I still don't know where she was. It was never for long and I managed to look after myself until she returned. She did leave a note most of those times so I knew, at least, that she intended to leave. And she would eventually come back."

Isn't it possible she left a note this time, too?"

"Surely I would have found it by now."

"Not if someone took it away. Perhaps she was planning to go somewhere and left a note, and someone forced her to change her plan and stole the note."

"That sounds a bit far-fetched. Who's going to break in to steal a note—and nothing else? But when I get home I'll have another look around."

Sara checked her watch and nudged him toward the door. "I think it's time for me to get my beauty sleep. And I have a few things to do before that happens."

"Yeah, I'm tired as hell, too."

"Thanks for looking after my little girl, Philip." She gave him a light peck on the cheek.

He tried to kiss her mouth, but got a mouthful of hair for his trouble as she turned her head to the side.

Eppie began to climb the stairs. As she went her spirits began to lift, too. At least Sara called me her little girl, she thought. Perhaps I will sleep in her bed after all. There may not be much more time.

CHAPTER TWENTY-FOUR

24

Bertha's head ached, and the incessant blinking of the television monitors stoked the blaze behind her eyes. The room was dark but the monitors provided sufficient light for her to see that she was tied in a chair inside a building and to recognize this small room in the barn by what remained of its stalls. She was worried. She felt sore and thirsty, and wondered if she was going to die here in this dark place. Life hadn't brought her much joy and she was tired. Death would perhaps be a blessing. If there was a Heaven she saw no reason why she shouldn't go there. Unless, even after all her prayers, she hadn't been forgiven for what she had done to Lynn.

The memories came flooding back.

She and her twin sister Lynn had explored Pox Island one warm, summer afternoon while the Cobans were away from the orphanage attending a business meeting. The twins and their friend, Marcel, had rowed across the narrow strait between the island and the estate in an old wooden boat they had discovered pulled up on the shore. They had brought a bag of sandwiches and bottles of milk stolen from the kitchen pantry. They spent a joyous afternoon just being children, exploring the island of their dreams, and playing tag and hide-and-seek in a huge empty barn. Until the previous year, this barn had been part of an active farm, but the farmer and his family had been bought out by the Cobans and had moved away.

Now Bertha had awakened to find herself a prisoner in the old barn that had been part of the best day of her life. She had been more afraid than this only once before but that had been a long time ago, the night her twin had died; the night she had lost her hand. But she had a bad feeling in her gut. Something told her this was just the beginning of something unimaginably bad.

She had sensed a rumbling vibrating noise in the background in the moments before she became conscious of her surroundings, and it continued incessantly. Bertha concluded she was hearing some kind of engine. The penetrating sound and the stench of diesel fuel did nothing for her headache and its accompanying nausea. If only she could get away from here and warn Sara and Eppie. Philip could survive on his own while she was away, but what would happen to the girls at Safe Haven now that she was gone?

She counted the screens of five television monitors in front of her. If she were able to stand up, they would be just above her eye level. So far nothing other than trees and water had appeared on the screens.

Her head throbbed. She recalled putting away the supper dishes at Safe Haven the night before and then going home. Or had she gone home? Everything in her memory was scrambled. What had happened to her? Why was she here? She'd woken up not long ago wondering who had brought her and tied her in this chair. She was cold—that damp penetrating cold that comes out of the soil and works its way inside your body to the bone. The room stank of stale manure, electronics, fuel and rotting wood. She had already become used to all that. But she would never adjust to the terror and hopelessness she was feeling.

CHAPTER TWENTY-FIVE

25

It was difficult to get Eppie moving the next morning. Her eyes were red from lack of sleep and she dragged her small feet reluctantly down the stairs, repeatedly pausing to yawn. Sara fixed breakfast for her: scrambled eggs, bacon, and toast with Bertha's strawberry freezer jam, but Eppie just pushed it around her plate. She refused to head out to the school bus, saying she preferred to stay home.

"You'll just go away and leave me," she announced and clung to Sara like someone drowning. "When are you going home to Halifax?"

Sara wondered how much of last night's conversation with Philip Eppie had overheard—the poor kid. She put her arms around the worried girl and hugged her. "Don't worry, honey, I can't go back for a while. There are things to be done. You'll never be left alone."

It took a lot to convince Eppie that Sara wouldn't run off to Halifax while the child was in school, but eventually she reluctantly boarded her bus. Sara considered locking the gate but decided there was no need during daylight hours. She went inside, picked up from breakfast and retrieved the book she'd cached under her pillow. Outside again, she took the book on a brief walking tour of the property, pinpointing each circled site indicated on the map inside. At almost every site she discovered signs of recent digging and careful efforts to hide any evidence that such digging had taken place.

"Dear Jesus," she said aloud. Who has been doing all the digging out here? What did they find? Her stomach was churning. Who should I call? Who can I trust? Philip is all right, I think. Unless ... could Philip be involved in some way? He didn't seem that upset about his Aunt Bertha. He's much more interested in a date with me than with the disappearance of the woman who raised him, Sara thought. What about Marcel? Jackie Cole?

"Speak of the devil," she muttered aloud, as Jackie's dilapidated blue Ford rattled across the crushed gravel on the lane. The policeman gunned the motor of the noisy truck and clattered to a stop beside her on the lawn. He rolled down the window, reached out, unlatched the door from the outside, and stepped down.

"Putting in a garden?" he said, grinning and gesturing toward the broken sods.

She tucked the little book into the back pocket of her jeans and laughed.

But Jackie wasn't finished. "You suppose they buried her under there?" He winked.

"What? Bertha! I can't believe you said that." The policeman might be a nice enough and cute enough guy, but she didn't find this at all amusing.

He could see that she was hurting. "Look, I'm sorry, okay? I guess this is no time to be making jokes. Bertha is missing and you're really worried. You know she was reported missing a few years ago—gone a few days. There was a big search and she was just away from home getting some kind of treatment. She didn't feel like telling the world about her problems. I've been thinking, maybe she did the same thing again. I came by to ask if you'd heard anything. We've got no signs of violence, after all. I've been making inquiries all over and no one has seen hide nor hair of her. I'd be completely convinced she just wandered off somewhere again if it wasn't for what happened to the minister's wife."

"Have you got a shovel handy?" Sara said and didn't wait for his answer. She bolted for the house. "I think there's one in the pantry off the kitchen."

"Hold on," he said. She stopped, waited. "There's one behind the seat in my truck, for worms. I like to trout-fish. I'll get it for you. You gonna dig some more?"

"I didn't do any of this digging. There are places just like this all over the lawn. It must have been dug after dark, because I haven't witnessed any digging since I arrived here. Some of the marks are fresh. What could they be looking for?"

"Captain Kidd's pirate treasure?" He smiled. "No, we're too far north. Maybe it was those kids out looking for dew worms."

"You might be right," she said, tossing aside the sods and digging into the gravelly soil.

"About the worms?"

"No. About the kids. I've seen kids out here late at night, in the rain. It was likely them that did this digging."

"What makes you so sure I'm not right about the worms, too?" asked Jackie Cole.

"I wasn't sure ... until now. Have a look." She moved to the side of the hole she had opened up with the shovel.

"All I see is a hole."

"Look again. Worms don't live in wooden houses."

The policeman dropped to his hands and knees, peering into the hole. Without the loose fill, the hole was rectangular in shape. Along its walls ran parallel lines that looked exactly like the fine lines between boards on the exterior of a house or a box.

"Jesus!" he exclaimed. "Are there any more of these?"

She led him to several others and together they removed enough sod and soil to confirm that the holes had also contained similar containers.

"Have you got time to come inside for a minute?" Sara asked of him.

"I guess so. What's up?"

"I just remembered something. I believe I know exactly what was in these holes."

She hurried to the house and led Jackie to the attic. She intended to show him the trunk with the sticks that looked like dynamite and the box of motors and electrical supplies she had found on her last visit, but they were no longer anywhere to be found—I'll be damned, she thought. Instead she took him over to the stack of butter boxes. Who had removed the dynamite and the motors from the attic, and when?

"I believe these are what fit those holes," she said.

"Yes, it looks that way. What do you suppose was buried in them? Drugs? Jesus, right on the ocean, this would be a perfect place for smugglers. Are the kids involved in drugs?"

"I don't think it was drugs," she said.

"What then?"

"I think I'll wait until I have more proof. I don't want to give any smart-assed policeman any more chances to make a joke out of this. And I'm not so sure whether to trust you, either."

Jackie raised his eyebrows at her. He was about to speak, then paused. He started again. "I am the police around here. If you have evidence of a crime, you have to tell me. Let's take a box down to one of those holes and see how close it comes to fitting. Tonight I'll ask my mother if she knows anything about boxes being buried at Safe Haven."

Sara picked up the box and headed for the stairs. Jackie reached out in an offer to carry it for her but she shook her head. "It's not that heavy," she said and headed down the dark narrow stairs. At the bottom she waited until Jackie had closed the door and then she hurried along the hall and on to the next flight. There was more light here so she picked up the pace. Halfway down she stumbled and the box crashed down the steps ahead of her. Jackie quickly grabbed the back of her sweater and tugged firmly backwards and she managed to grasp the railing. Otherwise she would have plunged to the bottom.

"Thanks, that was clumsy of me," she said. "I get excited when I get a break in a story. You saved my neck."

"Not at all," he said.

"You did. I would have fallen all the way to the bottom and possibly broken my neck. I was going too fast."

"That's not what I meant," he said. "I meant you weren't at all clumsy. Look at this."

He was bending down on the steps above her. She squatted down close beside him. She could smell his Old Spice.

"Oh, my god," she said.

"Rabbit wire. Someone was trying to trip us up." He untied the wire, which had been stretched across the stairs. "I'll have a look around the house. This wasn't here when we went up. It had to be done while we were upstairs. Stay close in case there's someone still here. "Where's Eppie?"

"In school. Why?"

"It could have been her, or one of her friends."

"Not Eppie," she said.

"Don't be too sure."

There was no one to be found in the house and no one in sight outside. They tried the box in the first hole and discovered it fit like a glove. Despite the gathering warmth of morning, the cold seemed to seep into her from the opening in the earth as if some spirit rose up out of it. She wished she had worn a sweater. She could feel the hardness of her nipples so she crossed her arms over her breasts and rubbed her prominent collar bones while Jackie tossed the box into the back of his pickup, along with the spade. Evidence.

"I'd like to go with you," she asked.

Jackie looked surprised and confused. "Huh? Are you nervous about staying here? I don't blame you."

"Not now. When you visit your mother ... Can I go? I'd like to meet her. I'm interested in speaking with older residents of Mussel Cove."

"I don't know. She has some dementia. Sometimes she can't remember much. But she's usually pretty good with the more distant past."

"I won't bite her. I'd like to hear what she has to say ... about the boxes." She also was curious to see if Jackie would actually consult someone who might know.

He hesitated only for an instant. "I'll come and get you before

I head over to the Manor. You be careful. Call if you need me. Do you have a cell phone?"

"No. Laura, my editor, said the reception wouldn't be all that good up here."

"You ought to get one. The reception is not digital here but if you go through Aliant it's not that bad. And maybe you should lock the gate." He climbed aboard the truck, slammed the door on the second try, and roared out of the yard.

She made a mental note to lock the doors every time she went in or out in the future. Perhaps she would lock the gate, too. And she'd better tell Eppie to do the same. She felt so alone. All her instincts cried out in favor of hopping in her car and driving as fast and far away as possible. This creepy, suffocating little place seemed to be turning darker by the second. But she simply couldn't. She promised Eppie she wouldn't leave. Not yet. Eppie needed her. With Bertha gone, even the pretext that someone else was in charge had disappeared. She had better call Children's Aid when she got a chance.

She was afraid. If she was to go any farther with this, she needed some sort of insurance. After a bit of thought she hit upon a solution that might work: she would photocopy the little book page by page. Then she'd fax a copy to *The Loyalist*. She'd call Laura and tell her what she'd discovered. She would send documents to Laura electronically and tell her not to run the story just yet. She didn't want to start reporters streaming into town. As appealing as "reinforcements" from the city might be, Sara thought of it as her story to break. A frightening and perhaps dangerous story, but still it was hers. She knew she needed a new career, and a strong performance here could establish her quite nicely. But her notes would be in Halifax just in case: instant insurance. She hoped.

She spent five minutes on a cover page and sent out what she could. She would transmit the maps and other information from the book from a regular fax in the village after she located a photocopier. Shortly afterwards, her screen told her that the pages and her files had been successfully sent.

Now to copy and mail the book itself, and bring a copy to

Marcel and ask him what it meant to him and the history of the orphanage. Sara felt safer already. At least for the present.

...

The phone rang, startling her. It was a woman whose voice she didn't recognize.

"Hello. Is this Sara Miles?"

"Who is calling, please?"

"Oh, I'm sorry. I'm Betty Holiday, acting secretary at Mussel Cove Consolidated Elementary. I'm doing Bertha Morris's job for a few days. Marcel Vertu, the principal, asked me to call you. He said you were a teacher and we seem to have an emergency here. One of our supply teachers had to leave suddenly and we need someone for the rest of the day. You'd be paid for the whole day, Mr. Vertu says."

Sara was confused. She had other plans but this was an opportunity to perhaps find out a few things from the children, and to get inside a classroom for a few hours. And she wanted to see Marcel anyway.

"What level?" Sara asked.

"It's a grade five/six combination. Your little Eppie is in the class."

"I'm sorry, Ms. Holiday, have we met? How do you know about Eppie?"

"It's a small village, Sara. Everybody knows things like that. I suppose I'd better tell you that this used to be Mrs. Stitch's class ... Are you interested?"

"How soon do you need me?" Sara wondered how Eppie would react when she walked into the room.

"Twenty minutes ago."

"I'll be as quick as I can."

"Great. See you when you arrive. Come into the office. I'll have the daybook and class list. It's a lighter teaching load than most days. There's a music class at the end of the afternoon."

Sara wasted no time getting there. She knew how such interruptions interfered with the smooth running of a school. Mussel Cove Consolidated Elementary was located on School Street, which curved up behind the Soup's On Restaurant. The parking lot was filled with yellow buses and the cars of staff members. She pulled into the space in front of a small sign that read "Phoebe Stitch." It felt odd parking there, but it seemed to be the only available spot.

Up the steps of the red brick school and through the large glass doors she hurried, entering a large lobby lit by an overhead skylight. It was a surprisingly new building with shiny terrazzo floors and pink cinderblock walls decorated with cheerful student art.

The office was easy to find. A large glass window looked into it from the lobby and she could see a small woman with gray hair seated at a busy-looking desk behind a waist-high counter. A sign on her desk said "Bertha Morris, Secretary." This was an aspect of Bertha's life Sara hadn't seen. Now a substitute secretary sat at her desk. Betty Holiday spotted Sara and rose, meeting her as soon as she came through the door. She handed Sara a green daybook, containing the lesson plan and a class list, a set of keys and a small booklet entitled "The Mussel Cove Consolidated Supply Teacher's Handbook."

"I'll show you the staff room where you can leave your jacket and then I'll take you to Room 104. Mr. Vertu is with them now."

"Thank you, Ms. Holiday," Sara said and nervously followed the woman who moved slowly and deliberately toward the staff room. Sara hung her jacket just inside the room and noted the comfortable furniture, the smell of stale coffee, the fridge and stove and the cluttered bulletin board. A sign read, "noon duty—Stitch sub."

"Are you ready?" asked the secretary.

"Sure," answered Sara. The secretary, who was probably a pensioner, led them in a slow march to Room 104 as if they had all the time in the world. The artwork on these walls was quite different from that of the lobby area. The colors were garish and unsettling. Sara wanted to look closer but there wasn't time. Perhaps at the end of the day while the students were in music.

Ms. Holiday knocked at the door and entered without waiting

for an answer. Marcel Vertu sat on the chair behind the teacher's desk, reading a newspaper. The students were working quietly and diligently. As Sara entered, a buzz of conversation began. Sara found Eppie's face among the thirty others and noticed that she didn't look pleased. Marcel dropped his newspaper to the desk and the conversation stopped. Instantly. Principals have a way of commanding respect. I wonder how they'll be after he leaves, she thought. The secretary gave Sara a pat on the back, turned and departed, closing the door behind her.

Marcel shook her hand, winked at her, and stood beside her.

"For those of you who don't already know, this is Sara Miles who is visiting with us for a while. She has agreed to help us out at the last minute and I expect you to offer her every ounce of respect that she deserves. Is that clear?"

"Yes, Mr. Vertu," the children answered in an enthusiastic chorus.

"Well, I'll leave them in your capable hands," he said and left.

Sara read out the children's names from the class list she'd been given and the children answered politely in turn. So far so good, she thought, surprised at how normal the whole thing seemed. She had been expecting some substitute-teacher-testing misbehavior. She had been presented instead with a more polite group of youngsters than she had ever experienced back in Maine.

"All right," she said. "You've been working on math. How long have you been working on this?"

"About an hour," one boy with large cheeks and bulging eyes answered.

"Thanks," she said. "That's about long enough. How about we go over a few of the harder math problems together and get on to our writing exercises for the day? But before we begin, perhaps we could get to know a bit about each other. My name is Sara Miles. I was a teacher in Maine, before I quit and moved to Halifax. I'm on a holiday from my job with a Halifax newspaper. While I'm here I thought I'd write something about Mussel Cove." Sara looked over at Eppie who was slowly shaking her head. Sara got the message. She wouldn't mention that Eppie was living with her. She paused.

"Now, what about you?" Sara and the boy with bulging eyes stared at one another while silence settled into the room like frost. She waited. After a prolonged and painful wait, the boy stood and stepped out from behind his desk. Even then he said nothing.

"First, tell me who you are and then say something about yourself, or Mussel Cove, or about your friends. I really am quite interested."

The boy laughed. She got a better look at this boy she had chosen. He wasn't a pretty child. His large eyes dominated his face. His lips were also uncomfortably puffed and voluptuously shaped. Sara was trying her best not to show that she was feeling uncomfortable about his appearance when he spoke.

"I'm Ira Black. My father is the Baptist minister. I hate my father and I hate Mussel Cove. I hate Safe Haven the most and I even hate you because you came here to write crap about us." He stopped speaking but didn't resume his seat. All eyes had been locked on him as he spoke. When it became obvious, after a few moments of uncomfortable silence, that he had finished, most of the class turned and focused their eyes on the substitute teacher. Eppie pressed her face against her wooden desktop and her arms were folded and crossed behind her head.

Sara was astounded by Ira's comments but stood her ground and tried not to look too upset. After all, she told herself, the boy did exactly what she asked him to do. This Ira Black must be the son of the woman who had drowned below Safe Haven. The child was obviously quite disturbed. He must be feeling unbelievable emotional pain. Her heart was pounding and she could feel its beat in one of the veins in her forehead. It would do no one good to overreact here, she knew.

"I have no intention, Ira, of writing bad things about you. I will try to find out the truth and then write about it. I am interested in helping Mussel Cove, not hurting it." She saw the anger and pain in Ira's fierce eyes. "Some of you have been hurt enough already."

Ira held her gaze a few more moments and then sat down.

"Never mind the rest of the introductions. I'll not put any more pressure on you. Let's get to the math problems," she said.

Things went along smoothly until, after printing an answer on the overhead projector, Sara heard one of the girls blurt out that she had worked hard on that problem but she didn't get it. "It's stupid," she said.

"Who had it right?" Sara asked. There was no answer at first, but to her surprise Ira Black's hand shot up, followed by several others, including Eppie's. She was sitting upright now, intent on what was happening. "Do I have a volunteer who would show this girl ..." She consulted the seating plan. "... who would show Josie how it is done?"

Ira stepped to the overhead and picked up the black erasable marker. Sara handed him a fresh transparency sheet and he worked out the problem quickly, in neat, clearly legible numerals. She smiled at him and thanked him as he sat, making a valiant effort to hide what to Sara was evident pride in his work.

Before she knew it, the bell rang for lunch and she was reminded from the lesson plan that she was scheduled for playground supervision in ten minutes. She hurried to use the bathroom located in the entry to the staff room. She filled a glass of water from the tap in the staff room sink, and picked up a slice of chocolate cake from a plate on the table. She went into the large workroom that connected to the staff room and stopped next to the photocopier. She placed the notebook from Safe Haven on the glass surface of the copier window and pressed the button. Nothing happened. A young female teacher she hadn't met recognized her plight, entered what must have been her personal code number and the machine went immediately to work. Sara made two copies of the entire notebook, placed the original in the mailer she had addressed and stamped the night before, sealed it, and hurried out.

As she made her way to the playground, several staff members nodded at her and said hello. She was in place out back of the school with a minute to spare. She set her bag, which contained the original and the copies of the book, on the ground beside her. She wondered if she should pay for the paper and toner she'd used but decided not to for the moment. She would prefer not to explain to anyone what she'd been up to. Not yet. She was also unwilling to acknowledge that she had brought the original of the book with her.

She was glad she'd worn the sweater. The school was set in an open area and the raw wind swept constantly through the yard, which was enclosed on two sides by the red brick school. The high walls of the building caused the wind to circle the playground, lifting bits of paper and junk food wrappers and spinning them around, along with clouds of gritty sand and the remains of last summer's leaves.

She watched the children, looking for some sign that they were somehow different from other school children. A group of older boys played soccer off on one side of a grassy field and two other groups played with basketballs around two nets placed side-by-side on the far side of the paved area. The majority of the children scurried around the yard while a few of the smaller ones climbed monkey bars and swung on swings in a small fenced-in section to her left. Nothing much drew her attention at first. She let her eyes scan lazily across the schoolyard a few times but mostly she looked over the afternoon's lesson plan. She wasn't watching the schoolyard when she heard a child cry out in a hurt voice. A small girl who had been standing between her and the swings turned to her with large brown eyes.

"Robbie fell off the swings again," she said.

Sara hurried across the low fence that was constructed of a heavy chain slung between short steel posts. A small chubby boy lay on the ground in front of a leather-seated swing that was slowly returning to the neutral position.

"Are you all right?" she asked as the children moved back to make room for her. Robbie scowled but the blonde-haired child readily took her hand as she led him out of the area toward the sunny spot where she had been standing. The small girl who had called Sara's attention to Robbie's plight met them.

"Hi, Robbie," the girl said.

Robbie didn't answer so she walked away looking hurt.

"Who was that?" Sara asked him. He didn't answer.

"You live out at the big house," Robbie said after a while.

How does he know this, she wondered? She had never seen him before.

"What is your name?" she asked.

"Robbie," he said.

"Robbie who?"

"Robbie Mahoney," he said. "My sister Kensey is in your class today. You're the substitute teacher."

"Yes." As she spoke she saw Ira, the boy with the wet, bulging eyes who said he hated everyone, walk by. He looked at Robbie and then Sara and hurried away.

"I think I'll go now," Robbie said and started to leave.

"Oh," said Sara. "I was hoping you'd stay and talk to me."

"What about?"

"Oh, I don't know. Maybe about the big house. How did you know I live at the big house?"

"Everybody knows that."

"Oh, I see. Did you also know, Robbie, that there are children outside the big house—sometimes in the middle of the night?"

Robbie didn't answer. His eyes looked frightened, as if he were about to panic and run. Sara wished she hadn't asked him that question. Too pushy. She had no right to frighten little children.

"Sorry," she said. "You don't have to answer that."

"It's all right. I didn't know you knew about the kids. The girl in the barn says you will help us find them. Ira said he didn't want you living in the house but he won't say it any more."

Sara felt alarmed. "Why not?" she asked.

"Because he hated his mother and she got drownded."

"Drowned," her teacher reflex responded. Is the child suggesting they all drowned Ira's mother to keep Ira from complaining about me living in the house? How could that be?

"Drowned," he said slowly, looking at her with large brown eyes. This is so weird, but he's such a darling, she was thinking, as his sister Kensey arrived and took his hand. She literally dragged him away from her. He looked back toward Sara as if pleading with her to say nothing of their conversation. They stopped beside Ira who appeared to be asking the smaller boy questions to which he replied with a vigorous, fearful shaking of the head. After a few moments the questions stopped and both Ira and Kensey turned toward her with deadpan faces and nodded. Sara's mind was racing. What had he said? The girl in the barn. Ira's mother drowned after he disagreed with the girl in the barn about whether Sara should stay at Safe Haven, or was it because he hated his mother? Sara felt her fingertips grow icy. She was more confused than ever.

On her way back to class Sara took a moment to explore the wall across the hall with its garish works of art on Bristol board. The pastel drawings were bizarre, many of them of houses burning with misshapen figures inside writhing in hellish anguish. There were a couple of paintings depicting a generic figure struggling to stay afloat beside an overturned canoe. One of these had been signed "Ira." Who would have encouraged these children to make such dreadful drawings? And then hang them on the wall? Was it supposed to be therapeutic? She shrugged and entered the classroom. She would definitely have to ask.

During the short afternoon class the students had a story to read and a series of homework questions, previously assigned. Ira asked if they could work on them for the remainder of the class and Sara agreed.

When the bell rang for the class to head off to music, Sara asked Ira to stay behind for a few minutes. The other students filed out of class looking back over their shoulders at Ira as they went. Ira showed no outward reaction. He simply sat at his desk holding his music book in his crossed arms.

Sara sat sideways in the desk in front of Ira's and turned to him.

"I'm very sorry about what happened to your mother, Ira."

He didn't respond in any way.

"I was looking at the drawings on the wall outside," she said. "Some of those are yours?"

He looked directly through her but she could see that his skin was losing color. He lowered his gaze and turned away toward the window.

"It must be terribly hard to lose a mother like that."

"She wasn't my real mother," he said.

"Oh ..."

"My real mother got sick and died."

"I'm sorry. My father just died a short time ago and I miss him a lot."

Ira didn't answer.

"I was looking at the pictures of the burning buildings and the people in them. Who asked you to draw these pictures?"

"Mr. Vertu. He has us for counseling. He's stupid, too. He thinks that drawing pictures of the things we're afraid of will help us. So we drew some pictures to make him happy."

"Oh, I see."

"Can I go now, please? Music is the only class I like."

She decided to gamble. "Just one more question: what is in the boxes that are being dug up around the old orphanage?"

Ira turned to her and looked at her with hard eyes. She could see his fear on the outside for the first time. He stood and said coldly and firmly, "I'm going now. Don't try to stop me."

Sara stayed and worked alone in the classroom until the final bell, when the temporary secretary arrived and asked her to sign a few papers. Marcel had sent a note. He congratulated her on her day's work and suggested they meet for a quick coffee at The Soup's On.

She scribbled an enthusiastic "yes" beside the question and signed it.

"Will you give this to Mr. Vertu?"

"Of course," the secretary said.

Sara handed over the math scribblers and the daybook to the secretary, then drove quickly to the post office, mailed the little book to Laura in Halifax and headed back to the restaurant.

CHAPTER TWENTY-SIX

26

Philip felt like his hair hurt deep down into its roots. The night before, he'd undressed for bed and had tried, with little success, to catch up on lost sleep. Too often lately he woke feeling more tired than when he went to bed. Something he was to have done for Sara was nagging at him. He tried to remember. Oh, yes, check for signs of Aunt Bertha's supposed "I'm leaving" note. He shivered, staggered into his gray terry housecoat, and stumbled down the stairs.

Aunt Bertha generally used the telephone in the downstairs front hall. If she left a note for him, this is where it ought to be. He picked up the note pad, which was blank, and strode into the kitchen for a pencil (on top of the refrigerator) and a sharp knife (the knife drawer beside the stainless sink). He hadn't listened to Aunt Bertha read all those Hardy Boys adventures for nothing. He'd never tried this trick, but he had always thought that someday he might. He poured himself a stiff drink of rum as an eye-opener. He smiled, enjoying the stolen moment of freedom. This was the only benefit he could see from Aunt Bertha's sudden, unexpected departure: there was no one around to nag him about his drinking, so he could do as he pleased.

He took another healthy swallow of the rum and scraped a fine dust of pencil lead onto the center of the top yellow page of the blank message pad. He held his breath and shook the black carbon powder back and forth across the face of the pad. He had expected to find nothing so the little he managed to read gave him some satisfaction. At least, it would be an excuse to call Sara. "I'm off to see ... " it read. He felt a sudden cold chill. The rest was too indistinct—wouldn't you know, he thought—but here was proof that Aunt Bertha had indeed tried to leave a note. Someone had likely taken off the top page and perhaps even the top two or three pages. "I'll be damned," he said aloud. Now he actually needed a drink. He swallowed the remainder of the rum in one gulp, relishing the burning sensation as it slid down his throat.

It occurred to him at that moment that there might be an additional benefit to his Aunt being on the missing list: now he had an excellent excuse to take a thorough look inside her precious locked desk. He had always wanted to do that. Perhaps he would discover some clue that would lead directly to her present whereabouts. He wasn't too worried about her quite yet, because of her past disappearances. But this was the first hint that something unusual might be involved. Please let her be all right, he thought. And let me have another drink to steady my nerves. The first one had only made him thirsty. Better still, bring in the whole bottle and some mix.

After the fourth stiff drink, he pried at several drawers on the desk and the slide-down front, but nothing wanted to budge. His glass slipped from his sweaty fingers and bounced on the thick rug under his feet. When he stooped to pick it up, he underestimated his level of intoxication and he crashed to the floor himself.

As he lifted his head from the musty rug and cursed his clumsiness, he discovered what looked like a cup hook that someone had carefully twisted into one of the gargoyle's feet, which served as legs for the solid desk. Hanging on the hook was a tiny key. There's a stroke of luck, he thought, and another genuine benefit of the drink. He rose carefully, removed the key, and inserted it into the lock holding the desk front in place. The lock opened on the first attempt and with a satisfying rattle, the slatted cover lifted up out of sight. Reaching inside he retrieved a fat cardboard accordion file of documents.

He carried his prize into the kitchen and dropped it with a satisfying thud onto the table. After he paused to push the start button on the coffee machine, he opened the file and sat. He turned and said to the machine, "I'll peek while you perk." He couldn't help chuckling at his cleverness.

He was immediately flabbergasted to discover statements detailing large sums of money paid to Aunt Bertha from The Halifax Trust Company. There were veritable stacks of these statements and deposit receipts dating back several years. The pay stubs from the school were there, too, but these were for shockingly small sums of money.

Once the coffee had perked and he had downed half a cup, Philip returned the cardboard file to the desk. If Aunt Bertha returned he could avoid a conversation about why he had been rummaging through it when she told him specifically not to. He searched the rest of the secretary but found nothing of interest. What was so crucial about the receipts?

Philip thought about his upcoming date with Sara. He was both excited and nervous. He had never wanted a date with a woman so much but he couldn't understand the intensity of his feelings. What was it about her that attracted him? She was pretty enough, but it was more than her appearance. Her voice was soft and warm and it got into his mind and spoke to him hours and days after he'd last heard it. It haunted him. His nervousness had nothing to do with her, other than the fact that she was a woman like the others he'd dated. Why did he always turn to alcohol when he was with women? At first he was all right and then he'd get so nervous. A drink would calm him, give him confidence. Another drink and he was the king of the world: his tongue loosened and he was so smooth. Another, and his tongue thickened and he became over-confident, even pushy. And on and on until he'd wake up in the morning feeling uneasy, ill, and certain that he'd behaved badly. He'd walk down the street thinking that everyone was talking about what he'd done. That was usually the end of the relationship.

The advice of some of the firefighters gave him the willies. They told him that women like to be mistreated. Treat them mean, they said. The more you mistreat them, the quicker they come crawling back, looking for more. Make them think you don't care if they live or die and they'll chase you all over Cape Breton;

you became "a challenge" for them. If you drank and swore and chased every skirt that came along, they'd want to reform you. The average woman, even among the ones who pretended they were liberated, was so dumb that the technique always worked. But if you were so foolish as to treat them decently by acting the gentleman, they wiped their feet all over you and treated you like the grub you truly were.

Damn it, thought Philip. It wasn't fair. If he had to be that phony with his feelings, it wasn't worth the bother. Why couldn't a guy just say what he felt right out, no matter how dumb it sounded? He couldn't be bothered playing silly games. That's what he wanted to say to the guys, but he couldn't say things like that to them. They'd laugh him right out of the department. But now he wasn't sure how he would behave with her. Could he ever tell her how he felt?

What if she suggested coming back to his place? Maybe she'd want to look in the desk, or, if things went well ... he'd better stop over after work, pick a few things off the floor, and mop the kitchen, just in case. Otherwise she would find out first hand what a helpless slob he was.

Despite the coffee and aspirins his head pounded all the way to the drugstore.

CHAPTER TWENTY-SEVEN

27

She found the principal sweeping dust from the sidewalk in front of his restaurant. He noticed Sara and waved. "Come on in and say hello. I'll get you that coffee I promised." Marcel's face became serious. "I hear you got along wonderfully with the children. Congratulations. Has there been any word on Bertha's whereabouts? We miss her around the school."

"No word on Bertha, unfortunately. I'm looking forward to the coffee. The day with the children was a bit stressful. I suppose partly because Eppie was in the class. Which reminds me, I hope you haven't forgotten about this evening."

"Oh, I haven't forgotten about watching little Eppie. A promise is a promise. I think you'll find me quite diligent at keeping every promise I make. I have a long and determined memory. I must say that I'm quite upset about what's happened to Bertha. I'm perplexed. Where the devil is she?"

"Me, too. I feel the same way ... I have something fascinating to show you, if you have a moment," said Sara.

"Wonderful. Let's get that coffee. I have just received fresh beans today. They're Ethiopian. Their odor is so delectable that it filled my whole apartment even before I opened the package."

"Sounds delicious."

"Come along then."

The moment Marcel began to grind the beans, a lush coffee aroma joined those of herbs and spices, wood and leathers, metals and fabrics, produce and perfumes. It reminded her of farmers' markets and organic food stores. The bitter odor of burnt wood, which had previously dominated Marcel's apartment, had already begun to fade into the background. While the coffee perked, Marcel settled into the large rocking chair opposite her.

"You had something to show me."

His hands were shaking. She didn't know why. Was he ill, or was it age? Nervousness? She handed him the fresh photocopies of the old book, hoping he wouldn't ask her where she'd made them.

"*Mon Dieu!*" Marcel gasped. "Where the devil did you find this? Where is the original? I must know!"

"I mailed it to a friend at the newspaper," she said, watching his face.

He hesitated an instant, then said, "This is wonderful. I can't tell you how important this document is to those of us who have a history at Safe Haven. It was right for you to stay. We have searched for this book for many years. But you have found it, you amazing child." He took another deep breath. "Jesus Christ! There is a map! Do you have any idea of how important a discovery you have made?"

"Yes. I think that this journal documents a list of orphans who died at Safe Haven and shows dozens of unmarked graves on the property where their bodies were buried. I also suspect that these deaths were never reported to the authorities. I am about to begin the process of checking. Am I close?"

"You are most clever, my dear. Beautiful and brainy. I suppose you have already begun to compose an article for your newspaper?"

"Of course. I've already forwarded the material to Halifax. But it will need some revision and editing."

"I wonder ..." Marcel appeared perplexed. "Would it be possible to delay the story a day or so? I'm not suggesting it not be published. The story deserves to be told. But once this story breaks and people discover how the orphanage covered up the deaths of these babies, and the profits they made from selling babies, we will be inundated by the media, the curious, not to mention thrill seekers and perhaps even police. It might be a real circus for a while."

Sara tried to look concerned. She had already asked Laura to hold off printing the story for a few days. But she thought it smart not to let Marcel know about that just yet. There was too much she still didn't understand, especially about the pack of children running around at night.

"The circus will come eventually anyway, Marcel. Waiting won't change anything. Don't you think we might as well get it over with? You said yourself that I should get away from here, that there was danger."

"You're right, Sara. But the people of the village don't know the full extent of the evil they once supported and will need time to absorb the initial shock before opening themselves to the outside world. The story will, and must, be told. You are completely correct in that. But I wonder if it might not be a better story if the community was properly warned. If they were given an opportunity to mourn and react privately—with you having the sole opportunity to witness their reaction, of course—before we bring in the professional news hounds. I have a proposal."

"Let me hear it," Sara responded warily.

Marcel licked his lips. "I suggest we plan a community gathering. We will invite anyone connected in any way to the history of Safe Haven. We will show them what you have discovered and I will tell them, and you at the same time, all that I have been able to learn over many years. That, I might add, is considerable. I'm certain your readers will be titillated by much of my material. It's not as illuminating as these pages you've just handed me, but it is darkly dramatic, and will startle even you, my dear. Does my little proposal hold any interest for you?"

"Give me a moment to think. It seems a bit overwrought. Do you really think it's worthwhile, or necessary?"

"Absolutely. Trust me on this and I assure you you'll see that it was most worthwhile and necessary. We have to think of the effect on the community. I think you may be underestimating how profound and disturbing these revelations will be."

"Okay. If you say so. Supposing I agree, where would you hold this event?"

"How about the scene of the crime, your present place of residence? Safe Haven itself. You can clear the idea of a slight postponement of your article with your editors if you like, though I'm almost certain that they will like it. It will make a better story. We will try to have the event as early as tomorrow evening. Then you can gather and organize your materials and get your completed story to your paper by the first of the week."

Sara's heart was pounding. She was just beginning to imagine the impact the story could have on her new career. Not that she was sure how much it mattered. Her heart was still set on returning to teaching, and even her day here with the creepy kids had done nothing to dampen that inclination. However, it couldn't hurt to have a second option, so this seemed like an opportunity she couldn't afford to let slip through her fingers.

"It sounds all right, Marcel. But won't we need more time than that to prepare for so much company?"

"No, we must not wait any longer. I'll get my restaurant staff working on some snacks, sandwiches and sweets. We'll have tea and coffee—I won't serve them my best, you understand." He winked at her. "But good enough to satisfy my regulars. And speaking of my regulars reminds me that you're not one of them," he paused and looked her in the eye. "When this is all over I assume you'll be heading back to Halifax."

"Yes, but there's still Eppie."

"Yes, our little Eppie, my babysitting charge for tonight." He looked away.

"Right. And I hope she'll not cause you any trouble. She can be a bit of a brat."

"You can be quite sure that she'll be no trouble to me. We school principals are quite adept at managing children. You and your young man will be free to go out and kick up your heels. 'Let us eat and drink,' so to speak, haha. I truly envy the two of you. Young Philip is a lucky fellow. I hope he appreciates you."

"How do you propose getting the invitations out in time for

tomorrow evening? I can't help you much unless I stay home tonight. I am quite willing to do that if I could be of any help. But I still think that tomorrow evening is a bit too soon. And we still haven't found poor Bertha."

"No, I insist. This book is a bombshell and the village must know, and prepare. You go out on your date. I have the restaurant staff and I'm sure some of my teachers will offer to help. As for Bertha, that seems out of our hands for now. Frankly, Sara, I think the affair must be concluded tomorrow night or not at all. If you've sent your notes to your editor, and your editor is worth his ..."

"Her ..."

"Sorry, my dear. If your editor is worth her salt, this story could break at any minute, and the press could be here smothering this village under a tidal wave of printer's ink and electrons before anyone gets the least warning. I can make some calls this evening. I have developed an excellent phone tree with which I can reach everyone within twenty minutes of the village by making half a dozen calls. Don't forget what a small place this is. I have plenty to do to help me pass the hours until you return from your romantic rendezvous." He stood up and strolled to the kitchen.

"I believe our coffee is ready," he said. Sara sat in silence while he poured two cups. "I hope you like it."

"Thank you," she said, and took several tentative sips. She smiled. "This is delicious."

"Look," said Marcel, "don't concern yourself about the work that must be done, or worry about the need to tidy up whatever mess we might make. My staff and I will see to everything. All that will be required from you will be your presence as hostess for the affair. At Safe Haven."

As he spoke, he pored over the book as if looking for something he couldn't find.

"All right, then," Sara said, although she was already having second thoughts. "If you think so. I'll let Philip in on what's going on. You don't object to me telling him about this, do you?"

"Of course not," he answered, his brow wrinkling.

"What is it?" she asked.

"Oh, it's nothing, really," he said, his voice belying his words, "I knew many of these children well, and it's hard seeing their names on these pages. It brings back many painful memories. I'm perplexed because there seems to be no grave marker for one of my best friends. Look here," he said, pointing at the list of names until he came to #16: Lynn Morris. He turned the pages to the map pointing at all the numbers in turn. There was no number sixteen. Every number on either side of sixteen was there, but no sixteen. Sara shrugged and handed the papers back to Marcel.

"Bertha and I watched her die," he said, water pooling around his pale blue eyes. "She was so beautiful. Twins are often like that. You knew she was Bertha's twin, didn't you? I've wondered, ever since, what they did with her body. Unfortunately, we may never find her."

Sara reeled—watched her die?—then collected herself. "You watched her die? How horrible. You must have suffered terribly. I think I'm beginning to understand. But are you sure this gathering is necessary. Aren't you over-dramatizing things a bit?"

"Pardon me?" Marcel said, puzzled and ruminating. "Over-dramatizing?" His face reddened and he appeared suddenly angry. His voice came across as distant and hurt. She wished she could retract her last few words. But it was too late for that. Words are like children, she thought. Once they are born into the world, they live their own lives. And create their own problems! She decided that now was not the time to ask how Marcel and Bertha came to watch Lynn die. She wasn't sure she wanted to know, truth be told.

Marcel held the photocopied pages to her. "Thank you very much for showing these to me. I wonder if I might make a copy sometime."

"No need," she said. "I made this copy for you. You can keep it. When the whole thing is wrapped up and I'm back in Halifax, I might be able to send you the original as a keepsake. You deserve it as much as anybody."

"Thank you," he said, his eyes softening. "By the way, would you mind if Eppie stayed behind after school with a few of the older children? They can help me prepare a little bit. I hope you don't mind. I took the liberty of informing the bus driver that she'd be staying behind with me. If that's a problem you can take her with you now. I've called the other parents and guardians and they've agreed. I can drive her home afterwards. I'll see that she gets something to eat. You can rest up a bit after teaching and get ready for your big date. But if it's a problem for you ..."

Sara hesitated for a moment. She still wasn't convinced that Marcel's plan was worth the effort. Why stir things up before the article was even published? But why should Eppie's staying behind be a problem? After all, he was the school principal and she had been willing to trust him as a sitter. Was the maternal instinct in her growing stronger than she supposed?

Five minutes later, she climbed into her Honda. Her mind shifted to Bertha's relationship to Marcel. Fate had tied their lives together in the brutal environment of Safe Haven. Was Bertha still alive? Where could she be? It should be impossible to move through Mussel Cove without being seen, especially since Bertha had no driver's license and required transportation wherever she went. Either she had left home on foot, or someone had taken her. Somebody out there had to know where she was. Perhaps Philip would have some answers tonight.

CHAPTER TWENTY-EIGHT

28

The policeman was waiting for her in Safe Haven's yard when she returned from school. So much for her nap. Sara set her books inside the door of Safe Haven and returned. She tossed an oily rag and a bundle of wrenches behind the seat of the pickup to clear away enough space so she could sit.

"I see you got rid of the butter box."

"I didn't exactly get rid of it," said Jackie Cole. "I stopped at Crawford's to pick up a pizza, and when I came back out I saw two kids running up the street carrying a box. I must have been in a fog, because I didn't make the connection right away. I figured they had found it somewhere and were going to build a soapbox racer or a fort. I really felt stupid when I realized that the kids had pinched the box off the back of my truck."

"Oh my God!"

He wrinkled his brow, surprised by the intensity of her reaction. "It's just an old box, for Pete's sake."

"But isn't it evidence, Jackie? I hope, for our sake, that you're right that it's no big deal. Did you recognize any of the kids?"

"They were pretty far away, and I wasn't exactly paying attention ... I think one of them was Kinsey Mahoney. Nice folks, the Mahoneys. Not the sort you'd expect to be causing trouble. Does it matter? Do you want the box back or something? There were those other ones, too. We're not out of evidence."

"I just wish I knew why they took it. You wouldn't expect kids to take a box out of a cop's vehicle for no reason at all. Maybe someone told them to take it. It must have had something to do with the digging at Safe Haven, and perhaps even those fires."

"And the murders, too, I suppose." He paused a moment, then laughed. "Don't you think you're being a little silly about this, Sara? Those kids don't see me as one of those awe-inspiring cops on television ... or the Mounties, for that matter. I'm the guy who gives a few speeding tickets, picks up a stray dog, or arrests someone who gets too drunk in a public place. The fact that I'm the cop makes stealing the box from me just a bit more fun. It will add a few more laughs to the discussions they'll have the next time they get together and smoke one of their parents' cigarettes. Just a bit of childish mischief ... defying authority ... the sort of thing I did a hundred times when I was their age.

He cleared his throat. "I'm here to drive you to see my mom, just as you asked." He grinned, turned on the ignition and off they went. As they braked to let an elderly woman cross the road, an empty coffee cup and a book tumbled from the dash. The cup bounced onto the floor and clattered down beside the door. The book landed in Sara's lap.

"*Independence Day* by Richard Ford," she read aloud. "Where did you get this?"

"The library in Sydney."

"This is a fantastic book. I can't believe you're reading this."

"Why can't you believe I'd read a fantastic book?"

"What else do you read?"

"I read whatever I happen to like."

"I mean what specifically do you read? Do you read poetry, for example?"

"Sometimes." He allowed himself to give full rein to his laughter as he stepped on the gas. The truck bounced ahead. Sara held on to the armrest. "What about yourself?" he asked. "Is it possible that you have a tendency to judge *your* books by their covers?"

By the time Jackie braked and pulled to a stop in front of the Manor, they seemed to have lurched and crashed through every pothole in the village. Sara tried her door but it wouldn't open. He hurried to her side of the old truck and opened the door from the outside.

"Your Highness," he said, offering his hand.

She took it and stepped as regally as possible from the cluttered cab. The coffee cup, which had fallen to the floor earlier, rolled onto the pavement behind her. They shared a good laugh as Jackie picked it up, tossed it onto the seat and slammed the truck door shut.

Sara tried the heavy glass door of the Manor, but it wouldn't budge.

"The blue button to the left of the door at eye level," Jackie said. "There are buttons for coming in and going out. I could never figure out why there's a button for going in."

Sara turned her head and found it. "Push button below and pull open the door following the buzz," she read aloud. "Couldn't the patients read this?"

"It stops the ones who shouldn't open doors. Mom could read the words when she first came in here, but for some reason she couldn't do what they said."

As they made their way along the corridors, Jackie greeted all the bent and misshapen patients, most of them by name, and they responded with broad smiles or warm, enthusiastic handshakes. Sara was impressed. A very social nursing home.

The gleaming cleanliness almost masked underlying odors of stale cigarettes and urine. Mrs. Ophelia Cole's room sat wedged into the far south corner of the dementia ward. This area housed patients who suffered from Alzheimer's disease or other forms of mental degeneration. Several elderly residents bashed their arms and legs against restraining chairs and called repeatedly for help. Jackie's mother, though, rested quietly in her high, narrow hospital bed.

"How are you doing, Mom?" asked the cop in a gentle voice Sara'd never heard him use. "I've brought a friend to meet you."

His thin mother reached out a pale bony arm and took his strong freckled hand in her skeletal grip. He placed his other hand across hers and held on tenderly as if caressing delicate china, then rose to lean and kiss her forehead. As they sat in silence, he removed one hand and ran its fingers through her wispy hair. Sara watched, intrigued and a bit jealous. She couldn't picture herself being so tender with her own mother, or her mother sitting still for it. She wondered where the cocky, jock-like, village-idiot cop persona had gone. He turned to her, grinning and a little sad.

"I don't think she'll talk too much this afternoon. Sorry."

"Does she always know you?"

"Sometimes. And sometimes she thinks I'm my father."

"Is your father still living?"

Jackie took a deep breath. At first he didn't speak. He rose and moved away from his mother's bed. He moved close to her and spoke in a quiet voice.

"My dad shot himself when I was seven years old. I didn't know why until I was in my twenties. He was an orphan from Safe Haven. I don't know what happened to him there but he had lots of problems with depression. He tried to be a good father to me but he didn't know how. He was afraid to touch me."

There were tears in Jackie's blue eyes when they said good-bye to his mother. Sara wiped hers and hugged him. They didn't speak.

On the way out they stopped at the nursing station where Jackie held a whispered conversation with his mother's pretty nurse. The young woman was obviously fond of the policeman. Sara waited and soon they left the home without another word.

"You in a rush?" he asked, as they re-entered the village proper. "I make a mean Caesar."

"Salad?"

"If you want. I meant a drink. But, yes, I'll fry up some steak, pop a spud in the microwave and toss you a salad."

She looked at her watch. She had a date with Philip later to-night and Marcel was already looking after Eppie. "What did the nurse say ... about your mother?"

Jackie raised an eyebrow and paused before speaking, "Mom took some kind of turn and fell earlier today. I'll go back and sit with her a spell later. She's all right now, but she gets agitated at night. I have some time now though, and I hate eating by myself."

She checked her watch again and sighed. "All right, sounds good to me."

"My place is a mess. I hope you don't mind."

"I'm in your truck, aren't I?" They laughed. "Could we stop and pick up my car on the way to your place? That way I can leave when I'm ready. I have plans for later." She already wished she didn't.

...

The meal pleased her and he protested when she first offered to help with a couple of days' dirty dishes. She had drunk two Caesars. When she dropped her second empty glass into the sudsy water of the sink their hands touched and she felt a deeply sexual connection that surprised her. She picked up the dish towel to dry her hand and stayed by his side, drying dish after dish. He said nothing. Several times their bare arms brushed and once his elbow slid softly across her breast. Neither could recall the moment just before they kissed.

His bed shocked her at first—more a nest than a bed. It wasn't fresh or clean, but it seemed to suit the moment perfectly. They climbed its high sides fully dressed and he immediately found her mouth with his. His hands, still damp from the sink, were inside her blouse on her back and all the while he kissed her like she was ambrosia—the most delicious thing he had ever tasted.

She was the first to open a button, and while he kissed her, she slowly unfastened each one. She left his shirt open, sliding from his broad shoulders. She ran her hands up his sides and across his back, enjoying the firmness of the muscle. He continued to kiss her.

Most of the feelings she was experiencing were familiar: the elation and excitement, the pounding of her heart, the heightened sensitivity of her skin, the joy of being so alive. But there was something new here in this room with Jackie. Before there had always been a sense of foreboding, a fear of what came afterwards. This time Sara felt safe. She was not afraid. This good man was strong and gentle at the same time, totally confident. She could let herself go, knowing somehow that he would never do anything to harm her. When their eyes met there was none of that anger to which she had become so accustomed, in Tony and throughout this town. Jackie's eyes seemed to smile at her, their blueness a small copy of the bits of sky she saw from time to time through the high window beside his bed. All her fears melted away and she felt pure joy.

She kicked off her shoes one by one and found the end of his belt. She felt him suck in his waist and the buckle was soon undone. Slowly she lowered his zipper and reached for the elastic of his undershorts. He was wearing none. He laughed and then purred like a cat as her fingers encircled the shaft of his stiffened cock. His hands slipped up her back and in an instant his big hands were supporting her breasts, weighing them like warm ripe melons. Still they were kissing hungrily and kneeling face to face. She lowered his jeans and played her hand along his penis as she plunged her tongue deeply into his mouth before pulling away and lowering her mouth onto his cock and stretching out on the bed. He slipped off her slacks and underwear, gently pulling them down and off and slowly buried his face in the warm sweet flesh and moistness between her legs.

It was Sara's turn to moan. He gently and expertly worked tongue and fingers until he sensed she was about to explode, then rolled on his back and lifted her above him like he was horse and she his rider. She lowered herself onto his erection and pressed herself down using hands against the sloped ceiling as a fulcrum. Anyone passing the small house a few moments later might have heard them loudly express their mutual climaxes.

For a while they lay breathless and silent, her right hand in his left until Sara was almost asleep. Sometime later she was startled by the sound of a flushing toilet. She glanced at her watch.

"Oh my God! I have so much to do. I've got to run."

He kissed her long and hard before she dressed. It was all she could do not to forget her promise to Philip and her concerns about Marcel's plans for the next few hours. It would be so lovely to stay here with this beautiful man.

"Oh no," she moaned despairingly as she drove away. "How am I ever going to keep my date with Philip?"

...

Eppie and Marcel did not arrive at Safe Haven until after Sara had had time to shower and dress. She was in the kitchen when the front door opened and Eppie stepped inside, holding the door for Marcel who entered, field of vision obscured by a mound of parcels.

"I thought Eppie and I might decorate the house for the gathering. A bit of pleasure before the pain of the revelations. Mitigate the disturbance. We'll make punch and later the girls from the Soup's On will come over to make up trays of hors d'oeuvres. Our guests can snack and enjoy their coffee while they await the fall of the guillotine. You don't object to my using the telephone? I have a few calls yet to make."

"Of course not," Sara replied. "Whatever you need." Sara thought Marcel was going to a bit more trouble than she would have. But it was his "party" and it was obviously a bigger deal to him than it was to her. Then again, she hadn't been a ward of Safe Haven. Eppie had detached herself from Marcel and now clung to a large fistful of the fabric of Sara's dress. He smiled at the girl.

"Don't wrinkle your lady's dress, child. Come over here. We have work to do." Eppie obeyed. "She'll be perfectly safe here with us." He turned to the child. "Won't you, Eppie?"

Eppie appeared to relax instantly. She began removing packages of balloons from one of the parcels Marcel had carried in.

"Oh," he said, "I've brought some more of my special coffee and teas to freshen your personal supply and a few fresh croissants for your breakfast. That is, if you get back in time." He winked. Eppie frowned.

Sara laughed. "You needn't worry. We'll not be out all that late."

As she spoke a knock came on the door. "That'll be Philip," she said with a sigh.

CHAPTER TWENTY-NINE

29

"Where do we start?" Sara asked as she slid onto the passenger seat of Philip's Crown Victoria. The dome light flooded a spotless interior and the lights and dials glowed in welcome. She smelled fake lilacs and looked out the windshield where the silver paint of the hood glistened in the moonlight. Suddenly it was prom night again and with that thought rolling through her mind she looked back to watch Philip gallantly and carefully closing the door beside her. For just a moment Jackie Cole left her mind.

"Start?" asked Philip as he dropped behind the wheel and closed his door, "You look fabulous."

"Thank you, you are looking quite posh yourself. But wasn't this supposed to have something to do with finding poor Bertha?"

Even in the dim glow of the instrument panel, and under the flood of a passing street lamp, Sara could see that Philip was blushing. She found his awkwardness disarming.

"I've been to most of the houses in town asking questions. I've called all the usual numbers: police, hospital, school. They've hired someone to do her part-time secretarial work at the school. Didn't take Marcel long to replace her."

"I know, I was substituting at the school today."

"How did that go?"

"Great." Images of the school flooded her mind, followed by the inevitable warm surge of memories of Jackie Cole. She shuddered slightly, recalling the high points of her passionate late afternoon.

"Nobody has seen hide nor hair of Aunt Bertha," Philip reported. "I'm at the end of my rope. Either she's done one of her disappearances or something bad's happened. I can't help but think of Shirley Black's drowning. Do you really think we'll make progress driving around tonight?"

"No. And you might as well know that the shit's about to hit the fan."

"I don't understand. What shit?"

She told him about finding the book and her meeting with Marcel, including his plans for the "party."

"Wow, that'll blow a few minds."

"Did you come up with anything interesting?" Sara asked.

"I managed to get inside Aunt Bertha's desk this morning."

"What did you find?"

"Surprisingly little, bills and the like. Strange, since she told me never to open it. She has kept pretty tight financial records. She isn't, or wasn't, hurting for money. Someone set up a trust fund for her."

"Oh ... Who?"

"I don't know."

"Where are we going?" she asked, distracted by the rolling scenery of Cape Breton lit by a full clear moon and a velvety mist suspended above the rolling sea.

"I thought we'd head over to Sydney for dinner, if that suits you. It's your night out so you're the boss. I know we have to talk about Aunt Bertha, but we might as well enjoy ourselves while we do it."

Sara decided she didn't want to be the boss. She'd leave the decisions up to Philip. Maybe for once he wouldn't defer all the decisions to her. However, she had second thoughts when she realized that his first stop in Sydney was the liquor store, where he bought a bottle of Captain Morgan dark rum. But she said nothing. His next stop was the Irving Mainway where he filled the gas tank and purchased a large bottle of Coke, plastic glasses and a bag of ice, which he dropped to the pavement to loosen and separate its congealed cubes.

"You look like you've practiced this procedure," she said.

"I'd say," he responded.

He opened the trunk and pulled out a Styrofoam cooler, which he placed in the back seat, setting the Coke carefully and reverently in the bottom beside the rum and dumping the entire contents of the bag of ice over them. He then adjusted the cooler so he could reach it from where he sat in the front seat. The cooler was new. Its tag read "Clem's Hardware, Mussel Cove, $4.99."

Philip parked the car in a space overlooking the harbor and poured two glasses of rum and Coke. He didn't measure the drinks, pouring the rum directly over the cubes and filling the remaining space with Coke. Sara managed to force down the strong drink. She had no problem with having a few drinks, but she knew what could happen when a small body swallows too much drink too quickly. She had no interest in making herself sick or losing control of her faculties. When her glass was empty she agreed to a second one but insisted he mix it weaker. She held the empty glass and told him when to stop. He didn't add much more than she wanted.

"No ice," she said and held the glass while he filled it with Coke. Philip by then had managed to pour himself a generous third drink. It was becoming obvious she would have to drive back home. Philip was probably already well over the legal limit.

When they finally arrived at the restaurant Philip had chosen, "The One-Eyed Cormorant," Sara found that she stumbled a bit on one of the steps out front. She giggled like a schoolgirl.

"This place is probably overpriced," she whispered and awaited his reaction.

"Not to worry, my love," he answered gallantly. "I don't spend money often, so I've got a healthy nest-egg. Order whatever your heart desires. Just as if you were a queen, which you are to me."

Why are drunks so charming? Whether he meant it or not, it felt good to be flattered.

"Why thank you, kind sir."

The maitre d' stood waiting, his professional smile already wearing thin. "Table for two?" he asked.

"*S'il vous plaît,*" answered Philip in his best high school

French. "A table with a view," he said, pointing toward windows that looked down over the south arm of the Sydney River.

"*D'accord, monsieur. Suivez–moi.*"

When Philip hesitated Sara said, "Follow him."

"Oh yes, of course. I was waiting for you."

Sara resisted the urge to comment. She hastened after the maî-tre d' and Philip caught up and possessively placed an arm across her shoulders. He helped her into her chair. A waitress arrived at once and Philip ordered a Moosehead Dry. Sara asked for water.

The meal was a bit too heavy for Sara's taste but she managed a polite portion. She would have preferred one of Bertha's meals. The restaurant meal reminded her of the frozen entrees available in the frozen food section of the Mussel Cove IGA for less than three dollars.

The exaggerated flow of Philip's gallantry was beginning to ebb into a dreary drunkenness. Before he had quite finished his beer, he ordered a liter of Australian Chardonnay and proceeded to consume most of it himself. Gone was the pretext of chivalry. Here was the reality of alcoholism. The wine was disappearing and he was apparently afraid he wouldn't get enough of it. He poured her a few drops and filled his glass again and again. The look in his eyes hinted that the evening was unlikely to end well. A question was forming in the back of Sara's mind, and she decided it was now or never if she hoped to get any answers out of him.

"Philip," she said.

"Yes?"

"Do you remember dropping a prescription off to Bertha at Safe Haven when I was in the village."

"Yes. Why?"

"Did you notice a stray boot in the kitchen?"

"Boot? Like for your foot? Why would I notice a boot?"

"You'd notice this one. It was filthy ... slimy and would have been sitting on a counter or a table, although I suppose Bertha might have set it on the floor someplace."

"No, I don't recall seeing a boot, especially a slimy boot. I can't see Aunt Bertha letting anything slimy or dirty into the house. Why do you ask?"

She looked into his vacant eyes. The redness of his face revealed nothing other than his present condition. She assumed he was telling the truth. His face was even more of an open book now that he was drunk.

"Oh, nothing." Silence reigned until the black-haired waitress returned.

"Dessert?" the woman asked, clearing away their plates.

"We'll have our just desserts won't we, Sara?"

"Pardon me?" asked the waitress, barely paying attention.

Philip gathered himself, speaking carefully, "What sort of desserts do you have?" In spite of the care he took in forming his words, his voice made his intoxication obvious.

"Let's just go, Philip," Sara interjected. "I've had enough."

"You've had enough to eat?" he said, looking hurt. "But we haven't talked about Aunt Bertha yet. Except for that question about the boot."

"Let's find a more private place to talk. We'll take the bill now, if you don't mind." She tried to smile at the waitress but she felt too much tension to pull it off.

"Sounds good to me," said Philip. "Could you bring our bill to me?"

No sooner had the waitress left than he asked, "Are you mad at me or something?"

"Or something. You've had too much to drink, you bonehead."

"Don't worry about me. I'm still not what anybody'd call drunk. I'll admit I've had a bit more than I should have, but I'll be all right in a few minutes—just you wait and see."

"All right. As long as we agree that I'm doing the driving from here on."

"Are you fitter to drive than me?" he asked incredulously.

"Is the Pope Catholic?"

"Huh?"

"I'm definitely more fit to drive than you, mister. I didn't have much of that liter of wine we supposedly shared."

"Very funny."

She ignored him. "Let's go find a quiet place and sit for a while. We'll let some of this booze burn itself off. How does that sound?"

Philip nodded. He hated being patronized. But the idea of spending some time in a parked car with Sara, in "a quiet place," interested him mightily. He quickly forgot that he had felt insulted. He marched to the cash register, stumbling over his feet enough to see that perhaps Sara was right about his being too impaired to drive. He pulled two fifties from a large roll of bills before stuffing it back into his pocket. He took the change and carried it back to the table where he left it as a most generous tip.

Sara drove a short distance and parked near where they'd stopped to drink the rum before dinner. Philip reached for the bottle, but she shook her head "no." "We don't need that. We were going to talk, remember?"

"Okay. I just thought a little drink might make the talk easier."

"If you get any drunker, Philip, I'm leaving. I mean it. Even if I have to pay for a cab ride home. I can handle you as you are but no worse. Nobody likes spending time with a slobbering drunk."

"How about a kiss?"

"Perhaps later. Right now we have to talk. Where did Bertha get to?"

"I haven't got a clue," his voice betrayed the fact that he resented her refusal to kiss him. Sara decided not to notice.

"Would anyone have a reason to abduct her or harm her? She's a lovely woman but not what you'd describe as young and desirable. She may have some funds but she's certainly not wealthy, is she? And I wouldn't expect she has an enemy in the entire universe."

"Why did they murder that frigging minister's wife, or burn down those houses and fry Mrs. Stitch? It seems to me that logic doesn't have much to do with any of this."

"I think Bertha is alive, Philip. She's out there in trouble, but she's alive. And my intuition is usually pretty good. I think there is some logic behind all this. It's just that we haven't figured it out yet. Neither we nor the cops." She stole a thought about Jackie Cole.

"If she's alive, where is she?" demanded Philip, sliding over against Sara. He put his left arm over her shoulder and with his right reached across her tummy and held the softness of her waist under his cool fingers. He moved his face up close to hers. "Kiss me, please," he implored.

She couldn't help sympathizing with him but she had no desire to kiss him. She had barely left Jackie's arms. It had been months since she'd felt Tony's demanding hands on her and the touch of Philip's strong fingers did feel pleasant. Her short time with Jackie had awakened a powerful hunger. She wished he were here. "I don't know," she whispered.

Encouraged by the ambiguity of her response, Philip continued, drawing her warm body closer to his and kissing her tenderly. At once her head began to spin. Then she felt him reach up under her skirt, where he fumbled with the elastic of her panties. His hands brushed against her tender abdomen, and he unintentionally pinched her. Immediately she became aware of the ache of the slight hangover that was forming in the wake of the heavy drinks she had downed earlier. Still holding the kiss, she reached down and withdrew his hand.

"Uh-uh," she grunted, then broke the kiss momentarily, "Kiss me if you want, but go nice and easy. Please be patient."

His reaction was immediate and startling. He pulled away from her angrily and sat pressed against the passenger door like a dejected puppy. His confidence had completely vanished. She was immediately aware that Philip was not and never would be a proper substitute for Jackie Cole. She slid back behind the wheel and they sat unmoving in suffocating silence.

"I'm sorry, Philip," she eventually continued. "Your kiss was nice. It made my head spin. But you were a bit clumsy and I couldn't help but feel rushed."

"It doesn't matter, I'm used to it. Let's fuck off out of here and do something else, okay," he snapped, his tongue sounding sticky and thick.

"You're still angry."

"Yes," he replied. "But not at you. I'm pissed at myself. I'm clumsy just like you said. I'm only trying to do what a guy's supposed to do. You're a sophisticated woman, and I'm just a clumsy hick."

"Come on, Philip! You're a university graduate and a registered pharmacist. You're a great guy. The only thing lacking in you is a realization of all the things you are. You need to like yourself more. You've got everything going for you except that you drink too much. Way too much."

"You're making fun of me."

"Chill out and be yourself. Relax."

"You're not making fun of me?"

"Look, do we have to do anything else tonight? It looks like our investigations on Bertha have turned up nothing. I'm tired and a bit hung over already."

"Yeah, I'd like to do something else. I think we'll start to feel better if we get away from this place."

"Okay then. What should we do?"

"Let's do what we planned in the first place. Let's go looking for my Aunt Bertha. We'll assume she's somewhere close to home. Makes sense, doesn't it? If she is near home, then it's got to be somewhere out of the way, off the beaten track. Because in the village, somebody would have seen her by now and it would be all over town. They would have phoned me in droves, those tongue-waggers. Or, they would have called the cops, or you, or Marcel, or someone who knew her. So we should begin a search and look in all the places a person could hide, or be hidden. Because if we don't start looking, how are we gonna find her?"

"Sounds sensible to me," Sara replied. "But I'm doing the driving." She was glad to be heading back to Mussel Cove. She could have asked Philip why he had changed his mind about the value of driving around the village looking for Bertha. But she knew the answer. He didn't want to end their date. He was willing to do a sham search for Bertha if it meant they could spend a bit of time together. She was flattered by the thought, even though she was anxious to get the night over with. And the journalist in her was driving her on besides.

"Go ahead and drive," Philip eventually responded. "I'd likely break the breathalyzer." He laughed.

Sara enjoyed the sensation of driving. Philip's Crown Victoria wrapped her in almost womb-like comfort. It was a smooth ride, and they set their sights on Mussel Cove.

...

She woke with a start, dangerously close to the guardrail. She jerked the car back onto the road and turned anxiously toward Philip.

"Would you like me to drive?" he slurred and laughed. She glared at him. To her disappointment he had the rum bottle on his lap. He grinned sheepishly and a quick glance at the level of the liquid confirmed her suspicions.

"I'm getting really tired, Philip. Let's head home." She sighed.

He uncapped the bottle. What the hell, he thought. I'll show her. He consciously took a much longer swallow than he knew was wise, aware it was already far too late to salvage anything from the night. No more action this evening, alas.

"Let's fuck off home, then," he said drunkenly. "You can go back to your place and visit that old bastard, Marcel. He's more your type anyway."

"Philip! You're such a self-destructive jerk!" She jammed down the accelerator. She was awake now. It was as if someone had poured ice water over her head. Her anger would keep her on the road. Getting Philip back to Mussel Cove and out of her life became the priority of the moment.

"What about Aunt Bertha?" whined Philip. He began to sob, and knock his head against the side window. Sara glanced toward him, now afraid. Tony was violent but not crazy and pathetic like this. "Why can't I do anything right?" he asked. "Oh, Sara, I'm so sorry I screwed up our date. I can't drink. I never could. I shouldn't have bought the booze." He paused and waited for her reaction. He got none. "I'm going to quit. That's it. I quit. Will you ever forgive me, huh, Sara, will you?"

It was a full minute before she answered. When she did, her voice was cold, impersonal and firm. "All I know is that I'm getting out of this godforsaken hellhole and never, ever coming back. I'm getting my story tomorrow and then that's it." No sooner had she spoken than she thought of Eppie and Jackie, and knew she wouldn't leave, not yet.

They were entering Mussel Cove. Aunt Bertha's house was up the hill next to the Mussel River with the bridge on one side and Mahoney's house on the other and just across the road from Safe Haven. As they approached, Philip spoke, "Why don't you take my car home with you. Let me off here and I can walk up and clear my head. There's not much use in my going to your place. I'm not fit to drive myself home. Just park it there and I'll send someone for it in the morning. Okay?"

Just ahead, Sara saw, or imagined, shadows or dark shapes crossing the road.

"Are you sure?" she asked, deciding not to mention the shadows. What would be the point anyway? And she wanted to do nothing that might delay his getting home to bed where he belonged. She wondered if he could navigate the short distance to his house without getting lost or falling on his face.

"I'm fine, for Christ's sake," he said. As he stepped from the car he apologized one final time. Sara might have been more impressed if she hadn't seen him stuff the rum bottle into his belt before getting out.

She burned up the asphalt in her haste to get away. However, she didn't drive directly home. She felt immense relief to be on her own again and decided on a quick spin past Jackie Cole's house before returning to Safe Haven and the party preparations. You never knew. She smiled—he might still be up. You know, up.

As she neared her destination, she saw a child run out of Jackie's door, pause for a moment, then, spotting Sara's car, dash away toward the ocean. Sara pulled quickly into the driveway, jumped from the Honda and dashed into Jackie's house through the open door.

"Jackie?" she called. There was no answer.

Out she ran, slamming the door shut behind her—hurrying off in pursuit of the child she had seen. The chase was no contest, even though the child was strong and quick as a cat. Sara's long legs, and hours of running at the fitness club in Halifax, paid off. Three minutes later she had the kid. The youngster was small and wiry, but once captured, went limp as a dead fish. There was something familiar about her. Sara yanked off the mask. She gasped.

"Eppie! What the hell were you doing in the policeman's house? It's almost midnight. What's going on, young lady? Does Marcel know you're not at home?"

Eppie shook her head and scowled. "He's too busy to know or care where I am. I had a job. I had to go to the cop's house and look for his notebook. I was supposed to steal it but I couldn't find anything. He must have it with him."

"Who told you to go steal the notebook?"

"The ghost girl sent me a note. She said the cop was getting too nosy. He was going to ruin everything. He is going to be punished soon and she didn't want his notebook left around for anyone to read."

"How is he going to be punished?"

"I can't tell you."

"Let's go home. Come on, or I'll drag you."

Sara wondered why Jackie wasn't at his house, but then she remembered he planned to spend time with his mother at the Manor. At that moment, as Eppie rose and began to walk with her toward Philip's car, the town's fire horn shrieked, followed quickly by the whooping siren of the first engine. She wondered if Philip heard it. It didn't matter. He was in no condition to do much about it anyway.

"Let's go see where the fire is," she said to Eppie. With a rapidly beating heart, Sara pulled the frightened child to the car.

CHAPTER THIRTY

30

"Where did Jackie get to?" asked Mrs. Ophelia Cole. She lay in bed. Jackie had untied the bands the nurses had used to secure the old woman's limbs to the frame of her adjustable bed. When she became agitated, as she normally did toward evening, she flung herself around and wandered about getting into all sorts of mischief, taking items from other patients' rooms. So every night when Jackie couldn't be with her she had to be secured, and she thrashed about in her own personal hell.

"I'm right here, Mom." With him by her side and the restraints loosened she began to relax. The evening agitation, known as "sundowning," was a common occurrence with Alzheimer patients. It seemed like the sun acted like a solar source, powering the patient's ability to keep their agitation in check. When the light faded there was this urge to go somewhere, or do something. One theory that Jackie had heard was that most people associated the daylight hours with working hours, hours away from home, and once the light dimmed there was an urgency to get home to the familiar place. With the Alzheimer patient, the familiar place was always out of reach. "I'm right by your side," Jackie repeated.

"Not you, silly. I was wondering where our boy, Jackie, got to. Is he playing outside with his friends?"

She thinks I'm my poor father, Jackie thought. I wish she'd just go to sleep. I'm so tired. He took his mother's hand and held it. He decided to humor her, and make her happy. "He's outside playing in the yard. He's building a fort."

"I hope Jackie doesn't hurt himself. Is he using a hammer?"

"Yes, but he's always careful. You know that. I'll watch him. You get some sleep." He squeezed her weary old hand. It was surprisingly soft and warm.

After she fell asleep she relaxed her grip and he was able to sit back in his chair. The moon projected a rectangle of light across her bed. He glanced at the window. The glass was so clean he could make out the stars adjacent to the moon—or were they planets? He didn't know. He dreamed of Sara.

...

He awoke suddenly, confused by the memory of a loud crash. Had he dreamed it or was it real? A shadow flitted across his mother's bed between him and the window. She was awake, too, and shouting. She stopped and leaned toward his ear.

"Let's go home," she whispered conspiratorially. A certain bizarre quality in her voice sent shivers through his body. "I don't know why we ever come here. It isn't worth it. This is the part I hate—those poor children. Take me home."

Jackie had never heard her talk like this. He was eavesdropping on something from the past; a conversation between his young parents, perhaps—a nightmare that his mother had kept silently to herself until now. Jackie had been an accident, he knew, born when his mother was supposed to be past child-bearing years. He knew nothing about their youth.

He glanced toward the nursing home window, through which the shadow had been projected a moment ago. A sense of deep foreboding crawled like an alien fetus into his stomach. Someone had installed a heavy wire mesh screen across the window as he and his mother slept. The mesh hadn't been there before, right? He sensed a movement and heard a series of sharp raps outside against the wall. He rose to investigate and hurried around the bed. As he moved, his mother slid out from under the covers near where he had sat and shuffled to the door, trying to get out. He changed direction and hurried after her, also trying the door. Locked. The loud hammering continued outside the window. What the hell was going on?

"Easy, Mom, easy. You have to settle down." He eased her into her chair and clamped the restraining tray into place. There was a loud, persistent rumbling in the distance, moving ever closer. "I'll be right back, Mom," he whispered.

Whoever had been at the window was now standing on the ground, and another small person was carrying away a stepladder. As the rumbling outside increased he discovered the source. A large truck was approaching—a fuel tanker. Menacingly it veered off the road and climbed the lawn, stopping directly below the window.

Jackie watched, heart pounding, his mother caught up in the mood of terror, yelling like a banshee from her chair. A short man, or perhaps a child, of indeterminate sex, wearing a rubber mask, scampered from the passenger seat of the tanker. She/he walked to the rear of the truck, unrolled several meters of hose, then turned to the truck and pushed a switch, causing the motor of the truck to increase its revolutions. The child swung the hose toward the building several times. Jackie heard the unmistakable sound of breaking glass and watched as the better part of the hose disappeared into the building below him. The child walked to the truck again, did something else that changed the timbre of the engine and, within seconds, Jackie began to smell gasoline fumes.

CHAPTER THIRTY-ONE

31

There's a certain inexplicable, irrational pleasure in staggering up a sidewalk, Philip was thinking just before he stumbled and crashed headlong onto the ground. He landed hard on the narrow strip between a hedge and the concrete sidewalk. "Almost there," he mumbled aloud, embarrassed in spite of there being no witnesses to his drunkenness.

Instead of heading home he had changed his mind and started back into the village toward the fire hall. There might be some fellows at the bar. But he probably wouldn't go in. It would be good for him to walk some of this off. He reached for his waistband and found, to his relief, that the bottle of Captain Morgan had survived the fall. His rum, and his dick, were both intact. He yanked the bottle from his belt, unscrewed the cap and took a long swallow. There was no woman around to tell him what to do.

He was almost on his feet, giving the bottle cap a final twist, when a group of children, wearing grotesque Halloween masks, crossed the parking lot next to the Mussel Cove Baptist Church.

Fear swam through his sodden mind. Had they seen him fall? He remembered seeing a similar mask the night of the fire at the Stitch house. Are these creatures coming to set me ablaze like they did the old schoolteacher?

He breathed a sigh of relief when they passed by him without a glance. Where were the little buggers going at this hour of the morning? He waited until they were almost out of sight before he dared to move. Could these little brats have had something to do with his dear Aunt Bertha's disappearance? He shuddered.

"Holy gentle Jesus, I'm pissed," he said aloud, then scanned the moonlit starry sky, unable to spot a solitary cloud. He had promised Sara he was through with booze, but he might as well not waste the last little bit he would ever drink. Not that he always drank a lot. What appealed to him was alcohol's potential to draw upon the mystical part of his nature. It seemed almost sacramental in its power over him. Aboriginal groups used substances to bring on sacred visions. Rastafarians smoked ganja while they awaited repatriation to Ethiopia. Booze carried the mind away from the humdrum concerns of the mundane world. Stumbling drunkenly up a darkened street was a sort of free dance. The beauty of being pissed was that it required so much concentration to merely stay in the upright position that the mind had no time to worry about trivial things. Booze was his only break from work—his recreation, his hobby, his art, and his romance. Sara turned him on all right, but he'd never behave well enough to suit her prissy nature.

He sipped more rum as he stumbled along, and began to sing aloud. In his stupid condition he became careless and lurched out into the open with the main body of children just ahead of him. They loped past in well-practiced near-invisibility inside the shadows cast by random electric lighting. His position was flooded by moonlight, his profile outlined in the glow of the village behind him. Suddenly aware of this, he dragged his unsteady silhouette behind the Baptist church until he was sure they had gotten almost to the bridge. He decided then that he had best turn around and go home. It wasn't safe wandering around like this.

By the time he arrived at the lane that turned up to Bertha's house, there was no sign of them. He waited a moment in silence, rocking back and forth, listening for some indication of where they had gone. He heard nothing. He might as well go home and get some rest. He turned and headed up the hill toward Aunt Bertha's empty house. He was dog-tired and his bed would feel good.

Then he heard the voices behind the wall of Safe Haven. Damn. What were they doing in Sara's garden? Did she know they were there? He couldn't go home now. Sleep would have to wait.

Whether she cared for him or not, he couldn't leave her now when she needed him. Not to the mercies of these little peckers.

He followed the well-worn path to the break in the stone wall. Looking into the large, empty yard, he wondered where the rascals had gotten to this time. Perhaps Sara would know. He ought to see her anyhow. Perhaps that old bastard, Marcel, was gone by now and she would be happy to see him. Maybe it still wasn't too late. He would never forget the moisture of her mouth and the silken softness of her flesh under his fingers.

He looked at the house. Good, there were still lights. Something large came suddenly out of the darkness and thrust him to the ground; a man or a large animal or a heavy child, which then ran like a frightened elephant out of the yard and into the night. Philip's heart pounded as he staggered to his feet. What the hell was that thing? What was it doing in here? Poor Sara, to be living in such a place.

As he hurried up the steps toward her door, he sensed more movement behind him, lighter feet or paws coming at him from several directions at once. Before he could turn around to look, he heard the town's fire horn howl throughout the village and, at that exact instant, his head exploded and he was falling. He didn't land. There was nothing. Blotto.

CHAPTER THIRTY-TWO

32

The wing of the Manor containing Jackie's mother's room was now an inferno. Flames leapt thirty feet in the air. Sara pulled her car to a halt as close to the burning structure as possible, shut it off and leapt out.

"Stay here!" She screamed at Eppie above the roar of flames and engines, the shouts of firefighters, and the hiss of wind and steam. She ran to the main door but was held back by several firefighters.

"Jackie Cole and his mother are in there," she yelled and pointed.

"So are lots of others," one of the firefighters told her, his mouth almost touching her ear. "My mother was in there, too. We've gotten everyone out of the other wings, and most of the folks out of this one. We can't do anything more in this end until the flames are completely out, the gas fumes are gone, and we cool her down a bit. I'm sorry, but it would be suicide to go in there now."

Sara collapsed on the edge of the lawn and sobbed. Eppie disobediently had come out of the car and knelt beside her. Sara opened her arms and they held tightly to one another.

The fire was soon brought under control. The Manor, despite its age, had been retrofitted with a sprinkler system. Several fire-fighters with airpacks entered the building. After a few minutes they staggered back out shouting and others entered with stretchers and first-aid equipment.

"Go back to the car, Eppie. I'll be there in a few minutes."

Sara looked left and right and ran inside. Someone shouted from behind her, and she knew she hadn't much time. The corridor was scorched and blackened. She arrived at Mrs. Cole's room and found the door bolted from the outside and two large nails driven through the door into the frame. It was the only door on this corridor that was closed.

"You have to get out of here, Ma'am. This place is still full of gasoline fumes. They could re-ignite without warning."

"No!" she shouted. "There's someone inside this room. You've got to check this room."

"It's closed. They may have closed some rooms because of government cutbacks."

"That was the hospitals, not the nursing homes," Sara said. "They didn't close this room. Someone else did, whoever set fire to this place." She pointed at the nails whose heads protruded at an angle near the edge of the door. Then she sped back up the hall toward the exit, stopped at a glass case in the hall, broke the glass with her shoulder, and yanked out the heavy fire axe. She hurried back up toward the closed door.

"No, wait!" yelled the firefighter. But Sara had already delivered a couple of heavy blows to the door with the awkward red-headed axe, concentrating on the lock and a spot near where the nails had been hammered in. Then she kicked hard and the door flew inward. She found no one in the room. She ran to Mrs. Cole's bathroom and pushed open the door.

Jackie must have placed a wet towel along the bottom of the door to keep out the heat and fumes. It hadn't helped much. Jackie sat holding his mother protectively in his arms as if she was alive, but the scalding heat, or the poisonous fumes, or both, had gotten to them both. Sara waited until the medics arrived to tell her what she already knew, and then she dragged her feet slowly out to the waiting Crown Victoria and Eppie.

...

Both the main gate and the front door were locked when Sara and Eppie arrived at Safe Haven. Sara felt as empty as a discarded shell on a fishing wharf. Her short, sunny time with Jackie Cole had opened a new window in her life and now it had been slammed shut, boarded over and then set alight. Try as she might, she could not make herself feel anything other than some vague buildup of pressure and it seemed as if her head would burst at any moment.

Marcel met them at the orphanage door as she was fitting the key. She decided when she saw him to tell him nothing. She could not bear to discuss it no matter how understanding he might be. He'd hear it soon enough. His jaw dropped when Eppie scurried through the door from behind her temporary guardian.

"Sorry, Sara," he apologized. "I have been quite busy with the telephones. I'm afraid I assumed Eppie was asleep upstairs. But that's no excuse. I'm so sorry."

Sara shrugged and Marcel continued.

"I've managed to make a few preparations for tomorrow evening's little affair. I hope you won't object to the temporary rearranging of the furniture. I'm not only mortified by my extraordinary incompetence as a babysitter, but also about how presumptuous I've been. If you wish things returned to normal just tell me, and it will be done. I'm frankly quite surprised to see you home so early. I had assumed that you might take advantage of my presence here to the fullest."

Sara sighed. "It's a long story, Marcel." She had to struggle to control her feelings, which finally seemed on the verge of cascading from her like a salty waterfall. She turned to Eppie and spoke firmly to the child, "Get up to bed. I'll deal with you tomorrow."

She marched Eppie to the bottom of the stairs and was astonished at the changes Marcel had brought about in the relatively short time they'd been gone. The huge front drawing room had been lavishly decorated, as if for a wedding feast or a grand ball. The tables were arranged in a circle, covered in exquisite lace fabrics, upon which sat decorous candelabra, some she recognized as having been in Marcel's apartment, and others she had seen covered in dust in the attic. The candleholders had been polished and filled with fresh candles for the occasion. The guests for Marcel's "information party" tomorrow night were sure to be impressed.

In the center of the ring of tables, dominating the space, stood the heavy oak altar from her bedroom. It looked like it belonged there. Tables from every corner of the house had been carried in to hold food and drink for perhaps the largest party the house, or Mussel Cove for that matter, had ever known. Or, at least the largest party since the time of the Cobans.

Sara walked to the altar and placed her hand on the surface. Her fingers tingled and for just a moment she recalled Jackie's mouth and his fingers. Then that pleasant memory was replaced by the image of his lifeless body protectively holding his mother. Tears welled up anew but she forced them down. There was too much for Marcel to do and no time for tears just yet. "This was in my room," she said with shaking voice.

"Yes, I have been quite presumptuous. I thought it necessary to have the altar here. It has a role to play in our adventure. It will have huge meaning for several of our guests. You will understand tomorrow evening. Still, I know how upsetting it must be to have strangers invade the privacy of your sleeping chamber."

"It's all right, Marcel. I'm glad to have something to distract me. And I'm happy to have this monstrosity out of my room. The thing gave me the creeps. How did you ever get it down here? It must weigh a ton."

"Some of my staff were here with food and drinks. Your refrigerators and the pantry are filled to the brim. I had help to move the heavier items. Almost strained my back. You can look around. I think you will agree that we are almost ready. I must admit to a bit of excitement on my part. I so love a party."

Something like a shadow slipped past her, heading deeper into the darkened house. She felt suddenly cold. She wondered if Marcel noticed it, too. But she didn't have the strength to ask.

CHAPTER THIRTY-THREE

33

The first clue to Philip that he was alive was a sound like rain; the second was the eerie flickering light of the television monitors. His throbbing head seemed to be pulsing at least one hundred-fifty beats-per-minute and his eyes stung as if they had been bathed in sweat or tropical seawater. Close to panic, he struggled to breathe slowly and deeply until gradually his composure returned. He turned his head slowly, sensing a rat-like movement in the near-darkness behind him. He fought for control of his mind as memories of his drunkenness and shame returned. Nausea came in spasms and, with it, the urge to vomit.

"Damn," he attempted to snarl, but all he managed was a muffled grunt. Someone had taped his mouth shut, so vomiting would mean almost certain suffocation. He sat perfectly still, focusing on one of the monitors, while his stomach settled and slowed once more. After a second glance across his shoulder, he realized he was beside Aunt Bertha. She was alive! For a moment he was elated but quickly realized that though he had found her they were now both among the missing.

He attempted to distance himself from his thoughts; to deal with them as a disinterested observer; to let them flow dispassionately through his mind. Had he been here an hour, many hours, or maybe days? He turned jerkily toward Aunt Bertha and his whole body spun as if in orbit. He repeated the action and realized he was roped in a secretary's chair with a swivel base that creaked as it turned. A few more snaps of his head and he was facing Aunt Bertha, who was tied to a Captain's chair.

He recognized her strait-jacket as the type they'd used on her more than twenty years before, when she had had her breakdown. He was ten years old and angry at how she'd been changing before his eyes. Philip had never been able to learn what had been turning her from the contented woman who performed every chore with whistling cheerfulness, into the tormented and agitated malcontent who had to be carted off to "The Provincial." All he ever got out of her was that she and Marcel had been "recalling the old days."

Across from him now in her Captain's Chair, Aunt Bertha moaned. Does she recognize me? He stared into her reddened eyes until he could stand it no more, and had to close his. It looked like she was completely out of it.

He tried to sleep. Perhaps sleep would ease the pain brought on by his stupid drinking. Somewhere on the back of his head he felt another kind of ache. He recalled approaching Sara's house in the darkness, and then nothing. Was he conked on the head and brought here? Likely. But by whom? The little punks? Probably. But why? Panic welled up again. He could imagine no worse death than being burned alive.

When the tall hooded person dressed like a monk entered the chamber, Philip had fallen, exhausted, into sleep again. The visitor loosened the tape on Bertha's mouth and jammed in a drinking straw. She took a swallow of warm ginger ale and then, when she found her voice, tried to say something to the sleeping Philip, but the monk yanked out the straw and pressed fresh tape firmly across her mouth. The hooded figure undid her bindings, helped her to stand up, and led her, past Philip, through a door. As they proceeded, the throb of a small engine grew louder and the smell of diesel fuel grew strong. She was shoved into the tiny bathroom and the door was slammed shut. The first time this had happened she had been embarrassed and terrified, this time she was merely grateful. A few minutes later she was led back to her chair and bound up once more.

Philip woke up as a blindfold was tightened across his eyes. Something bit like the sting of a wasp in the muscle of his arm. He too was led roughly to the washroom and back, too lethargic and in too much discomfort to struggle. He stood while someone unzipped his pants and withdrew his shrunken penis. The person poked him in the ribs. Even without the prodding, Philip knew what to do. He had been holding on a long time and he was happy to let fly, even blindfolded. Whoever was helping him aimed true and he could hear the stream landing in the water of what must be a toilet. He smelled the pungent aroma of hot piss rise in his nostrils and he sighed. His kidnapper waited until he had expelled the last few drops and tucked him away. By the time he was back in his chair the liquid from the hypodermic had taken full hold and he dozed again. He was drugged so heavily that he didn't think it odd, until later, that some stranger had handled his cock and he had not given the slightest resistance. He hadn't even thought twice about it. He wondered what drug he had been given.

...

In the monitors, Bertha watched as the children's boats approached the island, then as they walked toward a large, dark building. Ah, they're arriving here at the barn, she thought. Bertha watched them go behind the building and disappear from sight.

Moments later they reappeared in the two monitors that displayed the interior of the barn. The children surrounded tables heaped with junk food: chocolate bars, potato chips, pretzels and cheese fritters, coolers of soft drinks in crushed ice, boxes of candies, cakes and cookies, stuffing their mouths and jamming their large pockets to overflowing.

As Bertha watched, some invisible hand switched all but one of the monitors to activities inside the barn, leaving a solitary screen to survey the approaches to the island. She stared in amazement as the lights dimmed and a young girl materialized out of the fog at the far end of the barn. Could it be? Long-buried memories exploded violently into her consciousness.

The moment of her twin sister's death was burned indelibly into her subconscious. And now, it seemed, here was Lynn's very body resurrected, upstairs in this barn—even the voice. Chills of painful recognition raced along Bertha's aching spine. What in Jesus' name was going on with all this madness?

"The day we've worked for is finally here," the ghost girl/twin sister said to the children. "You will finally be free. Your pain will be over forever and the evil destroyed. Children will no longer live in fear of evil. You know what this village has done. You uncovered the bones of the children of old, uncovered the sins of your parents and grandparents. Now atonement will be made for those sins. When the guests arrive, we begin. You have been obedient and loyal, and without you we couldn't have succeeded.

"Tonight, our job is the most important yet. We must take all the boxes we've unearthed to the basement of Safe Haven, where we can show them to tomorrow's guests. I will be going now. Good luck and thank you."

But this was *not* her sister, Bertha insisted to herself. That was impossible. It must be a doll or something, one of those computer, holograph things she had seen in movies. A camera trick, maybe with mirrors or something. Something ... but not her poor, precious—and long dead—Lynn. As the image and the voice faded, Bertha watched the children, who, like a flock of well-managed sheep, turned and poured out of the barn. She knew now that the girl was a fake, an imposter, an agent of manipulation, but obviously these children did not. Her drugged mind struggled to put the pieces together. What was going to happen?

She took no comfort from Philip's presence here with her. She was afraid for him. His being here meant that he, too, was in great danger. It only added to her despair and sadness.

Moonlight danced across the face of the dark water when the frenzied, sugar-pumped children finally paddled toward their homes. Bertha had no choice but to sit while the hours passed, feeling more powerless and confused than she had ever felt in her tragic life.

CHAPTER THIRTY-FOUR

34

Sara was too tired and upset to clean up dishes or gather crumbs. Marcel had offered to tidy up before he left, but she said she would look after it in the morning. She had cut short the conversation over cups of Sleepy Time tea. Grogginess came shortly after the first sip. The tea had been well-named.

Now in bed, almost asleep, she recalled walking with Marcel to the door before dragging herself upstairs. She had never felt so drowsy.

She fell asleep and dreamed about being back with Jackie in his little house. His kiss tasted of raspberries; he seemed to know exactly what she wanted, without being told, and he took his time, beginning with the lips, the ears, her face and neck. She abandoned herself to passion.

The dream dissolved, but a delicious eroticism remained as an aftertaste as she hovered between sleep and wakefulness. Try as she might, she couldn't remember how, or even if, the Jackie-dream ended. She fought the urge to pee but could put it off no longer. Summoning the will power to force herself upright, she lingered hypnotically, groggily in the sitting position on the side of the bed, wondering if she had the energy even to stagger across the room to the bathroom.

On the dresser to the left of her bed, the clock read 6:45 a.m. She was surprised how much time had passed. She seemed to have dozed for only a few minutes. Pushing her drowsy body upward, she strained to lift its leaden mass and shuffle across the room. She stumbled past the mirror above the dressing table, saw her reflection, and realized she hadn't even undressed. She used the toilet and returned to bed, pulled off her sweaty, smoky-smelling clothes and tossed them to the floor. She closed her eyes; sleep came again instantly.

On the way back upstairs, Eppie, too, felt like dozing. She was very tired. The bones of the lost children had been deposited safely in the cellar of Safe Haven. She had been told it would require several trips using all the canoes to get them across the water from the island. Her latest job had been to keep watch and make sure Sara didn't wake up and discover the others coming in and out of the house.

But the job was finished now. Eppie had tiptoed down to the cellar to view the line-up of boxes in the large granite-walled enclosure. There were lots of them. She had met Marcel on the stairs.

He had been watching through the window as the children streamed in and out and finally towards home to climb into their beds before their parents awoke. "See you all later," he had said aloud as the last of them passed by.

"What will happen?" Eppie had asked when the others had disappeared into the early dawn.

Marcel was startled. He hadn't expected to hear Eppie's voice behind him. "Pardon me?"

"What will happen later?"

"The lost children of Safe Haven will be given a proper funeral send-off and all the guilty ones and their descendants will be in attendance to pay their last respects."

"What will happen to me and her?" she asked, pointing up to where Sara lay asleep.

"Be patient. Tomorrow you will know everything. But you must only concern yourself about the children. This is all about the children, my little lamb."

CHAPTER THIRTY-FIVE

35

The drapes were drawn and the room was shrouded in dark-ness. The clock on the dresser read 1:16 p.m.

Impossible. She couldn't have slept that long. She hadn't slept past noon since she was a teenager. She must force herself to wake up. Something important had been planned for today. What? It was hard to think. What a hangover! Sara couldn't remember ever having had such a bad time with booze. How much had she drunk? She did her best to recall details of the previous night. No, she definitely didn't drink enough to cause a reaction like this.

What was going on? A feeling, which bordered on panic, seized her, as if an enormous weight lay upon her and was suf-focating her. She remembered Jackie's lifeless body snug against his mother's, his face shiny and roasted from the intense heat of the fire around him, blistered like the paint on the bathroom walls. That sweet man, dead. The shock of that would account for part of her fatigue, but was there something else? Had Philip put something in her drinks? Of course not. He was inept but not evil. He wouldn't do something like that and, besides, she had driven home. Who then? Marcel? The tea?

Eppie appeared in the doorway with coffee. Her eyes were downcast as she handed the cup to Sara. "Mr. Vertu stopped his preparations for tonight's party long enough to help me make you some breakfast. It's ready in the kitchen. I hope you're hungry."

She hadn't expected Marcel back here until the evening. What had he been doing? Had he even gone home last night?

The coffee smelled heavenly and she needed a fix. She took

the cup and gulped a few mouthfuls of the hot liquid. Her head began to clear and her strength seemed to return as if by magic. Almost too magical. Was there something in this coffee, too? Was she being manipulated by drugs? The bastard! She must confront Marcel. But would he tell her the truth? And she had learned by now there was little point in questioning Eppie.

"Thanks, Eppie. I needed this. I don't suppose you got much sleep."

"Not really. I was too excited about the party. I've never been to a real party. I can't wait."

"Who said it was a party? I think it's more of a meeting. Rather a serious meeting, actually."

"Mr. Vertu had us stay after school yesterday to help. And people were decorating the whole house last night. Why else would they put up party decorations and get heaps of food and drinks ready if there wasn't going to be a party? Besides, I heard Mr. Vertu on the phone inviting people to come over."

"Hmmm. Sorry. I see what you mean. That sounds like a party all right."

"Can I go to it?"

Sara hesitated. Her head was much clearer, but it still wasn't right. Why couldn't she think straight? Could Eppie go to a party? Well, could she? It was a simple enough question. "I don't know what to tell you until I talk to Marcel ... Principal Vertu. Help me find my housecoat and we'll go downstairs."

...

Marcel was no longer in the kitchen. Sara stepped out the back door and watched the school principal pass by carrying one end of an extension ladder. A couple of children, not much older than Eppie, struggled with the other end. Was it usual up here in Canada for a school principal to have children and staff from his school help him with household chores? What on earth was he doing? The more she thought about it—struggled to think about it—the more Marcel Vertu seemed the central character in this swirl of small-town tragedy.

What had she let herself in for tonight? She took another sip of the coffee, hoping it would clear her head even more, and returned inside for a refill. It seemed to soothe her frazzled nerves. Eppie pulled out a chair for her. Sara shrugged and sat. The least she could do was show a bit of appreciation to the child for making breakfast. The questions could wait a few minutes while she ate.

She was confused by the relative darkness of the house. It was afternoon so the sun had to be out, yet the kitchen was lit by a single bulb of low wattage. All the drapes were drawn and no light broke through from outside. She started to rise to investigate, but the will to investigate left her and she slumped back into the chair.

What would become of Eppie after she left? Sara thought. Now that the story was on the verge of breaking, there would be no reason to hang around Mussel Cove. She had expected a visit from The Children's Aid Society, but nobody had ever come. She would have to make some calls. It still amazed her that Eppie had been left in her care. What did Children's Aid know about her? Wasn't this what the Mussel Cove story was all about? Who ultimately decided where unwanted children lived and who cared for them? Who was willing to make such an extraordinary commitment? The public seemed glad to have someone—anyone—care for these children, and would willingly turn a blind eye to small cruelties. It was easier than getting involved.

One thing was certain. Despite her own feelings of guilt, she knew there was no reasonable way she could look after a child properly in Halifax. She never knew where or for how long her job would take her away from the apartment. Sara looked up and found Eppie gazing at her as if the girl could read her thoughts. Sara quickly looked away. Eppie needed a real family who could put her interests first. What were the odds of Eppie ever finding such a family? Sara found her shoulders shrugging, her mind blanking.

The exterior door opened and Marcel entered, whistling "La Marseillaise." He had a leather carpenter's bag around his waist and a hammer in a holster attached to his belt. He smiled. "Well,

Sleeping Beauty, the glorious hour has arrived for the victims of this cruel house. I must say it is wonderful to see you up out of your bed like a lovely rose. I understand from Eppie that you don't, as a rule, sleep so late in the morning. I'm happy that you indulged yourself in the luxury of some well-deserved rest. I trust that by tomorrow morning you'll have your hands full, putting the finishing touches on the unbelievable but true story of the lost children of Safe Haven."

"I have been jotting down what I know already, but I have a number of questions for you. Important questions."

"Much of what you've written will require revision. Trust me, my dear, there is much more to the story than you could possibly guess. You have no idea of the surprises yet to come. When all the guests have gathered—and gather they will—countless untold stories could emerge under this large roof. The quaint community of Mussel Cove has many nasty secrets. It is a rare family hereabouts that bears no guilt for what transpired within these very walls. Think of tonight as a new *Book of Revelations*, full of confessions and realizations and atonement. When morning breaks next in Mussel Cove, the world will be a better place, and the lost children will finally be granted their eternal rest." Marcel removed the carpenter's bag and the hammer holster from his belt and dropped them, and a set of screwdrivers, into one of the kitchen drawers. "You said you had questions. There isn't much time."

Their eyes met and her face took on a serious demeanor. "Have you been putting something in my tea or coffee?"

"Pardon me?" he asked, looking away.

"Something to make me sleep? Some drug?" She sensed he was avoiding her eyes. There was a tightness forming around her chest.

"Why would I do that?" He turned toward the drawer again, opened it and removed a handful of screws from his shirt pocket. He spread his fingers and the screws cascaded into the drawer.

"To keep me out of the way, to slow me down, to confuse me—I don't exactly know why. What the hell is going on, Marcel?"

He smiled at her, his lower lip quivering. Then, he seemed to get himself under control. "It must be the pure Cape Breton air. I must go. The big night is drawing near."

"I'm not sure what you're up to. You have great expectations for tonight, Marcel. I hope you aren't too disappointed," said Sara, her voice flat. She was angry, disappointed and afraid. He had admitted nothing but she felt she knew the answer to her question. And you *will* be disappointed, she thought. Even the older folks in Mussel Cove were only children when you and Bertha were living at the orphanage. Many of the younger ones weren't even born, so what could they have had to do with the dark deeds? Was Marcel insane?

Marcel, Bertha and the other children had experienced unspeakable horrors. But did rubbing the collective noses of a population in the dirt of the past serve any useful purpose? Probably not. Marcel said the past had to be acknowledged. Perhaps he was right—maybe everyone would sleep better after tonight. But she doubted it.

Marcel put his hand on her shoulder. She was startled and jumped. "You seem so distant," he said. "Are you worried? You need not be. Tonight will be unforgettable. I am sure you will not be disappointed. You have no idea how much time I've devoted to thoughts of Safe Haven and its past, or how many hours I've spent planning such an event as this. You are not yet aware of my capabilities, but you will be soon. After tomorrow you will understand my abilities to make the earth move, in a manner of speaking." He blinked and licked his lips; his pale eyes burned.

Fear was energizing her, making her feel alive. "I hope it goes as well as you expect," she whispered. She moved a short distance away from him, then turned back, "Oh, yes ... I almost forgot. Eppie was wondering about 'the party'. Will the children be invited to this meeting? I thought about settling her into bed early. She's had enough bad experiences lately to last a child several lifetimes."

"Oh, well now, I thought I'd mentioned that," answered

Marcel. "I've arranged a separate affair for the children. They will be spared the tedium and the revelations of the adult gathering. Lots of treats, games and activities, and some light entertainment. I had hoped Eppie could lend me a hand with it."

"You seem to have thought of everything."

"I've been thinking of this for too many years to leave anything out. Don't worry, Sara. Everything will turn out as planned. You will have plenty to write about for months and maybe years to come. Perhaps a bestselling book. You will never forget this night. I promise." His hands shook, and his eyes danced. Sara had never seen him so excited.

"I hope you're right," she said, faking a yawn.

"Here," he said. "Let me make you a fresh coffee."

"Thank you, Marcel. I'll get it for myself." She cleaned up the coffee maker and added two level scoops of ground coffee from a container she pulled from the back of the cupboard. She sat and yawned for real while it dripped through. She sipped it slowly. Thoughts of Philip drifted across her mind like morning fog. What happened to him after she dropped him off? She was still angry and bothered by his actions the previous night. What a clumsy oaf. Yet, after what had happened to Jackie, she was worried about his safety. Whoever had killed Jackie and his mother could have easily done something to Philip. Especially in his condition. Had he tried to phone her, perhaps to apologize? No, if he had, Eppie or Marcel would surely have mentioned it. "I'm so sleepy," she said as she finished the cup.

"Well, my dear," said Marcel. "If I were you I'd take full advantage of your on-site babysitter and go upstairs and rest. Whatever is tiring you out will soon pass if you give your body a chance to recover properly. It's probably shock from all the recent unpleasantness. Or maybe you're just coming down with something. Everything is under control here for now, but once our guests arrive for the evening you'll have your hands full, greeting and playing the good host. Afterwards you'll be fully occupied recording the event for the reading public. I'd say this might be an opportune moment to take advantage of your sleepiness."

"You're sure you don't mind?" she said as her energy waned and the world began to spin about her. She couldn't help it. She was going to zonk out again.

"Certainly not," replied Marcel. "I was hoping to hang around until the guests arrived and now I have the perfect excuse. I would be delighted to keep an eye on everything. You run along and enjoy some sweet dreams."

Sara thought that nightmares were more likely but somehow she made it to her bed where she dozed off again. Several times from under the covers she imagined hammering and slamming sounds and the murmur of voices. She struggled to drag herself out of the comfortable nest to find the cause of the din. But, try as she might, she couldn't find the will or the strength. Now she was certain there had been something in her coffee. She had brewed the last cup completely on her own. Perhaps the drug had been mixed in with the ground coffee. Marcel had supplied some of the coffee, but what of the other drinks, the tea and cocoa? Had he supplied all of it? She dozed again.

Another dream. In it Sara called out to Eppie, who didn't answer right away, and when she did it wasn't Eppie at all. This child had a face that was indescribable in its radiance, skin almost transparent, cheeks like the petals of a delicate rose at the peak of its bloom, and eyes that tugged at the center of Sara's being.

"Be careful what you say and do, great danger lies in wait for you," the high-pitched, childish voice warned. "Run, run, as fast as you can, you can't escape the gingerbread man!" Sara laughed in the dream but the child didn't. The girl's big eyes welled up with tears and when she raised her arms to wipe them, the child's left arm ended in a bloody stump. Sara woke up drenched in perspiration. The clock on her bedside table said 8:20 p.m.

She stumbled out of bed and staggered to the window. She yanked aside the heavy draperies and tried to look outside, wondering if any of the guests had arrived. It can't be this dark outside. It was too close to the longest day of the year. She forced her eyes to adjust. Shutters. Someone had closed over the shutters. Her mind fought the shadows that dulled her thinking. Marcel and the ladder. He must have closed the shutters. Why? The only answer seemed to be to hide what's inside.

She heard voices. The house was already filled with people. She hurried into her clothes. She gathered up notebook and camera, a pen and a small, sensitive disk recorder. Her head ached dully just like before breakfast.

She descended with an otherworldly feeling. It was indeed a party, a celebration. Eppie had been right. These people were here for a good time. Most had a glass in hand, and several already showed signs of drunkenness. And she felt a little drunk and giddy herself, owing to the drugs. Philip should have been here by now if he was coming. She glanced around the large room. He was nowhere to be seen.

There was a large television monitor at one end of the main parlor. Wires were strung up high along the walls leading to Heaven knows where. Had Marcel brought in the television media people? Have I been scooped? There goes my fame and glory, she thought. Then she had another thought: without Jackie, this town had no police presence. Should she call in the RCMP? But what could she really accuse Marcel of? And wouldn't there be cops somewhere nearby, investigating the Manor arson—which was clearly murder? Police always carefully investigated the death of one of their own. But if she dialed 911, what did she have to say—that she was scared? What did it all add up to, and to whom could she turn for help if she needed it. No answers were forthcoming to her fogged-up mind.

And where was Eppie? Marcel would know. But where was he? Surely he was here. She'd have to find him.

She stumbled from room to room. There were so many strangers. Faces from behind all those locked doors in Mussel Cove. These strangers only increased her loneliness. She thought of Jackie Cole, who definitely wouldn't be coming, and how he had comforted his poor mother on their first visit to the Manor and then those stolen last moments in his arms. But the aftertaste of those memories was flavored by horrid images of that second visit, when she found him in the final embrace with his mother.

Sara wanted to scream out that it wasn't fair. She wanted a chance to mourn but knew there was no time for that yet. She had to find Marcel.

He was back in the dark kitchen, alone, his expression dark and grim. She stood in the doorway for more than a minute before he noticed her and waved her inside. He tried to grin, but the deep, dark lines on his forehead remained.

"Sara. Good, you woke up. I was about to send for you. It's almost time. Are you ready? You look awfully groggy."

"I could use a coffee, one that won't put me to sleep."

"I'll bring you one. This one will wake you up, I guarantee. I need you alert for this. Without the historian there is no recorded history."

For the first time since she had met Marcel Vertu she could see how time had taken its toll on him. He looked as if the frantic activity of the last few hours had drained him, not only of energy, but also of blood. All those wires and television equipment must have been difficult to install. What new questions would arise from all of this and which ones would be answered? As she sipped the bitter coffee that Marcel handed her, her head cleared like magic and she felt tense but alert, her senses painfully sharp.

"Where did Eppie go?"

"She's gone to help with the children. Our guests were encouraged to bring their kiddies along with them. I suggested it in order to solve the short-notice babysitting problems. Eppie is taking them across to the children's party I promised them."

"Where?"

"The abandoned barn just off shore below here. Your friend, Philip, suggested it when I told him I required a large space away from the house. I didn't want them to experience the evidence I plan to present to the parents. Ugly stuff. I met the young druggist down in the village early this morning. He told me he was walking off an enormous hangover. I've since obtained permission from the owner's agents and we're all set. So I've developed a grand adventure for the children that includes a canoe ride to the island.

They ought to have a hell of a time. Some of my girls spent half a day in the preparations. The children will be well-entertained."

"Will they be safe out there this late in the evening?" she asked, picturing unstable canoes crossing the deep water between the shore and the island in the dark, especially coming home. "Isn't that near where the minister's wife drowned?"

So Marcel *had* seen Philip and he was all right except for the hangover. Odd that he wasn't here. Or was it? Philip had nothing to do with Safe Haven, and perhaps was embarrassed about last night, or maybe Marcel was lying and something had really happened to Philip. She couldn't help but worry.

"What if a canoe tips over?" she asked.

"These children know the ocean. They are not like their parents, who never saw the need for swimming instructions. Mrs. Black was no swimmer, I understand. Even the fishermen can't swim. But their children are water babies. The Red Cross wasn't here to instruct the parents, who seem to think their children's lives are of more value than their own. Being around and on the ocean is second nature to these kids."

"Yes, but should they be out there alone at night? They are only children."

His smile faded. He snickered. "You don't know as much about children as you think you know. These are no ordinary children. They were born into Mussel Cove and it changed them. By the way, you were right about drugs in your beverages. I'm sure you're not surprised." He seemed to sneer at her.

"What!" Sara took a sudden step toward him. She was angry. She *had* known this but she hadn't expected him to admit it.

"I did it to protect you, to keep you out of trouble. All your black tea and coffee contained a powder made from Bertha's sleeping pills. Mogadon, I believe it's called, nitrazepan, ground up along with the beans. Your wake-up drinks, some of your coffee and the Earl Grey, all contained Ritalin. One of the children collected it from the other children who had supplies at home. The drugs work rather well, don't you think? I usually had someone at the house to make sure you got the right drink at the right time. And the chemicals are all perfectly safe. I have no interest in harming you. I checked out all the drugs by calling a pharmacy in Halifax on their 1-800 number before I gave any to you."

"How could you, Marcel? Who do you think you are?"

"The question is more, 'Where do I think I am?' my dear. It's time to go in. If the world were a different place, we might have been great friends, Sara."

"You jerk!" she said to his retreating back. "Now that I know what you're really like, I would never be your friend." Should she call 911 and report that she was drugged against her will? But she hadn't been assaulted or anything, and Marcel would certainly lie about the drugs when asked by a cop. What evidence did she have against him that would stand up? Damnation, she said to herself.

The party was swinging. Marcel mounted the platform near the large, flat screen television monitor and, with a twist of his head, indicated that she should join him. Sara shook her head slowly. She was not about to help him play his game. The crowd saw him step up on the small platform and the house went gradually silent except for the whir of cooling fans.

"You all know me," he began, his voice firm and clear. "And you no doubt have heard about our hostess, Sara Miles—over the back fence if you haven't had the privilege of meeting her in person. Although an excellent, professionally qualified and licensed teacher, she is presently an employee of *The Halifax Loyalist*. There she is, standing in the doorway to the kitchen, scowling at me. Don't judge her too harshly, she has more than ample reason to be angry. What you may not know about me—your consolidated school principal and restaurateur—is that I am a survivor of the institution that once operated out of this lovely old building, Safe Haven. I welcome all of you to what I promise will be the most memorable night of your life." He turned toward the screen on his right.

"This large, flat-screen monitor will play a major role in tonight's proceedings. The entire program will not take long, so I trust that all of you will stay with us until the event is over.

"Some among you inquired earlier about activities planned for the children, and I would like to show you." Marcel touched the palm pilot he was carrying and the lights in the room dimmed. The screen lit up. The picture instantly displayed a noisy space filled with excited children playing happily at video games, eating candy and potato chips and gulping soft drinks. The room was already a mess of discarded bags and wrappers and spilled drinks, but no one seemed to mind in the least.

Sara looked for Eppie in the crowd on the screen, but couldn't locate her. Something about the picture bothered her, but she didn't know what.

"Now, as to the affair before us," Marcel announced. The screen switched to the opening page of the book Sara had discovered in the secret door of the oak altar. "I would like to introduce you to some of my old friends, the luckless residents of Safe Haven. For those of us who lived there, there was nothing 'safe' about the place. Two of us, myself and poor, sad, Bertha Morris—who couldn't be with us tonight—are among the few survivors of the non-adopted rejects of this 'haven.' Many of the rejected children, who weren't so lucky, you will encounter later on tonight in a more concrete fashion."

The tips of Sara's fingers turned cold. The small hair at the back of her neck stood up, sensing danger. What the hell is he up to, she wondered? Some drinks sat unfinished on tables and mantle piece. Others, too precious to waste, were hastily swallowed. Irene and Alby Mahoney clutched one another and stared at the screen as page after page of names appeared and disappeared, while Marcel melodramatically read them aloud. Close by them, Ed Harding and Jane, his pretty daughter, stood in attentive silence. The whole crowd hushed its collective voice. Marcel turned up the lights as the sequence ended and the screen went blank.

"Next, we will go to the cellar to pay our last respects to the remains of the deceased. You will want to come along. This is a wake that is long overdue. Come, follow me."

From within the crowd a voice called out, "It's time to go home. I, for one, have had enough of this cruel charade. Marcel, you're off your rocker." This announcement was followed by a general rumble of agreement that threatened to shatter the spell Marcel had so carefully cast on the assembled crowd. He jumped back onto the raised platform.

"You will go nowhere!" he snapped, all pleasantness gone from his icy voice. "Until the entire evening's proceedings have run their course, nobody will venture outside of this building." His hand touched the palm pilot and once again the activities in the interior of the barn filled the screen.

"Take a closer look," he said. "These children are under my control. Nobody can provide them any assistance if I decide to act against them. Co-operate with me or else! I am in complete charge of your destiny, as your community was once in complete control of *my* destiny and those of my *friends*. There is no way out of this house without my help and co-operation, people. You will quickly learn how it felt to be a prisoner within these walls.

"Every window has been shuttered and bolted from the outside. All the doors are sealed by electronic locks and physical obstructions. This building, and the barn where your carefree children play so merrily, have been booby-trapped. Ferociously booby-trapped. Severely booby-trapped. Any attempt to tamper with what I have done, and the barn and its contents burn to the ground. Bye-bye babies. One touch of a button and the party ends. Ends with a capital 'E.' Poof! Do you understand? And forget your cell-phones. You know we get lousy reception around here anyway, and besides I'm running electronic interference." Sara saw some people, already ahead of Marcel, pound numbers on their cell-phones in obvious frustration. So much for 911, assuming there was a cop anywhere nearby in the first place.

There were a few scattered gasps—then a stunned silence.

Sara though to herself: why don't we all jump him? But then he had the control over the kids. Would he really kill them? Was he bluffing? Her experience with him suggested he never bluffed. He was a serious lunatic but not a bluffer. These parents wouldn't risk their kids' lives, and so what choice did they have?

Marcel stepped down and gestured for the guests—prisoners—to follow. Sara's head was spinning. He led them like sheep along the hall and down the stairs to the cellar. Sara followed as the crowd's movement suddenly slowed and their awful silence was replaced by gasps of horror and disgust. She pushed through to the bottom step. Nothing could have prepared her for the spectacle awaiting her. She had figured out what the butter boxes had been used for but seeing them complete with their bony contents was too much.

She raised her camera and began to shoot the butter box coffins and the expressions of pain and disbelief on the faces of the people of Mussel Cove. She had to do something, needed to focus her mind, to slow it down enough that she could think.

All around the circumference of the cellar were arranged rectangular wooden boxes just like the ones she had seen in the attic just a few days ago. But these were gray and weathered and stained by their years under the surface of the earth. The lids had been removed, revealing scores of small skeletons, many of them babies, only a few weeks, or even days old. A few skeletons were broken and twisted out of shape. Here were the lost children of Safe Haven. Finally there were witnesses to their having lived on the earth for a very short time.

CHAPTER THIRTY-SIX

36

Up above them in the barn the party was rocking. What did Philip call it? Hip hop; rap music—more like crap music. This cell, this black hole, had become a torture chamber and with the horrid strait-jacket Bertha was helpless to resist. Her nose and back itched in a million places.

Philip was awake, too. By rubbing his head across his shoulder he had managed, with great difficulty, to slip the blindfold from his eyes. It lay twisted across his nose. He sat gazing at the television monitors.

Not long ago Bertha had watched a convoy of children paddle those wiggly old canoes across to the island. Like mice in clothes, they scurried along the trails toward the barn. If she hadn't been so afraid she might have laughed at the way they moved, trying to be so adult and serious but unable to disguise their youthful strides. Her prison had been silent before the children came, too silent. She had longed for the stimulation of sound, the way she often turned on the radio or the TV for company when she was too long alone. But now there was too much sound. The little scamps were overhead whirling about as if controlled by some evil force. It occurred to her that they might indeed be possessed by the devil, especially if they were involved in the fires and her kidnapping. She had felt like she was possessed once before, in the bleak period after Marcel came back.

Above her the old barn vibrated and the relentless pounding of the children's feet loosened a fine yellow dust that cascaded down from the ancient rafters and joists and settled on her like some evil sorcerer's magic powder.

Bertha had to pee again. Usually the hooded man wasn't away so long. Why had Marcel dressed this way? Had he gone completely mad? She knew it could only be him. The image of Lynn had proved that. If he didn't come soon she'd have to let go. Philip would smell the warm urine and know what she had done and she would be shamed before him.

Despite her discomfort, she had been planning their escape. On her last night with Sara at Safe Haven, she had committed an unintentional petty theft. She had been peeling turnips for the evening meal and was called to the phone. When she returned to the cutting board, she couldn't locate the paring knife. It bothered her because it was nicer to use than the other paring knives in the kitchen—a tiny, black-handled Henckels. Later that evening she discovered the knife in the front pocket of her blouse. The next day she moved it over to the front pocket of her fresh blouse with the intention of returning it to Safe Haven. But that hadn't worked out.

She had thought it was Philip who slammed the door shut that last morning at home. She was dumbfounded to find Marcel standing outside the door to her room. First she thought something must have happened to Philip, or to Sara and the child.

He ordered her to grab a sweater and come along. She insisted on scribbling a note, then followed Marcel, heart pounding, in anticipation of discovering some disaster that awaited her at the end of this unexplained journey.

He led her to a private boat landing under the stone bridge, a wooden structure she had never seen before, where he helped her into a wobbly aluminum punt powered by an electric trolling outboard motor that whirred along the narrow waterway, passing Safe Haven on the left. They moved in near silence between tall grasses and reeds, leaving a narrow wake that expanded slowly, disappearing not long after they passed. When the river began to widen in anticipation of joining the Atlantic, Marcel switched off the motor and blindfolded her before she heard him switch it on again.

"I have a surprise for you," was all he said as the journey continued. There had been no eye contact and she asked no questions. For the first time in years, she felt afraid of him.

Something had happened to Marcel's mind, and something bad was in the offing.

What she had already learned of his past had almost destroyed her. His was a varied career throughout Europe. He had worked as a magician in several circuses, creating mind-boggling illusions. What he lacked in training he managed to make up for in ingenuity.

He entered the lives of the Cobans, once he found them, and began, at once, employing skills he had taught himself while working in Germany. In his mind he was the reincarnation of—who was it again—Manolesco, the great hypnotist. Marcel had previously moved to France, perfected his French, and set up a practice in alternative psychotherapy, massage and hypnosis, quickly establishing a reputation by willingly taking on cases that proved impossible to the traditional medical community.

His years of preparation and search bore fruit in France when he presented himself and his credentials to the elusive Cobans and they hired him to cure their insomnia and other personal problems. They had no idea that this sophisticated adult had once been a helpless child in their orphanage. Old age was upon them and they began to concern themselves with their destinies and the fate of their immortal souls. He'd gained their total confidence and trust, and guaranteed them a secrecy as sacred as that of the confessional.

He drained the cruel contents of the Coban's memories and assured them their sins were in the past, that they were born again as totally different people with new unblemished souls. Then he convinced them to sign over most of their enormous assets to the work he was doing for the glory of God. When he'd finished with them, they'd been tortured, then joyfully murdered. He served their flesh, which he'd carefully marinated and roasted to perfection, to several of their former friends, along with herbed rice and an excellent *Vin Nouveau*. The Cobans hadn't discovered his identity until their very last hours, when he wanted them to know *who* was about to kill them so nastily and why. Afterwards he had stolen the last of their money and sold most of their belongings. What he didn't sell, he shipped, along with their money, home to Cape Breton inside the cases of magic tricks.

He had expected Bertha to be grateful when he told her about all of it—with triumph and relish—but she had not handled the information well. Instead it brought back the loathsome day when she and her sister, Lynn, had touched Marcel's tiny genitals out of childish curiosity. The Cobans, informed of this by the staff, were titillated. That night the three children were taken into the Coban's evil-smelling bedroom. Although each of them had been there before, especially the beautiful Lynn, it was the first time that they were all there together.

It wasn't until the next weekend that the Cobans theorized that their lust had been caused by the behavior of the children, obviously sent by the devil to tempt them. Such evil must be properly punished. First the sinful hands were severed as proscribed in Matthew 5:30: *And if thy right hand offend thee, cut it off, and cast it from thee: for it is profitable for thee that one of thy members should perish, and not that thy whole body should be cast into hell,* and then the offending genitals.

Marcel's confession had brought it all flooding back. Bertha's sister Lynn had been a favorite of the Cobans. She had been showered with gifts and favors. It was only natural that the others should be jealous of her. But Lynn committed the ultimate sin a few days later when she escaped from Safe Haven. She set out to bring back the police, or anyone else who would listen to her. But it was all for nothing. She staggered into the village, still in shock from the amputation of her hand, and she searched until she found the police station. She collapsed in front of a man in uniform. She was showing him the bandaged stump when she realized where she had seen him before. He was a frequent visitor to Safe Haven, a close friend of the Cobans. He had actually been expecting her.

He carried her directly back to Safe Haven. A phone call had come to the station from the orphanage. One of her friends had snitched on her. That night she disappeared. But not before Bertha, Marcel and the others witnessed the sort of beating they would get if they ever dared to run away and speak "lies" about Safe Haven.

These memories—so brutal and scarring—had been too much for Bertha. She suffered a major nervous breakdown. Marcel visited her often, and after the professionals had just about given up on her case, he asked permission to attempt hypnosis. Reluctantly the psychiatrists and psychologists agreed to let him try, under proper supervision. He proved competent, and because the pros had heavy workloads, they left Bertha almost exclusively in his hands. She returned home and Marcel set her up financially so she would "not have to worry about money again," but she was never truly happy after that.

The one opiate to her painful existence was watching Philip grow from toddler to child, and from boy to man. Yet, even that had hurt. Like all children who endure long enough, Philip became an adult, a separate being and his tenderness and love—her sole comfort in life—faded to indifference and even sometimes to dislike.

The unfairness of it struck her like an angry slap. What would the children of Safe Haven have given for a sane and unselfish upbringing? Philip had outgrown the bitter teen years and as an adult was not unpleasant. Yet there was no pretense of deep affection. There were only memories of childhood when the small boy and the middle-aged woman adored one another. She sighed and Philip turned his head to look at her. A wave of nostalgia swept over her.

She finally caught the eye of her grown foster child. She glanced down, with exaggeration, at the pocket of her blouse, which showed above the top of her strait-jacket. He gave her a puzzled, dopey, drugged look and turned back to the television screens. Every once in a while they heard a click as switches were manipulated from some remote location.

Philip then heard a loud, insistent grunt behind him. He turned and stared at his Aunt Bertha. She had an odd expression on her plump face and was definitely looking down at those large, floppy breasts, bobbing her head like a chicken in a barnyard, while making grasping motions with her fingers.

Bertha's face was crimson with frustration. Her arms were firmly bound to the arms of the oak office chair. She could move her fat fingers but wondered if it was any use to try. She wished they knew Morse code, or sign language, or something. She let her hands droop at the wrists and spun them in small circles, watching his face for any reaction.

Was Aunt Bertha losing her mind? Would she be going back to the mental hospital if she managed to escape from here? She looked sane enough. Her eyes seemed normal. They pleaded with him to pay attention. He struggled against the haze to do so. She pointed with one finger at the front of his shirt, no, at the shirt pocket. He turned up his hand and bent it at the wrist, until his finger almost touched his pocket and Aunt Bertha nodded excitedly. She peered inside the front of her strait-jacket. Was there something in the pocket of her blouse? What?

She pointed to his legs. He lifted them into the air. She raised her leg a few inches and let it drop. Philip nodded. She used her left foot to slip off her right shoe. She lifted it, spread and closed her toes a few times, and gestured toward her pocket with grasping finger motions.

Philip opened his eyes wide and nodded. He removed his right shoe and lifted his stockinged feet near to Bertha's feet. She hooked her large toe into the elastic at the top of his stocking and pulled downward while he raised his foot. Now that his foot was bare he was certain of the plan. There was something in her blouse pocket that he needed to get with his foot.

He raised his leg in the air while she lowered herself as far as possible in the chair, nodding encouragement as she did so. Leaning back as far as he could, he raised his leg still higher and maneuvered his foot down the front of Bertha's strait-jacket. He twisted the foot around so the toes pointed almost downward. It hurt like hell. He was no contortionist.

Worse than the pain was the notion of playing footsie with his Aunt Bertha's massive tits. Blushing, he continued, as she urged him on with large excited eyes. His toes found their way into the narrow pocket of her blouse, and he felt something cold and hard against them. Wiggling them about in great discomfort he eventually caught the unknown object between his big toe and its neighbor. The next few moments were critical. Carefully he withdrew his foot. His entire leg was cramped, but there might not be another chance. Then, miraculously, it was out. His big toe bled freely from a pair of incisions, but he didn't care. They had a knife now and it was obviously quite sharp. What next?

Aunt Bertha grinned. Their game of charades had been a pleasant and encouraging distraction and it had been a success so far. She nodded toward the side of her chair and Philip moved his around using his shod foot until he was parked beside her. Perhaps he wouldn't need the knife. He slipped off his left shoe, removed that sock and began to work on the knots with both feet. After several long minutes, he realized he was wasting time. Philip picked up the knife, held it between his feet and began the process of sawing through the fabric. He dropped the knife on his first attempt and it fell onto Bertha's lap but after a few tense and em-barrassing moments, he resumed cutting.

Soon Bertha had her good arm free and she untied her remain-ing bonds, then Philip's, and, while he rubbed his wrists, ripped the tape from his mouth.

"Shit!" he yelped. "Jeese that hurt, Aunt Bertha."

"Sorry, dear. Couldn't be helped, eh."

"Let's get out of here." Philip moved unsteadily to the door on legs that had been idle too long, and then, when suddenly put to use, painfully cramped, but he found the door locked from the outside. He slammed his body painfully against it, but it wouldn't budge. Next he tried the interior door, which opened and allowed them to enter another dark, cramped room which contained two more doors, one of which was solid, locked and windowless. To Bertha's great relief, the second door inside the small room gave them access to the small bathroom. She opened this other door, flicked the switch and a light came on above the toilet.

While Bertha was in the bathroom, Philip hurried back to the monitor room and watched the children playing upstairs. On another monitor, which had just lit up, he recognized the interior of Safe Haven, where a huge room was decorated for a party—obviously the event Sara had spoken of on their disastrous date. The room appeared to have been recently deserted as he noted from the partly filled glasses here and there, and sweaters and jackets that had been tossed over the backs of chairs. As he watched, people with long, unpartylike faces straggled back into the room. At the tail of the procession, Marcel entered, followed by Sara whose pretty but drained face showed signs of panic. Marcel strode to a wooden platform and looked pontifically across the crowd.

"And now for the main part of the show," Marcel said. "Things are about to get unpleasant and I am afraid that I may no longer be able to count on your restraint. That's why I brought this along." He withdrew a pistol from inside his jacket.

"I used to begin and end each day by cursing ever having been born. But that was before my life's mission revealed itself to me. For many years I traveled Europe and America pretending I was a complete person, letting people think I avoided intimacy by choice, and not because this community cut away my manhood. Yes, my genitals were cut away in this very building while you all went on with your lives. Do you have any idea how that has affected my life? I lived with constant despair and loneliness, always on the run from myself. What work I undertook, or how I excelled in it, made no difference to the contempt in which I held myself."

There were tears in Marcel's eyes, which only served to accentuate his apparent madness and the fear that it engendered. The crowd reacted with cold, silent terror, all eyes on the gun.

"But then I made a pilgrimage to Jerusalem," Marcel continued, "and there, in that holy place, I suddenly understood what I must do. I would rid the world of an abomination. And I have been working on that plan for a number of years now. The final chapter is about to unfold.

"This charming old German pistol, a Luger, belonged to former friends of this community, the Cobans, a noxious pair who once begged me to quickly end their lives with it. I refused their request and employed it in ways that extended their suffering to the maximum."

"If I must use this old weapon again to keep you under control, I will not hesitate. It was you and your forebears who stood by and watched the Cobans commit their crimes—their mortal sins—against us. It was you who collaborated in the killing of the children of Safe Haven. It was you who permanently maimed those few of us who managed to survive."

Several voices protested anew. Marcel raised the Luger with a cry of fury and lunged and fired a warning shot. In their flight, the crowd pressed against the heavy altar behind them. Its solid mass held it in place a moment, but the combined weight of the crowd proved too much, and the huge furniture piece crashed to the floor and came apart. All eyes turned to the shattered altar. Even the roar of Marcel's pistol was forgotten in the moan of anguish that rolled like a wave across the room.

"Get back, you bastards!" he screamed. The top of the altar had broken away from the base and lay face down beside it. Between the top and the shattered base rested its macabre contents of bone, dust and fabric. A shadow seemed to lift and pass through the room as the air around them turned to ice.

Sara shivered as she elbowed her way close enough for a look. There on the floor lay the skeletal remains of yet another child; this one dressed in a dusty party dress. The skeleton was missing a right hand and the skull had apparently been violently crushed at the time of death. The bones of the tiny legs had also been shattered.

Tears streamed down Marcel's tormented face. He was torn between shock and anguish. He turned toward Sara who stood behind him. "I'd like to introduce you, Sara, to the last of the lost children of Safe Haven. This is Bertha's twin sister. Her name is Lynn." He turned and climbed the podium. His voice had turned flat, monotone and colorless. "As I said before, it's show time.

Don't expect to enjoy it." He waved the pistol around the room like a drunken cowboy in a cheap Western.

The uncovering of Lynn's bones had done further damage to Marcel's self-control. He, too, had begun to come apart before their eyes.

...

Back from the toilet and standing in the doorway of the control room, Bertha stood transfixed, staring numbly at the monitors. No single screen allowed her to glimpse the child's remains. Marcel's words to Sara resonated in her mind. There lay her twin sister. Why had they hidden her body, like some sacred relic inside that obscene wooden altar, instead of burying her with the others? Were they ashamed of being found out for their terrible brutality, or was it something else?

Marcel and Bertha had loved Lynn but their jealousy had led to her death. The guilt she felt over the phone call that led to Lynn's death had ruined Bertha's life. Everything had changed then. No new babies came to live at Safe Haven. Within months the Cobans left for good. She hadn't heard a word about them until Marcel returned decades later with his morbid tale of vengeance.

Marcel's voice on the screen broke into her reminiscences and she shivered as the meaning of his words arranged themselves in her mind. "I have been chosen to wreak vengeance upon the lot of you. Mussel Cove does not deserve children. Not in past generations and not in the generations to come. But before I introduce you to your fate, you will know how it feels to suffer loss. Watch the screen and weep. If you try to escape this building, you, too, will be destroyed. If not by me, then by the explosives and gasoline I've planted throughout the building."

Sara recalled the box of dynamite in the attic and the wires and motors. If only she'd investigated those things further at the time. Insisted Jackie look into them. She tried to think. She had to do something.

Someone pushed past her, driving her against a table, causing a crystal bowl of dill pickles to hang precariously over its edge.

She caught it before it fell, its briny contents wetting her fingers. Someone shouted above the crowd.

"For God's sake, let the children go free! They did nothing to harm you!"

Marcel turned angrily toward the voice. The Reverend Stanley Black eased through the crowd toward the platform. Father Doyle, the elderly priest from St. Dunstan's, followed him. Marcel's voice rang out, full of rancor and rage. "Those children are sprung from the evil loins of this diabolical community. They are already as evil as you and the generation that preceded you. There is no God in Mussel Cove. There cannot be, there is too much evil here." He swung the barrel of the gun toward the old priest. "You know that, don't you, Father? You heard all those confessions, and yet you did nothing. None of you did anything to help."

Marcel fired the Luger twice, and the clergymen dropped like sacks of grain to the floor. Blood seeped from dark holes in their astonished foreheads. He swung the gun threateningly around the frantic crowd.

"Watch!" he screamed above their terror, and the huge screen next to him lit up. He consulted his watch, raised his palm pilot, and selected a button. The barn appeared. Tongues of flame licked out around its foundation.

He aimed the gun at Sara's head. Her fingers, which still clung mindlessly to the crystal pickle dish, went white along its edge. Terrified, she felt this was the end. "You come with me," he ordered and guided her along ahead of him. She pushed back against his steady pressure. Marcel touched another button on the pilot. The front door swung open and he shoved her violently toward it. Most of the pickles and brine splashed out onto the floor. She looked for some surface upon which to set it down. At her back, anguished voices shouted above the moans and cries of others as they surged toward the door in an attempt to flee Safe Haven and do something to save their children.

Marcel turned the Luger on them, shouted and fired, forcing them back. He fired twice more into the crowd and turned to Sara.

She was ready. She focused her energy on what she must do.

With all her strength, years of repressed anger at those wasted years with Tony, anger at anyone who had ever hurt a child, anger at the violence that burned up Jackie Cole and his mother, she lifted her leg angrily, driving her shoe into Marcel's groin. The kick landed so hard it lifted him off the floor.

He only grunted and laughed. "No balls, Honey," he said with a mad laughter that was quickly replaced by enormous anger. He lifted the pistol, glancing momentarily across his shoulder to check the crowd behind him. She looked down at what remained of the bowl of pickles and she knew why she had held on to it so long. Without hesitation she slammed the heavy crystal bowl, pickles and what remained of the juice into Marcel's face. He screamed and tried to rub the acidic liquid out of his burning eyes. Sara pushed people aside and disappeared into the kitchen. Behind her Marcel roared, slammed the front door shut and fired the revolver again.

"Stay put," she heard him scream. "I've activated the explosives all around you. One push of the button and we all go up in flames," he shouted. "Watch the screen! Watch your children die!"

Sara got safely to the pantry, hurried inside, heart pounding, and slammed that door behind her. Too late, she realized she had trapped herself. She fastened the latch, and knowing that would never keep Marcel out, began stacking cases of canned goods, bags of flour, everything movable and heavy she could find, against the door. It mustn't end like this, she thought.

Marcel's frantic body battered the pantry door. Two bullets ripped through near the latch and rattled off something metallic in the near darkness. She dropped to the floor. Twice more his body slammed like an enraged bull against the door. His furious voice came muffled through the thick wood.

"Die in there. I don't care. There are others who will write about this, you bitch!"

She held her breath as the steps receded. She waited only a moment, then lit a wooden match she took from the metal matchbox holder on the pantry wall. She was startled by a sudden explosive scurry to her right. Nervously she lifted the heavy cover of the garbage chute, thankful for the moment that the sturdy wire mesh kept the rats on the outside of the pantry.

But could the chute provide her a means of escape? She had watched from a distance as Bertha raised the screen to dispose of garbage, so there must be an easy way of opening it. She felt around but couldn't locate the latch. If she could tear away the wire she just might fit through the opening and escape. There were still the rats and the filth, and the bin to escape from, and possibly the traps or explosives which Marcel might have installed. But, one thing at a time.

She lit a second match and a third. What could she do? She could use a hammer, but there was no hammer in the pantry as far as she knew. She held up the dying match and scanned the walls. Pots and pans and skillets. Of course. She snatched a heavy cast iron frying pan from its hook. Lifting it over her head, she brought it down with all her strength against the mesh. She surveyed the damage with her fingers and noted that the mesh had loosened. Taking heart, she brought the pan crashing down repeatedly onto the mesh. Her arm ached and the jagged wire tore at her tender hands and wrists, but she continued in near panic. Fear and anger invoked a strength she had never before known.

Something gave and the frying pan flew from her bloody hands. It clattered down the chute causing a further scurrying of panicked rodent feet. She didn't hear it land at the bottom. By feeling around in the dark she found that she could pry back the wire mesh enough to attempt fitting herself through the opening. If Marcel had considered it as a possible means of escape, it would be booby-trapped anyway, and it would all be over. But what choice did she have? She took a deep breath, climbed into the hatch and let go.

Almost instantly she landed. She had to get away and help Eppie and the others if it wasn't too late. When she lifted the heavy metal top she found that the sky was studded with stars. Quickly she rolled over the lip of the container and dropped to the ground, filling her lungs with fresh evening air tinged with wood smoke.

Suddenly she noted a rosy glow in the eastern sky above the trees near Pox Island. Quickly the red sky seemed to intensify. She had better hurry. "Eppie! The children! Oh Jesus, no. Marcel!" she screamed. "You demented bastard!" She ran quickly in the direction of the island.

...

Just moments before, Eppie's attention was drawn to Ira, the boy with the bulgy eyes, who stuffed his face as if this was his last meal. Eppie didn't eat junk food anymore. Not since her parents died. She didn't feel like a kid now. She did before, pushing countless handfuls into her mouth and swallowing them half-chewed until her tummy ached. Now she settled for ginger ale.

Ira stopped eating and stared at her, big red eyes filled with tears. He ambled across the room to where she sat on the floor. She wished she hadn't been watching him. His large head and those salamander eyes made her nervous. Outside at night in the dark she didn't mind being around him, but inside with the lights on, or in the daylight, like at the school, she tried to avoid looking at him. He was gross, and scary. She would get away from him now if she could, but it was too late.

"I know what's going to happen," he said. "We killed your folks and we killed my mother. Now all the other adults are going to die."

Eppie's thoughts strayed back to Sara in the big house with all the real parents. "You're crazy! The ghost girl didn't say anything about that."

"Something real bad is going to happen. I can tell. I can always tell." As he spoke, the lights dimmed and the wall at the western end of the barn began to rise. The ghost girl was going to speak to them again.

"I watched where Mr. Vertu locked up the drunk guy from the pharmacy the other night ..." continued Ira in the superior tone that aggravated Eppie to no end. "... and I know how to get out of here even when the doors are locked."

Eppie heard what he said. Then she asked, "What about the ghost girl?"

"It doesn't matter what she says," said Ira. "It's over. It's time to get out of here. I'll tell you all about how the ghost girl trick works, but you've got to come with me now."

...

Down below, Bertha and Philip watched the mechanical child appear on the television monitor. "This is the last time," she said. "Soon you'll all be free for eternity."

"Oh, my gentle Jesus!" gasped Philip. His eyes strayed from the child to an adjacent screen where he saw fingers of flame lick up the tinder-dry wall outside the barn. "God help us all. We'll roast in this blasted barn!"

Bertha simply sat and stared, her tired old face drained of all color, resigned to her fate, almost thankful it would soon be over.

CHAPTER THIRTY-SEVEN

37

Irene Mahoney clutched at Alby's sleeve. He'd taken a huge risk and slipped away while Marcel had been on one of his rounds. Alby had been trying to find some way out of the house without setting off any of Marcel's devices. He had arrived back without being caught. Thank God!

Alby Mahoney was an electrician who knew little about electronics and nothing about explosives. He reported to Irene. "There is considerable sophisticated wiring, and the shutters look to be operated by a system of motors, pulleys and heavy locks. It don't look like there's any way to get at them from the inside. The silly old bugger seems to know a surprising amount about bobby-trapping a house."

He handed Irene his linen handkerchief and waited while she dried her eyes. Alby's face looked as it had the day he'd given up on his dream of becoming the greatest heavyweight boxer ever to come out of Cape Breton. He wasn't good enough—not quite. He went to work for Irene's father. All in all it had been a good life, especially after the arrival of the children late in their marriage. Like magic, Irene, who had believed herself barren all through their early years together, agreed to adopt a girl, became fertile and gave birth to a son. The two children added great joy to their comfortable lives.

Alby and a few others had looked all over for an axe, a crowbar, or even a hammer—any tool to help rip or batter their way through the heavy shutters. They'd found nothing. They'd tried tearing at the thick oak with bare hands, but, aside from breaking fingernails and cutting ends of fingers, they'd accomplished nothing. Now he and Irene sat propped against the wall, completely discouraged.

Robert and Kensey Mahoney were in the barn with the other children. The parents watched the flames lick up its tinder-dry sides until the picture on the screen faded to snow. By now their precious children must have been destroyed in the flames.

Steeped in despair, the parents no longer thought of escape. Their cries of rage and the damning of Marcel Vertu had faded to an exhausted silence, broken only by the occasional sob, or muttered curse. Across from the Mahoneys, near the broken wooden altar, sat Edward Harding, owner of the drugstore, and his daughter Jane. They, too, were in shock.

Just a few hours before, they had loaded little Ashley and Cody into Ed's station wagon. The children were excited about the big party. During the short ride through town, they tried to imagine what would happen there.

Jane told her father she hoped Philip would show up so she could stop worrying. Ed was furious that he had had to call Louis Bigley, a retired pharmacist from Sydney, as a replacement. But by evening, Ed, too, was worried. Philip was often late but he had never stayed away all day without phoning.

Now, locked in the old orphanage, Ed had forgotten Philip and the drugstore. The grandsons were his pride and joy. They had had to win him over, of course. Initially, Jane's promiscuity had been beyond comprehension—and horribly embarrassing. She had always been a willful child. Such behavior would be understandable in a son, he told Philip. But daughters weren't supposed to act that way unless they were someone else's.

She had only one life, she had insisted, and no one would tell her how to live it. She had nothing against the concept of marriage per se, but she had no intention of marrying some jerk just to satisfy the gossips of Mussel Cove. Just because there was no one fit to marry in the village didn't mean she intended to deny herself the fulfillment of having children. Besides, most of the single moms she knew had been married for a while—for all the good it did them.

She had selected the fathers largely for their physical characteristics, as she saw little to choose from among their intelligence or personalities. Once she got pregnant, she dumped them and enjoyed the look of relief on their stupid faces.

Now her babies were gone. Jane had never been close to her father, but after she watched her children go up in flames with the old barn, she collapsed into his pudgy arms. The old man wasn't much comfort but he was all she had left. They sat on the cold hardwood floor, while a few of the more restless prisoners scurried about like blind mice in a maze.

Jane rose and placed her eye against the shutters. It took a moment for her sight to adjust. She could just make out a solitary figure in the distance, running toward the ocean. That reporter from Halifax. The girl stumbled and fell before rising and disappearing into the darkness. How did she get away from the house? If she got out, all of us could, too!

Something was happening inside the building. Jane could feel it. Did that American girl activate one of Marcel's explosives?

CHAPTER THIRTY-EIGHT

38

Sara dragged the only remaining canoe across the sand to the ocean and paddled desperately toward the island. Ahead of her loomed the inferno whose fierce hissing and crackling smothered even the crash of waves against the shore. The fire had created a mini-storm of violent air. Blood from the damage the wire mesh in the pantry had done to her hands had begun to harden; half-formed scabs broke, and fresh blood oozed from her stinging wounds to the salty paddle. She shifted it from side to side, driving it frantically into the water.

After what seemed an eternity, she dragged the canoe across the pebble of shore, and dropped it on sand just beyond the ocean's tidal grasp. She struggled along the path toward the burning barn. The upper level was engulfed in flames while sparks, polished to brilliance by the ocean wind, drifted everywhere, bursting like miniature fireworks and igniting smaller fires all over the island. Several sparks landed on her bare arms, biting like horseflies. She brushed hot coals from her hair and clothing. Burning was not how she wanted to die. The wind shifted as she approached the barn, and the smoke turned so thick she was swallowed in a dense gray sea.

Some solid creature slammed against her legs and sank powerful teeth into the inside of her thigh before jerking her to the ground. It snarled like a dog and she wondered if it were a coyote enraged by the fierce fire. Then a second creature came screaming hysterically toward her, but instead of attacking, it began pummeling the thing that had attacked her. Sara took the biting creature by the hair and yanked with all her strength. The jaws loosened, the pain eased, and blood seeped warmly down the inside of her leg. The wind shifted again, allowing the dancing flames to light up the space around her.

"Are you hurt, Sara?" yelled Eppie above the sound of the wind and the flames. "Did he hurt you?" Eppie held Ira by his foot, while Sara clung to his greasy hair.

"I think I'm okay," shouted Sara. "Are you all right?"

"Yes, we got everyone out before the fire got bad. Someone tried to burn us. Ira must have thought you were one of them, I guess. I'm sorry he bit you. He's kind of weird and maybe scared. Can you help us get the others out?" She turned towards the barn.

"Others?"

"Aunt Bertha and Philip. Ira saw Marcel put them in the barn."

"Where are they?"

Eppie pointed to a door on the lower level, a door someone had closed and locked since Sara's last visit to the island with Eppie. On the other side of it, she remembered, had been a small stable with a locked door on the inside.

"Where are the children?"

"On the outside shore. We told them where to go, and what to do if the entire wood went on fire. We couldn't go toward the house in case he came back."

"Marcel Vertu?"

"Yes."

Sara looked at the barn door. The heat this close to the barn was unbearable. "How do we get in? That door looks unbreakable."

"Can you boost me up? I couldn't reach. Ira wouldn't help me. There's a key on a shingle way above the door."

Sara had already begun to lift her. Eppie scrambled onto her shoulders and retrieved the key. Sara took it, unlocked the door, and swung it wide. She tripped over someone in the heat-filled blackness. She recognized Bertha mostly by her bulk and tried to move her. She hurried around the room but found no one else there.

Eppie and Ira together began to drag the large woman outside.

Sara next plunged through an open door, the one that had been locked on her last visit, into another smoky, darkened room. She was choking with the smoke and feeling dizzy and confused. There wasn't much time. Eppie said that Philip was in here. Sparks began to drop from the ceiling as the fire attempted to climb down through the floor. She felt along the wall until she came to a closed door and knocked violently, shouting Philip's name. She turned the knob, and to her surprise the door swung open. A small light bulb burned inside and Philip sat on the floor, in front of the toilet, whimpering. He saw Sara and sprang to his feet.

"Come on!" Sara shouted.

"Where's Aunt Bertha?" he shouted back, rubbing his eyes.

"Outside. Come on!"

When they came through the outer door there was no sign of anyone. Ira and Bertha and Eppie had all disappeared. Sara and Philip ran toward the shore.

CHAPTER THIRTY-NINE

39

Sara and Philip beached their canoe on the shore below Safe Haven. She jumped out and wished him luck as he paddled back to organize the children who remained on the island, and bring them back to the mainland. Sara worked her way through the narrow, wooded trail, and was shocked to discover Marcel ahead of her, moving away toward the orphanage. Gone was the frenzy that propelled him the past few hours. He walked as if blind to the world, as if time had suddenly dropped the burden of age heavily upon him.

Already the ruby red sky was fading to black, and the air was damp and heavy with the bitter smell of charred timbers.

Sara looked, with heavy heart, past the pathetic figure of Marcel, to the dark and sullen house. He didn't know his attack on the children was a complete failure. He had made serious mistakes. But he wasn't finished. His infamy might yet surpass that of his oppressors, the Cobans. What might the headline read? "Victim Turns Villain."

She considered calling out to him, wondering if he was still armed, and decided that didn't matter. She had no choice. He must be convinced to release the captives in the house. She hurried after him, but before she could say a word he stopped in his tracks and stared, spellbound, at the parlor window.

"Lynn," he called in anguish. "I did it. I did it for you!" He paused as if to listen and then answered the voice no one but him could hear, "I'm sorry, Lynn. I was afraid. I didn't want to tell on you. They made me do it, really. I was scared what they would do to you and what they would do to the rest of us. Please say that you forgive me."

Fear made of his face a landscape of remorse. "I'm sorry," he screamed. "It wasn't fair. They loved you. They loved you so much more than the rest of us ... Yes, I was jealous of you. But I was a child. It didn't mean that I didn't love you, too, just like everyone else. You were so pretty, so pretty and so perfect. I didn't think they would hurt you for running away. I never thought anyone could ever hurt you that much. How was I to know what they would do to you?"

Marcel fell to his knees and wailed, wringing his hands in front of his face like soiled dishrags. He was broken beyond control.

He staggered to his feet and loped toward the house, eyes glued to the parlor window. His voice, now low and tender, had taken on the purring tones of a lover in the presence of a loved one. "I'm coming, Lynn. I love you. I'm sorry! I've always loved you. I'm coming to you!" He raced toward the steps, pausing to enter a code into the Palm Pilot he pulled from his shirt pocket. The front door swung wide. He hurried up the steps with open and expectant arms, and disappeared into the building, leaving the door swaying behind him.

There was a shout of triumph from inside and a moment later the bulk of the population of Mussel Cove funneled through the open door, hurrying past Sara in the direction of Pox Island. Marcel was temporarily forgotten in the intermittent cries of joy and delight, as the children emerged, one after the other, from the trees below the house. Within minutes, the two crowds melted happily together. Bertha appeared out of the delightful confusion. There was no joy on her face. Without warning she bolted toward Safe Haven.

"Lynn!" she shouted, "Lynn!" She hesitated an instant, then ran like a schoolgirl toward the open door.

"Don't!" cried Sara, too late to stop her. She hurried after the older woman. By the time Sara caught up, passed through the kitchen and entered the parlor, Bertha stood rocking back and forth, whimpering before the broken skeleton of her sister. Marcel stood beside her, his finger poised above the Palm Pilot. In a pool of dark blood in the center of the room lay the pale, lifeless bodies of the two clergymen, all that remained of the invited guests. Marcel turned to Sara, eyes livid with anger. Bertha continued to rock.

"What next, Marcel?" Sara asked defiantly. "It's over."

"One push of the button and it's over."

"It's too late, Marcel. You've already failed. You've murdered two decent men and terrified a house full of others. You've accomplished nothing else."

"But I have destroyed their children," he said, a look of alarm in his eyes.

"Take a look outside."

He maneuvered carefully around bodies and furniture and stepped out the door. As he left, Sara crossed to Bertha and took her arm.

"Come on, Bertha," she said. "We have to get out now. The house is going to explode. Marcel intends to destroy Safe Haven, and burn himself up, and us in the process. We have to get out now."

"It doesn't matter. I don't care anymore. Lynn died because of me."

"Why do you say that? I thought you didn't remember."

"Marcel made me remember," she answered.

"How can you trust anything he told you? It's Marcel! Why should you?"

Marcel stumbled back into the room. "Trust whom?" he asked, his voice cold as death. "Are you talking about me? So the children of Mussel Cove are all free. The evil lives on, and it's all your doing."

"Bertha and I are leaving."

"That's what you think. In my plan you were going to write all about this. Instead, you've made my whole life a joke. My mission lies in ruin. Why should I let you go?"

"If you had a shred of decency left in you, you wouldn't have to ask," Sara said angrily. "You say the evil still exists in Mussel

Cove, and you're right. Think about it, Marcel. You told us not many minutes ago how you had ended the evil of the Cobans with your gun. But did that end the evil? Think. Who else do you know that tried to kill innocent children? Who else do you know who has shown a total disregard for human life and human dignity?"

"Shut up!" Marcel pulled out the Luger and pointed it at her.

"Don't, Marcel," said Bertha. "None of this was her fault. It was you and me who caused Lynn to die. I don't care about me any longer, but please let the girl go. Lynn would want that; I know."

"You don't know anything, Bertha. You're such a stupid old cow. You had nothing to do with what happened to Lynn. It was I who told on her. Lynn was the favorite. She always got everything." He turned to Sara.

"You ruined everything. All those years of planning. All those dreams are nothing because of you."

"Come on, Bertha, let's go home." Sara steered Bertha toward the door.

"Stop!" Marcel screamed, pushing the gun right into Sara's face.

"No, Marcel, it's over," said Sara, grabbing his arm. Bertha stepped forward and looked sadly into his eyes as he fired. Sara felt, rather than heard, the deafening concussion of the Luger as Bertha tumbled to the floor.

"Bertha!" cried Marcel. He dropped the pistol and pulled the Palm Pilot from his pocket.

Sara's face relaxed in resignation. She held his gaze unflinchingly and slowly shook her head from side to side. What must be will be.

"Get out, you bloody bitch. Now!" shouted Marcel. "You have ten seconds. One, and two, and ..."

Sara walked to where Bertha lay sprawled on the floor. She looked for a pulse. "Thank God," she said. Sara spoke softly as she helped the old woman get slowly to her feet. She did her best to hurry Bertha out the door. Marcel didn't even look at them anymore.

At the bottom of the steps they stumbled and fell. Behind them, a series of loud shuddering explosions threw several shutters open, allowing clouds of black smoke to curl up into the sky. Instantly flames appeared here and there in the building and dark smoke merged and rose skyward.

Sara helped Bertha to her feet and as she led the old woman away from the house she glanced back over her shoulder. Flames devoured the tinder dry house as if it were paper.

Suddenly Eppie appeared and jumped into her arms. The child was blubbering like a baby. "I want my mommy!" she said. "I want my mommy!"

CHAPTER FORTY

40

Sara found Eppie sitting alone by the pond dangling her bare feet in the cool, sooty water. She was sobbing and asking for her mother. All around them people were gathering their families and friends together and leaving the Safe Haven property in droves. Minutes before, an ambulance had arrived and hurried Bertha away to the hospital. As she was being placed on the stretcher, Bertha handed Sara the key to her house.

"You'll need a place to sleep," she whispered. Sara spoke briefly with Philip, assuring him that Bertha would be all right, and he told her to take Eppie to Bertha's house. He'd stay out of their way for the night. He planned to remain at Safe Haven with the fire fighters until things were finished here, and on Pox Island, and then to catch some sleep at the fire hall. Sara was grateful. Otherwise she probably would have driven to Sydney River to find a motel for herself and Eppie.

In the morning Sara got up early and placed several phone calls. She told Laura that she would finish the story after she got back to Halifax tomorrow. She explained briefly the events of the night before and Laura told her she'd already gotten most of the feature story laid out. The weekly would go to press in plenty of time. Next Sara had called Children's Aid and made the necessary arrangements. She woke Eppie and explained to the girl that she was returning to Halifax right away. Eppie made little protest. She, like everyone else, was too exhausted. Sara helped her get cleaned up and they exchanged good-byes as they awaited the arrival of social workers. Eppie cried a great deal and frequently asked for her mother. It was as if some magic spell had been broken, as if things could go back the way they were before all of this had happened. The poor child, and all the children of Mussel Cove, had a long and difficult road ahead of them. When they finally said good-bye there was no great show of emotion, no regret, no thank you very much.

"Goodbye Eppie," Sara said. Sara's eyes were damp and she felt a tinge, just a tinge, of guilt. But she knew this was how it had to be. Mostly, though, what she felt was an enormous sense of relief.

Eppie just looked at her blankly and said a subdued, "Good-bye."

Shortly afterward, Sara visited Bertha at the hospital. The woman was heavily sedated and Sara could only sit a while and hold her good hand. She told the old woman good-bye and thanked her for all the good food and for her kindness.

"None of this was your fault," Sara said. "Take care of yourself." Bertha looked at her with sad eyes. Part of Sara yearned to ask the woman about the drinks and drugs she had been served at Safe Haven, but decided it would serve no useful purpose. She assumed it had all been part of Marcel's manipulation of the people around him for his own purposes. From the hospital she drove quickly out of Mussel Cove. The sun was shining and she felt at peace. There was nothing to pack and carry away. The few things she owned, including her computer, had been destroyed in the fire. It was just as well. She wanted nothing tangible to remind her of her terrible time in that accursed place.

It's odd, Sara thought, how often life snatches us up into a tornado and tosses us down somewhere we never intended to go. Life stories so often come down to landing in a place where history is about to be made and, like it or not, you are in it.

She knew now that moments of joy and scenes of unforgettable beauty alternate with times of unbearable pain and ugliness. Most of what comes between these extremes fades into a dense fog. Days or even hours are too often all we can recall of a season, a year, or even a decade.

There were things she would never understand. What sort of poison infected gentle, loving human beings and turned them into insensitive monsters? What contagion turned abused children into the abusers of succeeding generations? How could Marcel have done what he did? After all the suffering that he'd undergone, how could he have contemplated inflicting such pain on the innocent people of Mussel Cove? How could he have manipulated those kids into starting all those fires—and then turn around and try to kill them himself with yet another fire? And why did so many of the kids do his bidding? Was it their childish ignorance? Did they think it was a game? Was it Marcel's status as their principal? Did they just lack a conscience?

How long had she been in Mussel Cove? This handful of days weighed more heavily upon her than all her years in high school or college. She could close her eyes and bring back all the faces in Mussel Cove clearer than when she had first seen them. She wondered how long they would take to fade away: the image of Eppie's burning house, old Father Doyle outside his church and later lying in the pool of blood beside the Reverend Black, Marcel at his happy, hospitable best or in the throes of his murderous madness.

As she drove along, Sara recalled the pleasure of brushing Eppie's hair in the big bathroom at Safe Haven; a sunlit afternoon gliding in the canoe on the way to Pox Island; the sweet morning feeling, sitting opposite the child at breakfast. Her dreams that last night at Bertha's house were littered with charred bodies and a woman's remains afloat on the ocean, her face obscured by a feeding starfish and crowds of children who roamed in the deep of night, aware that nothing in the world could stop them.

She wondered what she'd gained from it all. She had cut herself away from a good life because of a relationship that might have destroyed her. Tony had found her and attacked her and she had run again. Now she was returning to Halifax to face him and wondered if he had gone back home to Maine. Perhaps he had given up. Perhaps not. But she knew she wouldn't run again. In Mussel Cove she had met an interesting older man who turned out to be a monster. Another man had been attracted to something he imagined he saw in her. The third she had known the shortest time, though love might have been a possibility with him. Last night she had also dreamed of Jackie Cole. They made love in the musty bed in his small house. Then she dreamed of him sitting beside his mother, comforting her until they died.

Sara realized that something was different about her. For the first time in her life, she had been confronted with a serious problem—and she hadn't run away. She was astounded to discover how strong she could be when she had no other choice. Life in the future looked more exciting now.

The sun was setting over Bedford Basin as she crossed the MacDonald Bridge high above Halifax Harbor. Tonight she'd stay home alone and listen to some Debussy; perhaps have a bubble bath and a tall glass of Wyndham Estate Bin 444 Cabarnet Sauvignon, then sleep comfortably with the familiar sounds of anonymous sirens and the noisy traffic of complete strangers on the streets outside her window. She couldn't wait for tomorrow.